# "Dad, can I stay up late tonight?"

"Not on a school night," Mitch said. "Now, why don't you go show Granddad your drawing, then get to your homework?"

Sam grumbled something unintelligible and went inside with his head hanging. By the time he'd greeted their yellow Lab and shown his grandfather his drawing, he was in a better mood.

Mitch watched the two most important people in his world for a moment. But a part of his brain refused to focus on the scene. Instead, it kept pestering him to check out the car in the lot near the park's rose bed. Unless he missed his guess, it was a red compact. And as far as he knew, there had only been one red car there today.

But Tessa Masterson was supposed to be safely ensconced in her room at the River View, not sitting in a dark parking lot on a wet October night.

"I'm going out for a quick run," he informed Sam and his grandfather.

"It's raining," Sam observed.

"Your dad's losing his marbles, going out for a run on a night like this," Caleb said, drawing circles on his temple with his index finger.

Maybe he *was* crazy, Mitch thought. Crazy enough to have to see for himself if the car in the parking lot had California plates and a pregnant, sad-eyed woman inside.

Dear Reader,

Over the past year and a half, Riverbend, Indiana, has become very real to us. It has come to life in a manner we would have never thought possible when we were first asked to help create this wonderful little town and the people who inhabit it. And along the way, we've gained new friends of our own—the other authors in the series.

We've come together from across the country to find that even though none of us has ever been to Riverbend, our visions of what we wanted it to be were very much alike. No matter where we grew up, north or south, city or country, we all hold a place much like it in our hearts.

We hope you enjoy reading Tessa and Mitch's story as much as we enjoyed writing it, and that all the Riverbend stories will find a permanent place in your hearts.

Sincerely,

*Carol and Marian* (writing as Marisa Carroll)

# Last-Minute Marriage
## Marisa Carroll

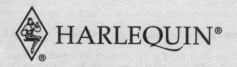

# HARLEQUIN®

TORONTO • NEW YORK • LONDON
AMSTERDAM • PARIS • SYDNEY • HAMBURG
STOCKHOLM • ATHENS • TOKYO • MILAN • MADRID
PRAGUE • WARSAW • BUDAPEST • AUCKLAND

ISBN 0-373-70942-0

LAST-MINUTE MARRIAGE

Visit us at www.eHarlequin.com

**Printed in U.S.A.**

## CAST OF CHARACTERS

**Mitch Sterling:** Single father, owner/operator of Sterling Hardware and River Rat

**Tessa Masterson:** Unmarried, seven months pregnant, stranded in Riverbend

**Sam Sterling:** Mitch's ten-year-old son

**Caleb Sterling:** Mitch's grandfather, lifelong Riverbend resident

**Brian Delaney:** Father of Tessa's child

**Tom Baines:** Prize-winning journalist, estranged father and River Rat

**Lynn Kendall:** Minister and newcomer to Riverbend

**Ruth and Rachel Steele:** Tom's twin maiden aunts, operators of Steele's Books

**Kate McMann:** Manager of Steele's Books and Lynn's best friend

**Charlie Callahan:** Contractor, temporary guardian and River Rat

**Beth Pennington:** Physician's assistant, athletic trainer and Charlie's ex-wife

**Aaron Mazerik:** Former bad boy, current basketball coach and counselor at Riverbend High

**Lily Bennett Holden:** Golden Girl, widow, artist and River Rat

**Abraham Steele:** Town patriarch and bank president, recently deceased

# CHAPTER ONE

SHE WAS LOST.

There was no getting around it. She was thoroughly lost on the back-country roads of rural Indiana. Lost, almost out of gas, and totally shaken by her near miss with a gargantuan piece of farm machinery at the last crossroads.

Tessa Masterson got out of the car and took a couple of deep breaths. It wouldn't help her baby if she went into a fit of hysterics. And even if she allowed herself to give in to the urge, what good would hysterics do in the middle of nowhere?

And she *was* in the middle of nowhere. She looked around. Cornstalks nine feet high lined both sides of the narrow road. They stretched away, ahead and behind her, like a long golden tunnel, blocking the view of the tree-studded, nearly flat landscape. Overhead the sky was a bright autumn blue, not a cloud in sight. But she knew the blue sky and the warmth of the October afternoon were an illusion. The air would grow cold when the sun went down, and storm clouds were gathering along the western horizon. She'd watched them piling up in her rearview window for the past couple of hours.

Grasshoppers whirred around her, leaping in the dry

brown grasses growing along the banks of the shallow ditch that paralleled the road. It was a much smaller ditch than the one she'd nearly driven into trying to avoid the huge green combine with its wicked-looking, spear-tipped attachment that took up almost the entire road.

The wizened farmer in the cab of the machine probably hadn't even seen her predicament. If he had, he didn't bother to stop and help. By the time she'd righted the car and stopped shaking enough to drive on, she'd lost track of the directions the highway patrolman had given her as he'd waved her off the main highway to detour around a jackknifed eighteen wheeler. She reached into the back seat, took a map out of her backpack and spread it open on the hood of the car.

Was she supposed to go left at County Road SW-6 or stay on this county road until she came to E-7? She should have written the instructions down, but there'd been cars behind her, their drivers impatient and obviously more familiar with the area than she was. She knew she needed to keep heading east, and she was doing that, but in this part of the state, major highways were few and far between. As was just about everything else but cornfields and silos.

Tessa pushed a strand of her shoulder-length, honey-blond hair behind her ear and looked around. No landmarks of any kind could be seen, dwarfed as she was by cornstalks. A large brown grasshopper landed on a fringed circle of Queen Anne's lace by her foot. He swayed there for a minute, surveying the world from an even more limited viewpoint than

Tessa's, and then hopped away, leaving the flower swinging in his wake.

No help there.

She had to find a town, or at least a gas station, or she and her temperamental car would be stranded out here in the boondocks for the night. The Wabash River ought to be somewhere to the south. If nothing else, she could head in that direction until she ran into it, and then turn east. But she didn't know how far south the river was.

She'd caught a glimpse of a blue water tower just before the incident with the combine, but it had disappeared behind the distant line of trees by the time she reached the next open field. If she was reading her map correctly, the water tower belonged to a small dot on the map called Riverbend.

Already the sun was riding low above the cornstalks. The shadows were long, and the whirring of the crickets and grasshoppers had slowed in just the short time she'd been standing at the side of the road. She folded the map, getting it almost right on the first try. She had to find her way to this Riverbend place. And soon. For all she knew it was so small they rolled up the sidewalks at five-thirty and the whole town went home to supper, including whoever ran the filling station. But evidently it was the only town for miles around.

She was so tired. She'd driven most of every night and half the next day for the past four days. She'd gotten into the habit when crossing the desert, because it was cooler driving. But by the time she'd reached the plains of Kansas, she was doing it to save money.

Motel rooms were expensive. Even the cheapest, no-frills ones cost more than she could afford. She couldn't—*wouldn't*—arrive at her sister's home in Albany seven months pregnant, unmarried, and with nothing but the clothes on her back.

*I'm going to have a baby in two months.* As always, the thought gave her a little shock of anxiety mixed almost equally with joy.

She might have picked the wrong man to be the father of that baby. She might have made a mess of her life in a lot of ways. But she was determined to be a good mother, even if that meant going home to Albany in disgrace, putting up with her older sister's I-told-you-so's and going on welfare until the baby was old enough for her to get a job. Even if it meant giving up her dream of teaching history to spend the rest of her life working to keep food on the table and a roof over their heads.

She already loved this baby. She was going to keep it. And she was going to raise it the best way she knew how. But she didn't dare think too far ahead, because the enormity of it all scared her to death. One day at a time. One step at a time. That was how she'd made it so far. It was how she intended to keep on.

And the very first thing she needed to do was buy gas for her car.

"LOOKS LIKE RAIN," Ethan Staver said, lifting a finger off the steering wheel to point at the horizon. "Clouds been piling up all afternoon."

"Radio said it would start before sundown," Mitch

Sterling replied. "Supposed to rain all night and all day tomorrow."

"That'll have the farmers on the move."

Mitch surveyed the fields of yellowing corn that bordered the county highway through the bug-splattered windshield. "None of them like to get bogged down in wet fields."

"And the longer it takes for them to get their corn in, the later it'll be before they can take off for Florida for the winter."

Mitch grinned. Ethan hadn't lived in Riverbend, Indiana, all his life the way he had, but the police chief knew farmers.

"What did you think of the renovations to the regional jail?" Mitch asked him. They'd spent the afternoon touring the facility—Ethan as the representative of Riverbend's small police force, and Mitch as a member of the town council.

"The place looks pretty good. Not that we send a lot of people there, but it's good to know there's a secure facility when we need one."

Riverbend was the seat of Sycamore County, Indiana. It had its own jail in the courthouse, but these days it was pretty much just a holding station for prisoners. There was no way the county, or the town, could afford a state-of-the-art facility like the regional jail.

"And the extra revenue we get from renting our unused bunk space to the guys from Indianapolis is a shot in the arm to my budget," Ethan said.

"Amen to that," Mitch answered. Keeping the town budget balanced while juggling the needs and wishes of a population bordering on nine thousand was quite a job. Mitch enjoyed being on the council, but he also had his own business to run.

He glanced at his watch.

Ethan noticed. "I'll have you back at the lumber-yard before three," he said.

"It's Granddad's first day back since his hip replacement," Mitch reminded his friend. "I don't want him to overdo it."

"Sam going to the store after school?"

"He's got an art lesson with Lily Mazerik after school. I told him he could go home from there if I didn't come to pick him up. He's at the age where he thinks he should be able to stay alone."

"He's what? Ten? Eleven?" Ethan asked.

"Ten going on forty," Mitch replied. Sam was growing up fast, too fast, Mitch thought some days.

"How's he doing in school this year?" Ethan wanted to know. Sam was hearing-impaired. He attended regular classes and got good grades, but he worked hard at it. And so did Mitch. He spent a lot of time with Sam's teachers and his math tutor, trying to stay ahead of any problems.

"He's off to a good start. But he was really disappointed not making the Mini-Rivermen football team. He had his heart set on the starting-linebacker position."

"He's pretty small to be a linebacker."

"Yeah. And football is one sport where his handicap really holds him back." Even with his hearing aid Sam couldn't hear the play calls or the coaches' instructions. There was no getting around it.

Sam had done pretty well in Coach Mazerik's summer sports camp, Mitch had to admit, especially at swimming. And he'd played Little League baseball. The trouble was, as Ethan had just pointed out, Sam was small for his age. In football and basketball, his two favorite sports, that was as much of a handicap as his hearing impairment.

"He'll have a growth spurt in the next year or two, and then watch out," Ethan said.

That was probably true. Mitch himself had been something of a runt, the shortest in his group of friends until nearly eighth grade. And then he'd shot up six inches in a year. Maybe it would be that way for Sam, too. He wanted to see his son get as much fun and satisfaction out of playing school sports as he had.

Ethan's scanner squawked into life, interrupting Mitch's thoughts.

They both listened for a moment or two as the dispatcher and another disembodied voice discussed the status of the jackknifed rig ahead of them on the highway. "Sounds like the state boys are handling it just fine," Ethan said. "No need for me to get involved." He flipped on the cruiser's turn signal and headed off onto a county road that ran into the outskirts of Riverbend near the golf course. "We'll make better time this way."

Five minutes later they topped a low rise that brought a fleeting view of the Wabash winding away toward the west. The sky was blue, darkening to almost black on the horizon. The trees were shades of gold and yellow and brown, with a splash of maple red and the near purple of sumac here and there. Mitch could see tractors and combines working in half-a-dozen fields before they disappeared behind rows of unharvested corn.

Ahead of them a small red car was parked on the side of the road. A woman was standing outside it, looking at something spread out on the hood. She was wearing a long denim jumper and a pink blouse. Her hair was blond and shoulder-length, but since her back was to them, it was hard to pick out any further details.

''That's an out-of-state plate—can't quite make it out, though,'' Mitch commented.

''California,'' Ethan replied tersely. His eyesight was evidently sharper than Mitch's.

''Suppose her car's broken down?''

''Could be.'' Ethan turned on his emergency lights, but not the siren, and slowed as he approached the car.

Mitch saw his friend's lips tighten. He couldn't see Ethan's eyes behind his mirrored sunglasses, but he knew they would be steady and gray. Ethan was an ex-army Green Beret and all cop. The woman standing beside her car was probably perfectly innocent of any wrongdoing. But until Ethan proved that for himself, he wouldn't let down his guard.

The chief got out of the cruiser, his hand resting on the holster of his service revolver. The woman turned, surprise and wariness widening her eyes as she swung around, a crumpled road map held in front of her like a shield.

She was pretty, in a bland sort of way, Mitch noticed from his seat inside the police cruiser. Not too short, not too tall and very pregnant. Six months or so, at least, he estimated. She looked downright fearful as Ethan approached, his black police uniform, military haircut, and sidearm making him more than a little intimidating. She shrank back against the door of her car and swallowed hard. Mitch could see the muscles in her throat working from where he sat.

Ethan probably didn't mean to scare the living daylights out of a pregnant woman, but he was doing just that.

Mitch undid his seat belt and climbed out of the car. Ethan asked to see the woman's license as Mitch walked up. She cast him a harried glance and leaned into the back seat of the red compact to fumble in a pack that looked as if it had seen better days.

Come to think of it, the car had seen better days, too. The dust and grime of a lot of miles coated the bumper and partially obscured the numbers on the California plate. But the windshield was clean. And so was the back seat. Or what he could see of it, covered as it was with boxes and neatly tied plastic bags. Mitch would bet a week's profits from the lumberyard that everything she owned was in that car.

Ethan motioned Mitch to move behind him. His hand remained on his weapon, even though the woman he was confronting didn't quite come up to the level of his chin. She turned back, wallet in hand. A few freckles stood out on her cheeks and across her nose, and her eyes were big and blue and ringed with dark shadows.

Kara had been emotional when she was pregnant with Sam. She would have been sobbing openly by now. But not this woman. She was made of sterner stuff than his ex-wife, pregnant or not. She opened the wallet and offered it to Ethan.

"Here you are, Officer," she said, only the faintest hint of a quaver in her voice.

"Is this your current address?" Ethan asked, handing it back to her after a few moments' study.

"I...it was." She lifted her chin. "I'm moving back to New York. I was detoured off the highway by an accident and I've lost my way." She gestured to her car, the movements of her hands graceful and feminine. "I'm almost out of gas. Can you direct me to the nearest filling station?" She turned her head slightly to include Mitch in the query. "And I do mean the nearest."

"Riverbend's about two miles straight ahead," Ethan said in a friendlier tone, evidently satisfied they hadn't stumbled on some hardened criminal masquerading as a pregnant woman. "You can get your tank filled there."

"Thank goodness. Much farther and I'd have to push my car the rest of the way."

"I don't think you're in any condition to push a car, ma'am," Ethan said, hands on hips.

"I don't think I'd get very far trying," she admitted, the tiniest hint of a smile curving her lips.

"I would have offered my friend Mitch Sterling here to do it for you."

She turned to Mitch. She smiled just a little more, her eyes crinkling around the edges, and Mitch felt a surprising jolt of awareness. "That would make you a really good Samaritan, Mr. Sterling. But I've got enough gas to make it two more miles—I hope,'' she added under her breath.

''I can ride into town with you if you'd like,'' Mitch heard himself offer.

The wariness came back into her big eyes. ''No thank you.''

Mitch felt like an idiot. Where she came from, women did not accept rides with strange men. They didn't much around Riverbend, either, come to think of it. But he'd been brought up to offer his assistance to people in distress. ''No problem,'' he said to fill the awkward silence that followed her words.

''The first gas station is just three blocks inside the town limits,'' Ethan told her. ''You follow us and we'll have you there in no time.''

''Thank you.'' She got into her car and fastened the seat belt over her distended middle. ''I'm ready when you are.''

Ethan nodded, tipped the bill of his hat and walked back to the cruiser, Mitch behind him.

''She's pretty far along to be making a cross-country jaunt,'' Mitch said as they passed the little red compact and its occupant. Mitch watched in the side mirror as she followed them onto the road.

''Yeah, she is pretty big,'' Ethan agreed. He picked up the receiver of his radio and pushed the toggle switch. ''We'll just run a routine search on her license plate and ID.''

''Jeez, Ethan. You don't trust anyone, do you?''

''Nope. Ain't that why you hired me?'' Ethan retorted with a grin.

Mitch shook his head and settled back in his seat

for the rest of the trip into town. Ethan was a damned good cop. And good cops were suspicious cops. Yet anyone with half a brain and one good eye could tell that the woman in the car behind them wasn't a threat to anyone.

Except maybe a man's heart, with those big blue eyes and that lost-little-girl smile.

Mitch caught himself looking in the side mirror again, wondering what she'd look like if she smiled fully and without restraint. She'd be a real beauty.

Where the hell had *that* thought come from? He hadn't had the energy or inclination to look at another woman in a long, long time. He sure wasn't about to start now. She was a perfect stranger. She was pregnant. She was just passing through. In an hour she'd be gone from his life.

He leaned his head against the back of the seat and watched the clock tower on the Sycamore County Courthouse come into view, then the water tower and the elevator rising above the trees and the flat Indiana farmland he loved. The three tallest points in River-bend.

This was the place where his roots went deep into the dark fertile soil. This was home. But his mind wasn't interested in the familiar view. It was still focused on the pregnant woman in the red compact.

He turned his head enough to bring Ethan's profile into view. "What did you say her name was again?"

## CHAPTER TWO

TESSA LEANED BACK in the wooden glider located in the center of the little park and set it swinging with a push of her feet. She looked out over the Sycamore River to the far shore. It wasn't that far away, maybe a few hundred yards? She'd never been a very good judge of distance. The water was a mixture of shades, blue and green and brown, deep and slow-moving. It seemed tamer, more sedate, than its famous neighbor, the Wabash, of which she'd caught glimpses from the car.

A rowboat with a small outboard motor putt-putted its way to a landing across the river where houses lined the bank. Some were older and looked as if they could use a little loving care. Some were new, a few large and substantial, with landscaped lawns and big wooden docks jutting out into the river. But beyond the manicured lawns the land was claimed by corn-fields. Two-story white farmhouses and red-and-white barns stood in tree-filled yards as big as city parks. Cylindrical blue silos dotted the cloudy sky above pastures of black-and-white cows. For a moment Tessa wondered if she'd landed in her own private version of Oz. The town behind her looked like a Norman Rockwell painting. A town of her dreams.

She settled back in the swing and kept it going with a gentle push now and then. As she watched the reflections of clouds and trees in the water, she felt her eyes grow heavy. She wished she could stay here for the night. Catch up on her sleep, get her hair and her clothes really clean. It would be heaven. Certainly this little town, with the river at its feet and the late-afternoon sun and the scent of a few fading roses in a nearby flower bed, seemed about as close as you could get.

Her quiet reverie was broken by the sound of a car pulling into the parking lot behind her swing. She didn't turn around to see who it was. She didn't know a soul in Riverbend.

No one but the cop who'd eyed her so suspiciously and then escorted her into town. And the man who'd been riding with him. The one with eyes the same rich brown as the plowed earth and a smile that lifted the left corner of his mouth a littler higher than the right. Mitch Sterling, the cop had said his name was. She wondered if he had anything to do with the big hardware and lumberyard she'd passed on her way down to the river. It had looked like a going concern. Not as big as the Home-Mart she'd worked for in Albany, but impressive for an independent in this age of mega-chain stores.

"Hi there. Remember me?"

She turned her head to find the man she'd been thinking about smiling down at her. His voice was low-pitched and a little rough around the edges, but as warm as his smile.

She didn't smile back, although she was tempted.

You didn't smile at strange men in California. Or in New York, for that matter.

"Are you enjoying the view?"

"Yes," she said. This time she did smile. She wasn't in L.A. anymore. She was in God's country. Or so one or two signs she'd seen along the roadside had proclaimed. "It's very peaceful here."

"It's one of my favorite views."

"You come here often?"

He propped one foot on the rose bed's border, which was made of railroad ties stacked three deep. Real railroad ties, she'd noticed. Not those anemic landscape ties they'd sold at Home-Mart. This rose bed was going to be here for a long, long time. That was the way you built things in a place you never intended to leave.

"Most everyone in town does. But it's the same view I get from my kitchen window." He pointed down the way to a wide stream that emptied into the river. "I live in the yellow house over there."

Tessa turned to follow his pointing finger, but she already knew what she would see. The house wasn't yellow. It was cream-colored. Craftsman-styled, four-square and solid with a stone foundation and big square porch posts. Roses grew on trellises on either side of the wide front steps. Pink roses, with several still blooming, like those in the park.

She loved history. Not so long ago it had been her intention to share that love of history by teaching. Not ancient history, or Colonial history. Not even Civil War history. But the history of the century just past. The enthusiasm and hubris of the early decades. The heartbreak of the Great Depression and the sheer determination required to survive those years. The heroism and sacrifice of the Second World War. The optimism and opportunism of the fifties. Even the strife and intergenerational warfare of the sixties.

The house Mitch Sterling indicated had seen it all. She wouldn't be a bit surprised to find it had always been in his family. Riverbend seemed that kind of place, a town where families passed down houses and businesses and recipes from generation to generation. "It's a great house," she said. "How long has it been in your family?" The words had jumped off her tongue before she could discipline her thoughts.

"About ten years," Mitch said, not looking at her but at the house. "I bought it when my son was born."

"Oh." She tried hard to keep the disappointment out of her voice. Such a little thing, the house not being in his family for a hundred years.

"I bought it from the family my granddad sold it to in '74. My grandmother wanted something all on one floor, so he built her a ranch-style out by the golf course. But his grandfather built this house in 1902."

"Your great-great-grandfather built the house?" She didn't even know her great-great-grandfather's name. And she envied him the luxury of knowing who had owned this house, when, and for how long. It meant he had ties here, roots that went deep.

"Yup. I thought it should stay in the family."

"When I was growing up, I never lived more than three years in one place." What in heaven's name had possessed her to tell such a thing to a total stranger? She must be more tired than she thought. She stood up, levering herself off the swing with one hand on the thick chain that held it to the wooden frame.

Mitch Sterling leaned forward to steady the swing, but he didn't try to touch her. She was oddly disappointed that he didn't put his hand on her arm. She had the feeling his touch would have been as warm and strong as his voice and his smiling brown eyes.

She smoothed her hand over her stomach. The baby was sleeping, hadn't made a move in an hour. Perhaps she'd been lulled by the sound of the river and the rustle of the wind through the trees along the bank. Tessa hadn't let the doctor back in California tell her the sex of her baby. But she knew in her heart it was a girl. A daughter. Hers and hers alone. She raised her eyes to find Mitch watching her with the same quiet intensity she'd noticed the first time she'd seen him on the road outside town.

The silence was stretching out too long. "I have to be on my way. I want to make it to Ohio by tonight," she blurted.

"You've got a long way to go."

"I've come even farther." All the way from Albany and back again, with a detour through Southern California. But Albany was home, because that was where she and Callie had settled after their mother died. It was where she'd worked days at the Home-Mart and gone to school at night to get her history degree. Until she'd met Brian Delaney, a high-school friend of her brother-in-law's, and fallen head over heels in love with him, giving up everything she had to follow him to California.

She blinked. Lord, she'd been close to saying all

that aloud to this stranger. It must be something in the clean clear air, too much oxygen maybe, and not enough smog. She took a step away from the swing, trod on a stone and stumbled a little.

This time he didn't hesitate. He reached out and steadied her with a hand under her elbow. She was right. His touch was as warm and strong as the rest of him. "Are you sure you should be driving any more today? You look pretty done in to me."

He didn't mince words, obviously. Nothing like Brian, who tap-danced his way around everything—until it came time to tell her he was leaving her and the baby to follow his dream and play winter baseball in Central America.

"I'm fine, really," she assured Mitch.

He didn't look convinced. "It's going to be dark in an hour. It'll take you another hour after that to make it to the interstate. Why don't you stay the night here? The hotel on Main Street was restored just a couple of years ago. The rates are reasonable. And it's clean. It's even supposed to be haunted. And the restaurant's not half-bad, either," he added, deadpan.

"I don't believe you."

He made an exaggerated X on his chest. "Cross my heart, the food's good."

A chuckle escaped her. "I mean, I don't believe the hotel's haunted. I always thought ghosts were unhappy spirits doomed to wander the earth until they were set free. What could have happened in a town like this to cause a ghost?"

His face clouded slightly. She felt the same chill she had when the sun dipped behind a cloud a few minutes before he showed up. "Riverbend's not paradise," he said. "Most small towns aren't." Tessa waited, wondering what he would say next. He was silent a moment, glancing out over the river. Then his frown cleared and the sunshine came back into his face. "But this place is probably as close as you'll come to it. And as a member of the town council and the Chamber of Commerce, it's my duty to roll out the welcome mat. Get in your car and I'll show you the way to the hotel."

"That's not necessary." She had no intention of spending the night in Riverbend or anywhere else. She couldn't afford it even if the hotel rates were more than reasonable. They'd have to be giving the rooms away free.

She had no health insurance and less than two hundred dollars to her name. One hundred and seventy-nine dollars, to be exact. And her credit card. It was paid off, thank goodness, but she'd have to live on the credit line, and it was by no means a large one. It scared her to death to think about how nearly penniless she was.

But she wasn't about to tell Mitch Sterling any of that, no matter how warm his eyes and his touch. How could he know how truly desperate she was? And how determined she was not to be beholden to a man to whom she and their baby were just an afterthought? Mitch Sterling was a member of the Chamber of Commerce and the town council. He lived in the sort of storybook house she had yearned for all her life, in a town that was the embodiment of the American dream. In a place like Riverbend, a man didn't make a woman he professed to love pregnant and then leave her to follow his own dreams.

She had her pride left, even if she'd lost most everything else. And her pride wouldn't let her tell this confident, self-assured man that she had no intention of sleeping anywhere but in her car. So she let him walk beside her the short distance to the parking lot. She followed him out, onto Main Street, and then, after he waited for her to park her car, into the high-ceilinged, spotlessly clean lobby of the River View Hotel. She smiled when he introduced her to the clerk, a gray-haired woman standing behind an antique partners desk that served as a reception counter. He told the clerk that Tessa was a stranded traveler and to give her the best room in the house.

Then he had shaken her hand and said goodbye. "I'm late picking up my son from his art lesson. It's been nice meeting you."

"Thank you," she said, equally formal in front of the inquisitive eyes of the desk clerk. "I'll always remember your kindness."

"Goodbye, Tessa Masterson. Good luck in your journey." He turned and left the building.

Where had Mitch Sterling learned her name? From his friend the cop, she supposed.

"Now," said the clerk, "I imagine you'll be wanting a nonsmoking room."

"I..." She was going to say she didn't want a room at all. But she betrayed her resolve by asking what the room rates were, instead of turning on her heel and marching out of the building to her car.

"Fifty-nine dollars a night, plus tax," the woman

said, spinning the antique desk ledger toward her. More than reasonable. But still too much. "We take credit cards," she prompted.

Tessa was tempted. So very tempted. Just one night. She started to reach for the pen but caught herself. "I'm sorry. I've changed my mind. I really must cover some more distance tonight. I…I have such a long way to go."

The woman's smile faltered for a moment, then returned, polite but more distant now. "Certainly. I'm sorry you won't be staying with us. Have a safe trip."

"Thank you." Tessa turned and hurried out through the etched-glass double doors and down the steps to her car.

She did need to cover more miles tonight. She really did.

The sun was still shining even though the rain clouds on the horizon were moving steadily closer. There were only a few more minutes of the beautiful autumn afternoon left. As long as the sun was shining, she would sit in the park and soak in the warmth and dream a little more of what her life might have been if she'd grown up in a town like this, with deep roots and strong family ties, instead of in the run-down part of a city in a series of shabby apartments with a mother who searched for love in all the wrong places and a father she couldn't even remember.

She could do that. It would cost her nothing but another hour or so of her time. And it would give her back so much more. A few moments of peace and serenity that were worth their weight in gold.

IT STARTED TO RAIN just before sundown. The weather forecaster on the radio had said it would go on all night and most of the next day. Heavy fog was predicted for the morning, and school delays were a possibility.

If they canceled school he'd have to find someone to look after Sam, or else take him to the store with him. At ten and a half his son thought he was a grown-up. But Mitch didn't feel right leaving him home alone all day. Even in a town like Riverbend, a kid could get into trouble. Especially a kid with a handicap.

If school was canceled, he'd take Sam to the store and let him price the new shipment of Christmas lights that had shown up yesterday afternoon. He'd even offer to pay him double his usual rate of two bucks an hour. Mitch wanted that Christmas-light display up before the end of the week. The big chain hardware out near the highway had had its Christmas lights out for weeks.

People in Riverbend were loyal to Sterling Hardware and Building Supply, had been for the seventy-five years since his great-grandfather had first opened the doors. They knew it might take Mitch a week longer to get his shipments of such must-have items as icicle lights, but he'd get them. And he'd come damned close to matching the big store's prices. So they waited.

And Mitch tried his best to make sure they didn't wait a minute longer than necessary.

Thinking of the new store out by the highway brought a frown to his face. He'd lost his best employee, Larry Kellerman, to them just the week before.

Mitch was going to have to find someone to replace him soon. Trouble was, no one with Larry's experience or business training had applied for the job yet, and with the Christmas season less than a month away, Mitch couldn't afford to put a novice on the front lines. He'd have to take up the slack himself.

And then Sam would get the short end of the stick.

Not if he could help it, though. Sam had gotten the short end of the stick too often in his life. An ordinary sore throat when he was two had developed into a serious strep infection. His temperature had soared and for two days his life hung in the balance. Then when he'd emerged from the semiconscious state he'd fallen into, it had taken weeks for him to fully recover. And sometime, somehow, during the illness, Sam had lost a significant portion of his hearing.

Mitch's world had rocked on its foundation. Some days it was still a little wobbly. Kara had tried, she really had. But Sam wasn't an easy child to raise. There was the extra vigilance required to keep an inquisitive, hearing-impaired toddler safe, and all the therapy sessions and special preschool classes at the regional rehabilitation center forty miles away. If it hadn't been for Mitch's mother being there to help out…well, his marriage probably wouldn't have lasted as long as it did.

But when Sam was six, his parents had died in a car accident on the sort of foggy night tonight promised to be. Kara had called it quits soon after, taking off for the bright lights of Chicago, where she could be free to find herself without the impediment of a handicapped son and a husband she'd "outgrown."

Now it was just Sam and Mitch and Mitch's granddad, Caleb. And if it wasn't the ideal arrangement for raising a child or living your life, Mitch was mostly content with the way things were.

He coasted to a stop in front of Lily Mazerik's big old Victorian house and headed up the walk to the front door. He could have buzzed Sam's pager and had him meet him at the curb. It was a special one that vibrated, instead of beeping when a message came in. But he wanted to say hello to Lily and ask her how Sam was coming along, so he hadn't bothered. He turned the key on the old-fashioned metal doorbell and waited.

A moment later Lily appeared at the door wearing a paint-stained smock. Her silvery blond hair was pulled into a soft knot on top of her head. There was a smudge of paint on her cheek and a smile on her lips. "Hi, Mitch," Lily said, stepping back so he could enter the house. "Do you have time to see Sam's latest masterpiece, or are you in a hurry to get him home?"

"I've got time."

"Good." Her smile widened.

They'd been friends all through school and fellow River Rats, which was the name given the gang of kids who used to hang out together by the river. Over the summer Lily had fallen in love with Aaron Mazerik, the high-school coach and proverbial bad-boy-made-good. Aaron had also turned out to be the illegitimate son of Abraham Steele, the president of the bank and Riverbend's leading citizen, who'd died of a heart attack back in the spring. The revelation had created speculation and gossip that had lasted most of the summer.

Mitch followed Lily to the back of the house. Aaron was nowhere to be seen, and Mitch figured he was probably at the gym. Preconditioning for basketball season had started that week even though football season was still in high gear. Lily and Aaron's romance had had tough sledding for a while, but it looked as if everything was working out for them now. They'd been married in a quiet ceremony right after Labor Day.

Actually, when he thought about it, a lot of his old River Rat pals were pairing off. Charlie Callahan and his ex-wife, Beth, were back together after a fourteen-year separation. Mitch had promised Charlie he'd be best man when they retied the knot on Valentine's day. Lynn Kendall, the pastor at the Riverbend Community Church, and Tom Baines were seeing a lot of each other, and Mitch wouldn't be a bit surprised if something serious developed there.

He was the only one of the bunch left single except for Nick Harrison, who was now his lawyer, and Jacob Steele, Abraham's *legitimate* son. But for all he knew, Jacob could be married with a dozen kids by now, or he could be in jail, or dead. No one in town had heard from him in years, not even his aunts Ruth and Rachel. His old friend hadn't even come home for his father's funeral, and Mitch didn't have any idea why.

"Dad!" Sam looked up from the table in Lily's kitchen where he was sitting. "See what I did?"

"Hey, tiger," Mitch greeted him, moving past Lily to look down at Sam's drawing.

"It's...Mothra destroying Tokyo and...Godzilla's coming to the rescue of everyone in that building Mothra's going to step on." Sam smiled and shrugged. "How'd I do?" He'd made a hash of the monsters' names, but Mitch wasn't in the mood to correct him.

"Not too bad. We'll add them to your vocabulary list and practice later. Your picture's great." Mothra and his nemesis, the legendary Godzilla, were towering over the hapless Japanese capital, tiny human figures cowering at their feet. Perspective had obviously been the lesson of the day.

"He's one awesome dude." His son's smile reminded Mitch of Kara. Sam had his mother's blond hair, which turned almost white under the summer sun, blue eyes and one crooked front tooth. But Mitch also recognized himself in the boy. He had the Sterling square jaw and a nose that was going to be too big for his face for a few years to come.

He ruffled Sam's hair. He was a good kid—an antidote to all the lonely nights and lonely years that stretched ahead of Mitch. There he was, thinking about being alone again. "Tell me how you did this," he said a bit grimly.

"It's called perspective," Sam explained, enunciating as clearly as he could. Mitch shot Lily a grateful look. It was obvious she'd taken the time to help Sam with the word. "I'm learning how to make things look bigger and smaller just like you see them in real life. See, Mothra is fifty feet taller than Godzilla, but that doesn't mean anything. He's still going to get his ass whipped."

"Sam!" Lily's eyes widened, but the corners of her mouth twitched in a suppressed smile.

"Whoa, son." Mitch laid his hand on Sam's shoulder and applied some pressure so Sam would understand the importance of his words. "That's not a term you use in front of ladies. In fact, it's not a word you should be using at all."

Sam clapped his hands over his mouth. "Oops, sorry," he said, signing the apology for good measure. "It just slipped out. I mean, Godzilla's going to kick butt."

"Well, that's some improvement," Mitch said.

"You're forgiven," Lily told Sam. "How do you sign 'forgiven'?"

Sam showed her and she tried to repeat the swift movements of his hand and fingers. Mitch encouraged Sam to use spoken words as much as possible even though he knew sign language. It was a controversy in the world of the hearing impaired, sign versus speech, and Mitch had listened to both sides. But he'd decided that everyone Sam encountered would speak to him, and only a very few would sign. So they'd put most of their emphasis on speech therapy.

"Slow down," she said with a laugh. "I can't keep up."

"Practice," Sam teased, but the *r* sound slid away as it so often did. Consonants were particularly hard for his son to reproduce, since he'd lost his hearing before he was fully verbal, but Lily understood and rolled her eyes.

"Very funny. I'll practice signing. And you practice your perspective. Is it a deal?"

"Deal," Sam said.

"Okay. Your assignment for next week is to draw something you can see from your bedroom window using the proper perspective, okay?" She had been looking directly at him as she spoke. She formed her words carefully and didn't speak too quickly so Sam could read her lips.

"I promise. Can I take my picture home tonight to show Granddad?"

"Sure." Lily produced a heavy cardboard folder to protect Sam's picture from the rain on the trip home. "See you next week, Sam."

"See you. Come on, Dad. I want to watch *Unsolved Mysteries.*"

"Homework first."

Sam wrinkled his forehead into a frown. "I'm sick of school already."

Lily laughed. "It's only October."

"Tryouts for basketball are in four weeks," Sam told her. This was Indiana. Basketball season was as real an indicator of the passing year as falling leaves.

"You'll make the team this year, I know it," Lily said. "Aaron's told me how hard you've been working all summer."

"Really?" Sam brightened at the praise.

"It all depends on your report card," Mitch reminded him with a touch on his shoulder so Sam would look his way. "Now come on. Granddad is waiting for us, and he'll want to see your drawing, too."

Sam picked up his backpack where he'd left it beside the front door. "He's very talented, Mitch—before you know it, I'll have taught him all I can," Lily said, stopping Mitch with a hand on his arm. "If he keeps progressing at this rate, we'll have to contact someone at the university to work with him."

"Whoa. You've only been giving him lessons since school started. You're making it sound like I've got a budding Rembrandt on my hands."

"Well, I may be overstating things just a bit," Lily admitted. "But he's good."

"If he works at it," Mitch added.

"That, too. But he is only ten. Discipline comes with maturity."

"And he'd rather be Michael Jordan than Michelangelo."

Lily sighed. "Yes." She knew how sports crazy Sam was. And that his small size and his hearing impairment were holding him back from competing with the same skill and success as his friends. "You'll work it out."

"Yeah. We'll manage." Mitch shoved his hands in the pockets of his jacket. "We always do. At least with old Abraham's bequest to Sam, finding money for special lessons won't be a problem." He still had no idea why the town patriarch had left his son nearly $27,000, and he probably never would, although his grandfather Caleb insisted it had something to do with him fishing Abraham out of the river after he'd fallen through the ice when they were boys. "Tell Aaron I said hello."

"I will. Goodbye, Mitch."

"Goodbye, Lily."

"Bye, Sam," she called. But he was already halfway down the brick sidewalk and couldn't have heard her, anyway. "Tell him I said goodbye."

"Will do."

They didn't talk in the car on the way home. It was too dark for Sam to read lips, or sign and be seen, for that matter. They drove past the park, and Mitch caught the quick reflection of taillights in the parking lot as they made the turn. He wondered who was there after dark on a rainy night like this.

No matter. Ethan or one of his men would take a swing through the park later, and if the car was still there, they'd check it out.

He pulled the truck into the driveway, and Sam hopped out, holding his drawing carefully in both hands. He sniffed the wet air. "Smells like fog," he said, turning so that he could see Mitch's response in the fitful glow of the porch light.

Mitch laughed. "How do you know it smells like fog?"

"It just does. Granddad says he can smell rain and fog and snow on the wind."

"Granddad's good at predicting the weather. But he also listens to the weather report on the radio every hour on the hour."

"And he watches the weather channel a lot. Will it be bad enough they'll cancel school tomorrow?" his son wanted to know.

Mitch helped open the storm door for Sam to enter the back porch. The front of the house faced River Road, but almost no one except the mailman used the front door. Everyone else in Riverbend came down the driveway and around to the back.

"I'm not sure they'll cancel. But there'll probably be a delay and you can sleep in an hour in the morning."

"And stay up an hour later tonight?" Sam asked hopefully.

"Wrong," Mitch said. "Now, get in there and show Granddad your drawing and then get to your homework while I fix supper."

"But, Dad—"

"No buts. Or no *Unsolved Mysteries.*"

Sam grumbled something unintelligible and went inside with his head hanging. But by the time he'd greeted Belle, their yellow Labrador, and encountered his grandfather seated in the breakfast nook reading the paper, he was in a better mood. He held out his drawing for Caleb to see, explaining the finer points of the battle between Mothra and Godzilla.

Mitch watched the two most important people in his world for a moment as blond head and white were bowed over the drawing. But another part of his brain refused to focus on the scene. Instead, it kept pestering him to check out the car in the parking lot near the rose bed in the park. Unless he missed his guess, it was a red compact. And as far as he knew, there had only been one red car parked there today.

But Tessa Masterson was supposed to be safely ensconced in her room at the River View, not sitting in a dark parking lot on a wet October night.

"I'm going out for a quick run," he told his grandfather, who waggled his finger so that Sam could turn his head and watch Mitch repeat the words. "When I get back, we'll order pizza. How does that sound?"

"It's raining," Sam observed.

"I know. I won't be gone long."

"Your dad's losing his marbles, going out for a run on a night like this," Caleb informed his great-grandson, drawing circles on his temple with his index finger.

Sam nodded, repeating the gesture and rolling his eyes for emphasis.

The old man laughed, but he looked at Mitch with inquisitive eyes that had once been as brown as Mitch's own.

Maybe he *was* crazy, Mitch thought. Crazy enough to have to see for himself if the car in the parking lot had California plates and a pregnant, sad-eyed woman inside.

# CHAPTER THREE

TESSA SNUGGLED MORE DEEPLY into her big chenille sweater. It was the warmest thing she owned right now. She'd gotten rid of all her New York clothes when she followed Brian to California. Who needed parkas and wool gloves and snow boots in L.A.? But some nights it did get cool at the ballpark, so when she'd seen the sweater in a trendy boutique, she'd bought it without a second thought.

That had been seven months ago. Just about the time she got pregnant. The purchase was the second-to-last impulsive act she'd committed. The last had been to let Brian make love to her without protection one romantic weekend in Mexico, where he'd played a series of exhibition games. She'd been foolish enough to believe she knew her body's cycles well enough to get away with unprotected lovemaking. She'd been wrong. And she would never, ever be so impulsive or so foolish again.

She pulled the folds of the sweater more tightly around her. She didn't want to wake up from her half doze just yet and be confronted with reality: a bad choice in love, a nearly empty pocketbook and almost a thousand miles still to drive. She wanted to go on floating half-in and half-out of her dreams, the anxiety that dogged her every waking moment temporarily held at bay.

Knuckles tapped against the passenger window, and Tessa sat upright with a jerk. She turned her head toward the sound and at the same time reached for the door-lock button to make sure whoever was outside her car stayed there.

"Tessa?" She recognized the whiskey and honey voice, and the square-jawed profile outlined by the pinkish glow of a nearby street lamp.

It was Mitch Sterling.

"Oh, damn," she muttered under her breath.

She glanced past his concerned face. It was fully dark now, the kind of darkness a rainy night produced. She had no idea what time it was. She couldn't see her watch, and the clock on the dash didn't light up unless the engine was running.

She'd bought a cheese sandwich and a bottle of water at a place called the Sunnyside Café and brought them to the park. The storm clouds had rolled in while she ate. She'd watched the patterns the raindrops made on the river, watched the mist rise from its surface to writhe among the tree branches and creep forward to swathe her car. She'd only meant to rest her eyes, but instead, she'd fallen asleep. For a cowardly moment she thought of turning on the engine and driving away as fast as she could without saying another word to the man standing in the rain outside the car.

But she wouldn't take the easy way out. She wasn't that much of a coward. She lowered the window.

"Hi," he said. "Are you all right?"

"I'm fine." She wasn't really, of course. She was

twenty dollars poorer than she'd been when she encountered him the first time. She wasn't one foot closer to her destination. She'd lost four hours of driving time. It was dark and raining and getting foggy, and would continue to be that way for the next hundred miles or so, according to the weather forecaster on the local radio station. She was tired and discouraged, and she had to go to the bathroom. The last problem, a natural consequence of drinking an entire half-liter bottle of spring water and being seven months pregnant, loomed largest at the moment.

"You're sure you're okay?" He dropped onto his haunches in that infuriatingly graceful way men had, laid his arms along the open window and brought his face level with hers.

"I was a little sleepy, so I took a nap."

"Is your bed at the hotel that lumpy?" She couldn't see his smile but guessed it was there.

She was too uncomfortable and too embarrassed to be polite or equivocal. "I didn't take a room at the hotel, after all. Thank you for being concerned about my welfare, but please don't bother yourself anymore. I'm leaving town right now."

"You're not planning on driving in this weather." It wasn't a question, it was a statement. Tessa guessed the smile on his face had disappeared along with the one in his voice.

"I'll be careful."

"Careful might not be good enough."

"Look. I don't want to argue with you. You've been very kind and helpful today, but I really have to be on my way. My sister's expecting me."

"Not tonight, she isn't." His voice had taken on a hard edge, one she so far hadn't heard before. He reached inside the open window, unlocked the door and got inside.

Her car wasn't very big to begin with. Now it seemed even smaller with Mitch Sterling sitting beside her. Tessa forced herself not to shrink away. "Get out of my car." She wasn't afraid of him. Not really. But no woman with any sense let a strange man into her car. Even one who rode to her rescue in a police cruiser and came out in the rain to check on her.

"I will when you answer my questions." He folded his arms across his chest. He was wearing a T-shirt and sweats, wet from the rain, and the play of muscles in his arms and across his chest was just visible in the dim light.

"Look. What I'm doing here is none of your business."

"Maybe it isn't, but Ethan Staver or another of Riverbend's finest will be by any time, and they'll make it their business."

Tessa had no illusions at all that the grim-faced chief of police would even think twice about hauling her off to jail on a vagrancy charge. "Don't threaten me." She grabbed the door handle to get out of the car. But everything she owned in the world would still be inside with him, so she stayed put.

"I'm just trying to figure out what the hell you're doing sleeping in your car when you could have a perfectly good hotel room." He turned to lean against the door, and his face fell into even deeper shadow. Her face, she suspected, was perfectly visible to him.

She didn't want to tell him she couldn't afford a room at the hotel, but her bladder was screaming for attention. Suddenly she didn't care if he knew the truth about her circumstances or not. "I can't afford it," she said bluntly. "I have less than two hundred dollars to my name. I've been driving all night and sleeping during the day in my car for almost a week now. I'm probably as close to a homeless person as you ever see here in Our Town, Indiana. There, are you satisfied? Now that you know all the details of my sordid little story, will you please get out of my car?"

"No."

She laid her head on the steering wheel and fought tears of embarrassment and fatigue and discomfort. "Go away. Please. There's nothing you can do. I have to find a bathroom, and then I'm leaving this place as fast as I can."

"What?" He sounded bewildered and alarmed, no longer threatening.

"You heard me. I have to go to the bathroom. Don't tell me you didn't notice I'm pregnant. A lot pregnant. And pregnant women have to pee all the time." She didn't care how inelegant she sounded. She was desperate to be away from him. She sniffed, swallowing another lump of tears and looked around for the box of tissues she always kept on the seat. It was wedged half-under his thigh, the hard muscles covered only with a thin layer of cotton. She wouldn't have reached for the tissues if her life had depended on it.

"Hell," he said softly, not touching her with anything but the raspy warmth of his voice. He ran his hand through his hair, dislodging raindrops, which

splashed on his broad shoulders. His hair was thick,
she'd noticed earlier. Not too long or too short, and
the same rich brown as his eyes. "Don't cry. I didn't
mean to scare you."

"Well, you did," she said defiantly. "Hand me my
tissues, please."

"What?"

"You're sitting on my tissues."

"Oh, sorry." He looked where she was pointing
and handed her the box.

"Thank you." She took one and blew her nose.

"I'm not usually in the habit of bullying pregnant
women."

"Well, you're doing a damned good job of it." She
took another tissue and dabbed at the corners of her
eyes.

"My parents died in a car accident on a night like
this," he said quietly.

Now it was Tessa's turn to feel like a jerk. "Oh,
God. I'm sorry." That explained a lot about his actions
of the past few minutes.

"That's why I'm not going to let you drive out of
town tonight."

Lord, but the man had a one-track mind. "Thank
you for your concern, but—" She never got a chance
to finish the sentence.

"I know a place you can stay for nothing."

"I won't—" She wasn't reduced to the level of a
women's shelter yet. And she found it hard to believe
there was such a place in a town this size.

"Yes, you will. There's a dead bolt on the door.
And a bathroom." She could hear the smile return to

his voice. "And it's only a thirty-second drive from here. So you can, um, take care of that other need you have."

"I can't go home with you."

"It's not my home. It's my boathouse. Come on. I meant what I said. I'm not letting you leave town tonight. You can come with me or you can spend the night in the Riverbend courthouse jail. It's not nearly as nice as the boathouse."

"I've never set foot in a jail in my life," she said indignantly. The state of her bladder wasn't going to allow her to continue this argument much longer. She opened her mouth to give it one last try, then closed it again.

He let the silence stretch out for a few seconds. "Good. Then it's settled. I'll get you the key and in less than five minutes you'll be..." Mitch hesitated, and she could have sworn she saw his face darken in a blush, but of course, it was too dark to see any such thing. "Cozy as a bug in a rug," he finished lamely.

Tessa sighed and turned the key in the ignition. The prospect of a clean bed and a chance to shower and wash her hair was irresistible. She would figure out some way to repay him later. But right now it looked as if she was going to spend the night in Riverbend whether she wanted to or not.

"DAD! WAKE UP!"

Mitch's eyes shot open. Sam was standing a foot from his head. "Not so loud, tiger." He made a tamping-down motion with his hand.

"Sorry, Dad." Sam tried hard to keep his voice at

a conversational level, the way he'd been taught by his therapists. But it wasn't always an easy thing to do.

"What's up?" Mitch signed, stifling a big yawn.

"There's a car parked in front of the boathouse. A red car. With California license plates." Sam didn't bother signing. He had already bounded over to Mitch's bedroom window to look down at the brown-shingled boathouse below. He looked back over his shoulder to see Mitch's response to his news.

"I know. I let a lady stay in the boathouse last night."

Sam's blue eyes widened. "A lady? I didn't know you knew any ladies."

Mitch laughed and swung his feet over the side of the bed. He doubted if Sam's Sunday-school teacher, or Lily Mazerik, or Ruth and Rachel Steele would appreciate his son's last remark.

"Who is she?"

Sam had been doing homework when Mitch brought Tessa Masterson to the boathouse the night before. He hadn't heard her car drive in, of course. Neither had Caleb, who was dozing in his favorite chair in front of the TV with the volume so loud he was as oblivious to outside noises as Sam.

"Her name is Tessa Masterson. What were you doing looking out the window at dawn?"

"I wanted to draw the boathouse."

The answer surprised Mitch a little. "I figured you were checking to see how foggy it was."

Sam grinned. "I was doing that, too. School's going

to start two hours late. Tyler Phillips sent me an e-mail already. Can I come to the store with you?"

"Sure, tiger."

Sam looked out the window again. He was still in his pajamas, his blond hair sticking up in spikes all over his head. Mitch glanced at the bedside clock. It was a little before seven. He was due at the store in less than half an hour. He opened early, because contractors and farmers started work early. "Damn," he muttered, heading for the shower. He'd overslept because he'd forgotten to set his alarm. And he'd forgotten to set it because he'd had three beers before going to bed in an attempt to keep his thoughts away from Tessa Masterson sleeping fifty feet away in the boathouse. It hadn't worked.

"It's a good thing you remembered to set your alarm or we'd be late for work." Sam's alarm clock was connected to his bedside lamp. When it went off, the lamp flashed. There was also a vibrator under the mattress that alerted him it was time to wake up.

"What's she doing in our boathouse?" Sam wasn't going to be diverted from the subject he was most interested in. And his curiosity had saved Mitch from the indignity of rushing over to his bedroom window to see if she'd gotten up before dawn and left town without a thank-you or a goodbye.

"She was lost and needed a place to stay so she didn't have to drive in the fog." Mitch thought that was as good an explanation as any for a curious ten-year-old.

"How'd you find her?" Sam was looking out the window again.

Mitch clapped his hands sharply, bringing his son's head around. "I'll tell you all about it at breakfast. Is Granddad Caleb up yet?"

"He's still snoring." Sam grinned. Oddly enough, Caleb's snores were one of the things, like the clap of Mitch's hands, that Sam could hear. Probably because of the vibrations. His son wasn't totally deaf, but his impairment was serious and affected every aspect of his life.

Mitch had come as close as he could to getting over his guilt about the illness that had caused Sam's handicap. He and Kara had taken him to the doctor at the first sign of the fever that had escalated into a life-threatening infection. The doctor had prescribed the most effective antibiotic to treat it. But nothing had worked. And no one could be blamed. But Sam's life had been altered drastically, and and that fact had to be lived with. And worked around.

"I'm starved," Sam said. "Let's get breakfast or you'll be late opening the store."

"How come this sudden urge to be the fifth generation of Sterlings to run a hardware?" Mitch asked.

"No reason," Sam replied, trying to look innocent and angelic and missing both by a hair.

"Come on—spill it," Mitch demanded, sticking his head out of the bathroom so that Sam could read his lips. "What's up?"

"I want a new basketball, and you won't let me use my bequest to buy it."

Sam wasn't even close on bequest, but Mitch didn't correct him. "We agreed the money was to be used for special things. A basketball—"

"—isn't special. I know. But practice for fifth- and sixth-grade teams starts in two weeks. Tryouts are only a month away."

"I thought you were going to wait until Christmas to get a new basketball."

The glint in Sam's eyes intensified. "I'm going to make the team this year. The first team, Dad. Coach Mazerik said I was a hundred percent improved from the beginning of summer. I know to keep my eyes on the other guys. And I can hear the whistle sometimes if the ref blows it loud enough."

It was hard to take a stand against such determination. If Sam wanted to try out for the team, then Mitch would do everything he could to facilitate that. If his son made it, Mitch would cheer the loudest. If his son failed, he'd be there to pat him on the back and give him the encouragement he needed to try again the next year.

"Okay. It's a deal. Now hop in the shower and then we'll go invite our guest to breakfast."

"You'd better tell Granddad about her first."

"Good idea." Mitch's grandfather was as sharp as a tack and just about the most outspoken old coot in Riverbend. There was no telling what he'd say to Tessa if he thought he could get away with it. His nosiness was, in Caleb's words, "just being neighborly."

Mitch wanted his son and grandfather to make a good impression on Tessa Masterson. He knew it was foolish to care what she thought of the three of them, or what she thought of him. It wasn't as if she was going to make Riverbend her home. In an hour, maybe two, she'd be gone from his life for good. And with any luck the allure she held for him would dissipate as quickly as the fog would burn away under the October sun.

TWO PAIRS OF EYES watched her intensely as she sipped her orange juice. One set was blue, friendly and unblinking. The other was brown, faded with age, and they studied her with wariness and reserve.

Mitch wasn't watching her. He was standing and looking through the middle one of the boathouse's three double-hung windows that faced out over the river. A couch and a reading chair sat at right angles to each other a few steps behind him. To his right was the tiny kitchenette where she sat. It had white metal cupboards, a round-shouldered refrigerator and a stove and sink, both as old as the refrigerator. Against the outside wall was an equally small bathroom, and directly across from it, in a small alcove, was the bed, separated from the living area by a curtain hanging from a wooden pole. Above the head of the bed was another window, which didn't have a view of anything but Mitch's woodpile.

"More toast, Miss Masterson?" Mitch's grandfather asked politely. Caleb was a little stooped with the weight of his years, but in his youth he would have been as tall and broad-shouldered as his grandson. And as good-looking.

"More pancakes?" Sam added, watching his grandfather speak. Mitch's son was a slender boy, as blond as his father was dark. His blue eyes were fringed with long, luxuriant lashes. And because his smile was infectious and he looked so anxious to please, she intended to eat every morsel of overdone pancake and leathery egg on her plate.

Twenty minutes earlier the Sterling men had arrived at the tiny apartment over the boathouse bearing a breakfast tray loaded with food.

"Good morning," Mitch had said. "I'm glad we didn't wake you, but my son and grandfather wanted to meet you before we left for the store."

"I've been up for an hour," she'd told him. That was true. She'd been awake long before dawn. Twice she'd almost gotten in her car and driven away into the foggy darkness. But she'd made herself stay. Mitch had been right last night, and driving would still have been dangerous. It was foolhardy to put herself and her baby in harm's way for no better reason than to avoid seeing Mitch again.

He had stepped aside. "Tessa Masterson, I'd like you to meet my grandfather, Caleb."

"It's a pleasure, miss," the old man had said with a dip of his head. "Welcome to Riverbend." He'd held out the tray he carried. "We brought you some breakfast."

"Thank you." She'd stepped back so that he could enter the small apartment.

"Hope you were comfortable last night," he'd continued. "Hasn't been anyone staying in this place in a couple of years. Not since the last time my old army buddy from Florida visited. When was that, Mitch? Two, three years ago?"

"Three, I think."

"Hi. I'm Sam." Tessa had blinked at the forceful-ness of the boy's words.

Mitch laid a hand on his shoulder and squeezed a little.

Sam turned his head. "Too loud, Dad?"

"A little," Mitch had responded, making gestures with his hands. Signing.

That was how Tessa had learned Mitch's son was hearing-impaired.

Sam had chattered the entire time she was eating. She'd tried hard to follow what he said, but it was sometimes difficult. Certain words were slurred, others hard to recognize. But Sam didn't seem discouraged by her apologies for not understanding. He'd repeated himself patiently, as though it was second nature.

"Did you live in California very long? Did you ever meet a movie star? Did you go to Disneyland?"

"No and no and no," Tessa had replied, laughing. "I'm afraid not."

"That's okay. I've been to Disney World. That's in Florida, not California," Sam had told her. "It was great."

He hadn't commented on her pregnancy, although she'd caught him sneaking a peek or two at her tummy.

"Dad," he said now, watching her finish the last of her pancake. "It's time for the school updates. If they cancel school, I won't have to take my books to the store. Come to the house with me and listen for me."

His words were matter-of-fact, without an ounce of self-pity, but Tessa thought Mitch's eyes darkened a fraction, as though some old familiar sadness had stirred to life inside him.

"I'll be along in a minute," Mitch promised Sam.

"Take your time, son. I'll go along with the young one." Caleb held out his hand to Tessa. "It was a pleasure meeting you, young lady," he said courteously.

"Thank you," she said, and meant it. "And thank you for the lovely breakfast. I...I wish I could repay you somehow."

"No payment necessary. It was the neighborly thing to do. When I was a boy, my mother always had a meal or a dry place to sleep for a soul in need." He picked up the tray and moved a little stiffly toward the door. "Have a safe journey, miss."

"Thank you."

"Glad me and mine could be of help."

"Granddad!" Sam hollered from somewhere outside.

"That boy's got no patience, just like his ma," Caleb muttered as he left.

She was alone with Mitch. He was still standing in the same place, but he'd turned his back to the windows. Behind him she could see ghostly shapes of trees beyond the river. The fog was beginning to lift. It was going to be a lovely autumn day.

"Thanks for being so patient with Sam."

"No, you thank him for being so patient with me."

"Sam forgets strangers sometimes have trouble understanding his speech. His world is still small enough that, thankfully, it hasn't been a big problem yet."

"Do you all know sign language?" She shouldn't

be having this conversation. She shouldn't be giving in to the urge to learn more about him. She should be shaking his hand and picking up her backpack, then climbing into her car and driving out of town.

"Some of his friends are learning a few words and phrases. It's not just a translation of English words into ASL—American Sign Language—like most hearing people think. It's a complete language, with French derivation. The sentences are constructed differently from English. It's confusing sometimes. He's in regular classes at school, and none of his teachers have had the time to learn sign. His speech therapist uses it. Granddad and I sign with him, but mostly we encourage him to read lips. Actually, it's something of a controversy in the deaf world. To sign or to speak."

"I wasn't aware of that."

He raked his hand through his hair and turned back to the windows for a moment. "It's probably more than you wanted to know."

"I'm not that shallow," she defended herself, and was again surprised how much his good opinion of her mattered. "I just haven't had much contact with hearing-impaired people. And none with hearing-impaired children." She smoothed a hand over her stomach. "Was Sam born with his handicap?"

Mirch had turned back in time to see her instinctive protective gesture, and he raised his eyes to hers. "It's the result of an illness when he was two. It was just one of those things that happen from time to time. No one's fault."

"He seems happy and well-adjusted. You and his mother must be very proud of him."

"I'm divorced. His mother hasn't seen him in sixteen months."

"Oh. I...I'm sorry." Now she really had to go. They were moving into personal territory. She was a private person. She didn't talk like this to strangers. He seemed uncomfortable, too.

"And you don't want to hear about that, either. Look, I'm keeping you from being on your way. The fog will be gone in an hour. It's probably already lifted east of town. I have to get the store opened. My manager quit to take a job with one of the big chain hardwares. I've got to interview a couple of temp workers today." He'd channeled the subject away from Sam's mother with deliberate intent. The hard set of his face told her no questions about his ex-wife would be welcome.

"I worked in one of those stores for four and a half years," Tessa said.

"You did?"

"Uh-huh. While I worked my way through college. I'm a history major. I...I would have graduated in the spring." But now in the spring she would be taking care of her baby and trying to find a job and some sort of day care. Day care. Leaving her baby with strangers. The thought squeezed her heart.

"I would never have pegged you for a history major." Mitch shoved his hands in the front pockets of his khakis and took a step toward her. He seemed to fill the small room, and Tessa fought against the impulse to take a matching step backward.

"Twentieth-century history," she responded. "I had visions of getting my master's and teaching. High school, maybe junior college. But—" She shut her mouth with a snap. There she was, confiding in him again! "But now I have my baby to think about, and making a home for the two of us comes ahead of getting my degree."

"What about the baby's father?"

"I don't know how dependable he's going to be. So I'm not going to depend on him at all." Her chin came up a little and she looked him square in the eye. Somehow she couldn't envision any woman ever having to admit that about Mitch.

"How about a job?" Mitch surprised her by asking, one corner of his mouth turning up in a rueful grin. "A temporary job at Sterling Hardware and Building Supply."

"What?"

"I was going to pay the temp service eleven bucks an hour so they could give some poor guy seven and a half. I'll give you the same. Eleven, I mean. Not seven-fifty."

Almost five hundred dollars a week. She needed the money badly. But staying in Riverbend, even a couple of weeks, wasn't part of her new life plan. A plan as carefully worked out as she could make it. Nothing left to chance. No impulsive decisions. No acting on her instincts, which had proved so wrong, ever again. "I'm sorry. I couldn't possibly."

"Sure you could. What department did you work in at your old job? Paint and wallpaper?"

"I was the assistant manager," she said a little

sharply. "And I was the head of plumbing and elec-trical before that."

"Sorry, sexist remark," Mitch said with a grin guaranteed to melt a harder heart than hers. "I ought to know better. My grandmother and mother both knew more about the hardware business than I ever will. What do you say? It would help us both out. The son of a friend of mine, Mel Holloway, is getting out of the army just before Thanksgiving. I promised to give him an interview if the job's still open. I'd like to help the kid out. We need new blood in town. But until then I'm strapped. What do you say? It'd give you a little nest egg for your baby. And get me out of a bind."

"I don't have a place to stay."

"You can stay right here in the boathouse. The place is winterized. It's small, but it's got everything you need." She was tempted. Oh, so tempted. A few more weeks of independence, of not having to disrupt her sister Callie's household and routines. Of not being beholden to anyone. She was in danger of acting on impulse again. She'd heeded just such an overwhelming urge when she followed Brian to California. And look where that had gotten her.

"I can't. I have to get to my sister's. I have to find an obstetrician. I have to establish residence." So she could go on welfare. The words hung there unspoken between them. She felt her face grow warm. "It just wouldn't work out."

"Dad!" Sam's shout from the driveway cut through the tension in the little room. "It's time to go."

"I have to leave." Mitch came a little closer.

"You're welcome to stay here as long as you want. But promise me you won't go before the fog lifts."

"I promise."

"Drive safely, Tessa."

He held out his hand. For a wild moment she hoped he would try again to talk her into staying and taking the job in his store. But he didn't say anything more. He just stood there waiting, with his hand out.

She took it. "Thank you for everything, Mitch. Goodbye."

## CHAPTER FOUR

FOR THE PAST HALF HOUR Harvey Medford had been debating the pros and cons of buying a new lawn mower now, while Mitch had them at rock-bottom prices, or waiting until spring, when he really needed one.

"My old one probably has a good couple of Saturday afternoons left in her," he said, taking off his green John Deere cap to scratch his bald head. "It's already coming on to the middle of October. Supposed to get a hard frost end of the week. Probably won't have to mow again at all this year."

"Might not," Mitch agreed, laying both hands on the big lawn tractor, leaning his full weight on the sturdy housing, a gesture not lost on his potential customer. "Then again, it might stay warm for another couple weeks. You never can tell about the weather this time of year. Grass will grow some with this rain we're getting."

"You're right there." Harvey continued to ruminate, running gnarled fingers over the two-day stubble on his chin. He moved his cud of chewing tobacco from one cheek to the other, and Mitch couldn't help but think how much the old man looked like one of his prize milk cows.

"You got nearly two acres all told to mow, Harvey. You won't get this good a deal on next year's model in the spring." Mitch didn't let the slightest hint of impatience show in his voice or on his face. Dickering a little was part of the ritual of buying from the hometown merchants. If Harvey had wanted to plunk down cash for a lawn tractor without any conversation to go with it, he'd have gone to one of the big chain stores.

"I'll tell you what, Harvey. It's worth another twenty-five dollars to me not to have to store this baby over the winter. I'll give you as good a deal as you'll get anywhere on the snowplow attachment. And if it does up and freeze next week, you can run her over the yard and chop up the leaves so they blow over onto Roger Nickels's place."

Harvey's rheumy blue eyes shone with a wicked light. He and his neighbor hadn't spoken a civil word to each other since Mitch was in grade school. No one in town remembered what had caused the falling-out. Maybe not even Roger and Harvey. No one knew or cared anymore. But they respected the old codgers' right to carry on their feud. "You got a deal," Harvey said, then held out his hand. "Darned if you don't drive near as hard a bargain as your granddad."

"Who do you think taught him what he knows?" Caleb said, coming up to them. "I'll write up the bill for Harvey's mower, Mitch. There's someone wants to talk to you in the office."

"Thanks, Granddad." Probably another salesman, although Mitch didn't remember having any on his appointment schedule for this morning. He really had to get some more help. Too many things like this were falling through the cracks since Larry had quit.

His office was in the oldest part of the building. It was situated at the top of a flight of stairs, open to a view of the sales area below. The walls were bare brick, the ceiling beaten tin in a wheat-and-sheaves pattern that was worth its weight in gold these days. It was still up there on the ceiling, but not because his granddad or his father, or even Mitch himself, had known there was going to be a revival of such things. It was there because when times were bad, remodeling the office was the last place to spend scarce capital. And when business was good, like now, there wasn't time.

Mitch took the stairs two at a time and looked over the half wall, expecting to see a copper-tubing salesman or the guy who sold the new brand of tools. Both were due to call in the next week or so. Mitch figured they'd just gotten into town ahead of schedule.

But the figure seated in the chair beside his desk wasn't a salesman. It wasn't a man at all. It was a woman. A pregnant woman.

Tessa Masterson rose to greet him. "Hi," she said with that smile of hers, half shy little girl, half siren. The image had stuck in his mind like a burr since yesterday.

"I thought you'd be halfway to Ohio by now." He didn't smile back. He'd spent the last three hours attempting to forget he'd ever seen that smile or the woman who wore it.

He'd taken Sam to school the long way around when the fog lifted. He'd been determined to eat lunch at the Sunnyside Café and not go home to let the dog out, in case she was still there. He'd promised himself he wouldn't set foot in the boathouse until her scent had dissipated and the imprint of her head on the pillow was gone.

Her smile faded as she regarded him. She tugged nervously at the hem of the fuzzy sweater she wore over her denim jumper. Today her blouse was lime green. A bright cheerful color, he supposed. But somehow it only served to underscore the paleness of her skin and the dark bruiselike smudges of fatigue that shadowed her blue eyes.

"I came to see if the offer of a job is still open," she said.

"I still need help," Mitch admitted. "That hasn't changed since this morning. But since you're here, I'm figuring you've changed your mind about taking it. Why?"

"It's a woman's prerogative, changing her mind."

He walked to his desk and rounded it, facing her across the cluttered expanse of scarred walnut. "Not in this day and age."

"You're right." She took a quick little breath and spoke in a rush, as though she was afraid she'd lose her nerve. "I wanted to say yes this morning, but I needed to consider my options."

"You weren't prepared to act on impulse."

Her chin rose a little and her eyes narrowed. Then she nodded. "Exactly."

"I can understand that." He motioned for her to take a seat. She lowered herself carefully into the chair. She wasn't clumsy in her pregnancy, but neither had Kara been until the end. He wondered exactly how pregnant Tessa Masterson was.

"I've learned the hard way not to walk into a situation without both eyes wide open," she said, and he thought he heard sadness, laced with an undercurrent of resignation, in her voice. She looked past him for a moment, as though his scrutiny had made her uncomfortable. He didn't fool himself that she was looking at the Riverbend Farmers' Co-op calendar hanging on the wall behind him.

He waited for her to go on. It was quiet in the office area. Linda Christman, the bookkeeper, had gone to lunch. His granddad was still chewing the fat with Harvey. Someone was loading lumber out in the yard. He could hear Bill Webber's amplified voice calling for the yard boy to bring up the forklift. But Tessa took her time, ordering her thoughts, or gathering her courage, or both.

"I had every intention of leaving town this morning. But as I said, circumstances have changed. I called my sister from the phone booth in front of the courthouse. My nieces have been exposed to chicken pox. I've never had chicken pox." She was looking at him again, not past him, and he didn't have to guess about the emotion in her cornflower-blue eyes. It was plain to read. Fear. Not for herself but for her unborn child. "I can't take the chance of catching it from the girls and risk harming my baby."

Mitch nodded his agreement.

"I would have to find someplace to stay if I go on to Albany. I need money badly. Another job like this one isn't going to fall into my lap." She gave him another little half smile. "Not that I have much of a lap left these days."

He liked that about her, too. Her determination to see the lighter side of things.

"So you decided to stick around Riverbend as an informed choice and not on impulse. I'd probably do the same thing if I were in your shoes."

"I can't promise you how long I'll stay. My baby's due the middle of December. I need to be settled in Albany and to have found an obstetrician before then."

"What will you do about prenatal care while you're here?"

"I have my medical records with me. I saw my old doctor just a week ago. I'm healthy. But..."

"One of the docs at the hospital is a friend of mine. I'll give her a call and set you up with an appointment."

Her lips tightened almost imperceptibly, and her eyes sparkled with challenge. For a moment he thought she'd refuse his offer. But in the end she swallowed her pride. "Thank you. Does that mean I get the job?"

"I'm as desperate as you are, Tessa. I'm making an informed choice, too. Yes, the job's yours for as long as you care to stay. The apartment above the boathouse, too. Just like I told you this morning."

"I won't stay there for nothing. I'll pay fair rent. Is a hundred dollars a week enough?"

Mitch snorted. He couldn't help himself. For a moment the fear was back in her eyes and he was immediately sorry. She probably figured he was going to ask for more. "This isn't California. Three-bedroom houses might rent for a hundred dollars a week in these parts, but not the boathouse. I'll tell you what. I can't offer you any benefits. My insurance carrier won't cover you until you've worked here for six months. And they won't cover your pregnancy even then."

"I understand that."

"Consider the use of the apartment the only fringe benefit I can offer."

"I—"

"Take it or leave it."

Once more she surprised him, this time by not arguing. "I'll take it. Providing I can start work as soon as possible."

"First thing tomorrow." Mitch stood up. She did, too, and he motioned with his hand for her to precede him down the stairs.

She stayed put. "I want to start today. Now. Or the deal's off."

"You drive a hard bargain." He didn't want to push her any further, or she might bolt and run. She was going to be staying in Riverbend for at least a couple of weeks. He felt like a kid who had made a wish on a star and had it come true.

The only thing he had to remember now was not to get too close to that star, or he might find himself blinded by the brightness.

"SHE'S GOING to be staying in the boathouse," Caleb told Sam as they were setting the table for supper. He stopped putting down forks and spoons so that Sam could watch his lips. "She's going to work at the hardware for a couple of weeks."

"To help you and Dad."

"That's the idea." His great-grandfather's lips were pulled into a tight line. That meant he wasn't happy.

"It's hard working at the store," Sam said. "She's going to have a baby. Should she be doing that work?" He'd noticed she was pregnant right away. It was pretty hard to miss.

"Having a baby is a natural thing. As long as we don't let her lift anything too heavy, she'll be okay."

"Where's her husband?" Sam set a glass of water by Caleb's plate. He didn't sign much with his great-grandfather. Caleb's arthritis was too bad.

"I don't know she has one."

"Why not?" The pregnant ladies he knew in Riverbend had husbands.

"Haven't got the foggiest notion why not." The old man shook his head and frowned. "The world's changing fast. In my day a pregnant woman didn't go gallivanting around the country by herself. She stayed home and let her husband take care of her. Women don't think they need husbands to raise kids these days, more's the pity."

Sam couldn't catch all the words. Caleb liked to ramble on to himself, and he didn't always remember to look at Sam while he did it. Granddad Caleb was losing his hearing, too. Pretty soon, he said, he and Sam would be in the same boat.

Except Granddad Caleb had been able to hear things all his life. He didn't have to guess what a bird singing sounded like. He didn't have to wear a hearing aid and use an augmenter in class and feel like a geek.

"She's pretty," Sam said. "Her hair's the same color as Mom's."

"She doesn't look anything like your mother." Caleb rounded on him with narrowed eyes. With his big nose and white hair, he looked just like an eagle when he did that.

"I know. Mom's shorter than her. And skinnier."

"Yeah, I guess she does have the same color hair now that I think on it. But that's all they've got in common, I hope." Caleb turned away as he said the last words so that Sam wouldn't see him. But he was too slow. Granddad Caleb didn't like Sam's mom. He'd never said so out loud, but Sam knew. He couldn't hear everything people said, but he was pretty good at figuring out what they didn't say.

"I hope she stays awhile. If she helps out at the store, maybe you and Dad won't be so busy all the time." He was worried that if he made the basketball team this year, his dad would always be working and never be able to get to the after-school games.

"It would be nice to slow down a bit. But your dad up and hiring a woman practically off the street isn't my idea of the way to go about it. I don't see any good coming of this." Caleb saw him watching his lips and abruptly stopped talking. He motioned to the refrigerator. Sam took his cue and went to get the sliced ham and homemade baked beans that Granddad Caleb's friends Ruth and Rachel Steele had brought over for them two days ago. They'd also brought an apple pie. But that hadn't lasted long.

"Do you suppose she knows how to bake apple pies?"

Caleb shrugged, looking at the clock. "Danged if I know. Probably not. Women these days don't like to cook no better'n men."

"Dad's a good cook."

"By necessity, not temperament."

Sam wasn't sure what his great-grandfather was talking about. "What's temperament mean?" He tried hard, but he knew he didn't get it right. Sam sighed. Another word to add to his practice list with his therapist.

"I'll explain later. Let's eat. It's been a long time since I had my lunch."

"Do you suppose the lady in the boathouse has anything to eat for supper?" He'd seen her red car drive in a little while ago. He could see lights in the boathouse from the kitchen window.

"I reckon she got herself all this way from California, she can find her way to the grocery and buy some food."

"And milk for her baby. I know that women who are going to have babies are supposed to drink a lot of milk so their babies are big and strong."

"Who told you that?"

"Tara Webber's stepmom had a baby last spring, remember? She told me."

A lot of his friends' moms were having babies. He wouldn't mind a baby brother or sister himself. Except his mom didn't live with them anymore. He could hardly remember when she had. She'd moved to Chicago so long ago. Chicago wasn't all that far away.

He'd looked it up on the map once. But she hadn't been back to Riverbend since a year ago last Fourth of July. She hadn't even called him on the phone for weeks and weeks. Not even since he'd got his own phone. The one with the special earphones so that he could really hear her voice.

She didn't have a computer, so he couldn't e-mail her. She said she'd get one if his dad sent her the money. She said she couldn't afford to buy one on her own, and she wasn't allowed to e-mail him from work. Sam wanted to believe her. But the truth was, his dad did send her money, and she always had something else to spend it on.

He was almost getting used to it—his mom not doing what she said she was going to do didn't hurt so much anymore. Most of the time. But it would be nice to have a mom again. If he couldn't have his own mom come back to live with them, maybe his dad could find another woman to be his mom.

Sam bent his head and pretended to study the piece of ham on his plate. Only he really wasn't checking out the fat on the edge of his ham slice. He was thinking. Thinking real hard.

His dad must like the lady in the boathouse. If he liked her some, maybe he could learn to like her a lot. And if he liked her a lot...well, wasn't that how grown-ups sometimes fell in love?

When Sam's mom had first left, he hadn't wanted his dad to have any girlfriends. He figured if his dad had a girlfriend, then his mom would never come back. But as a guy got older he saw things differently. In January he would be eleven. Practically a teenager.

Almost a grown-up. He could share his dad now. With the right woman. Maybe Tessa was the right woman.

She didn't have a husband, as far as Sam could tell.

And she was already going to have a baby.

That was good, too.

Once, just before his mom left, he'd come into the room while she was arguing with his dad. Her face was all red and scrunched up like it got when she was going to cry. His dad had seen him and tried to make her be quiet, but she wouldn't. Sam was getting pretty good at reading lips by then, and he'd seen what she was saying before she figured out he was there. Sam had never forgotten that one sentence. She'd said, *No more babies, Mitch. No more babies like Sam.*

But Tessa's baby wouldn't be like him. Her baby would be able to hear.

Tessa didn't have a husband. His dad didn't have a wife. And Sam didn't have a mom, or a baby brother or sister. If he could get his dad and Tessa together, he'd have everything he needed to make a family again.

# CHAPTER FIVE

"I DON'T KNOW, Ruth. I can't decide whether I want stripes or a floral pattern in the bathroom. I wish you'd tell me which you like best."

"I don't think stripes will work, Rachel," said Rachel's twin sister in a tone of long suffering. "The house is as old as we are and the walls aren't all that straight." The two women sat surrounded by sample books at the old-fashioned oak library table in the middle of the hardware store.

Rachel pursed her pink lips. "But this one is so pretty."

Everything about the two old ladies, Tessa had noticed, was pink and white. From the tops of their curly white heads to the tips of their toes.

Rachel Steele—they'd introduced themselves the moment Tessa walked up to ask them if she could be of help—was dressed in a pink sweat suit, with colored bands of rose and mauve on the sleeves. Ruth wore a raspberry sweatshirt and matching sweatpants. Both were wearing identical pairs of pristine white tennis shoes. They were small and plump and looked like two pieces of candy that had somehow found their way out of their gilded box and into the wallpaper-

and-paint department of Sterling Hardware and Building Supply.

"Rachel. Ruth." Caleb looked over the waist-high wall that blocked off the view of the office on the upper floor. "Good morning, ladies."

"Good morning, Caleb." Rachel glanced up from the sample book, the frown that had marred her face disappearing in a smile that deepened myriad tiny wrinkles around her mouth and eyes. "The search goes on. I'm almost in despair of ever finding the right wallpaper pattern for my bathroom."

"The paper on the walls now is just fine," her sibling insisted. "We've got better things to do this morning."

"You always say that. I'm determined this time to find just the right paper."

"Perhaps a floral stripe?" Tessa suggested, pulling sample books from the shelves. She'd told Mitch the day he hired her that she didn't intend to spend her time in paint-and-wallpaper, but that's where she'd ended up.

Working for Mitch, she was finding, wasn't the same as working at Home-Mart, because Mitch's hardware store was different, and so were his customers. Some of them had been coming to Sterling's since long before he was born, she suspected. Many of them were friends and contemporaries of Caleb's, like the ladies she was helping at the moment, and probably of Mitch's late parents'. The men smiled politely, tipped their feed-company hats and headed for Mitch or Caleb for their electrical and plumbing needs, or sought out Bill Webber in the lumberyard.

The women did the same if they were buying hardware. But if they were looking for paint or wallpaper, they brought their questions to her. Riverbend was a traditional place, she was coming to learn. And one of the traditional things about it was the unwritten rule that men didn't like to look at wallpaper books or paint-chip cards. Even men whose business it was to know about such things.

So Tessa smiled when she was approached with a request, and debated the merits of vinyl versus grass cloth, and enamel versus latex, flat finish or semigloss, from morning to night.

And she liked it.

Mitch's customers weren't workaholic boomers with high blood pressure who'd been told to get a hobby. Or people who'd spent three hundred dollars on tools and how-to books and still couldn't miter a corner. Or thirty-something couples, with two precocious, ill-mannered children in tow, who were looking for just the right lighting for that dark corner of the study.

They were hardworking farmers, factory workers, housewives and professional people with pride in their homes and deep roots in the community. They did most of their own work and didn't want or expect a huge display of home-decorating magazines by the cash registers or weekend classes in sponge painting and plumbing 101.

"Do you think a floral stripe will work, Ms. Masterson?" Rachel asked, looking over her shoulder as her twin drifted away to continue her conversation with Caleb. "My sister's correct about one thing. The walls aren't quite as straight as they could be. Miriam Harris is going to hang the paper for us. She said not to worry, to buy what I want. She's very good.'' Rachel paused. ''Have you met her yet?''

''No, I'm afraid not. I've only been working here a week.''

''She's a lovely person. Widowed so young, poor thing. I'm sure you'd like her. I don't want to make the job harder for her than it has to be.''

''The floral stripe you were looking at in this book,'' Tessa said, tapping her finger on one of the open sample books on the table as she brought the conversation back on course, ''has a straight-across match and it's wide enough that your paper hanger can compensate for any problems she encounters with an off-plumb wall whenever she comes to a corner.''

Rachel Steele peered at the pattern over the top of her glasses. ''Why, yes. I see what you mean. And it is lovely. I liked it immediately. My eye keeps going back to it.'' Tessa had noticed that. ''The roses look real enough to pick. And I can accessorize around those little yellow and blue forget-me-nots. I'll buy new towels. They have such lovely thick ones at Killian's department store. Have you seen them, Ms. Masterson? You'd be pleasantly surprised, I think. But perhaps not. Caleb said you lived in California. I expect Killian's is very small potatoes compared to the stores you shopped in there.''

''I only lived in California eight months,'' Tessa said, closing several of the rejected sample books so as not to distract Rachel further. ''But yes, the stores were very chic. And very expensive.''

"Well, Killian's has excellent value for your dollar. You really should give them a look see when you decide on a permanent home." The old lady sounded as if it was a settled thing that Tessa was staying on in Riverbend.

Tessa didn't know quite how to respond. She had no idea what explanation Mitch had given for hiring her. His other employees had been polite and helpful, but none of the men had asked her about her private life. And the only other female employee, Linda Christman, the bookkeeper, was expecting her first grandchild to be born in February. The few conversations they'd had over the past week centered on babies, not Tessa's past or her future plans, which suited Tessa just fine.

"I'll be sure to do that." But of course, she would probably never set foot in the old-fashioned department store on Main Street. She wasn't going to be living in Riverbend permanently. She'd be gone long before she needed towels or new curtains. The well-worn leather sofa in the boathouse could use a little sprucing up, though. An afghan in camel and gold, maybe, and a couple of throw pillows to hug close on a cold winter night. A nice thank-you gift to Mitch and his grandfather.

Rachel ran her finger over the wallpaper sample. "Ruthie, come here, dear. What do you think of this one? Ms. Masterson believes it will do nicely."

Ruth came back to the table, along with Caleb Sterling. "You've chosen from the most expensive book," she said.

It was easy to see which of the twins had the more

forceful personality. Ruth looked and sounded just like
a teacher Tessa had had in third grade—the way Tessa
herself might sound forty years in the future if she
realized her dream to teach history. The thought tick-
led her fancy, and she raised her fingers to her lips to
brush away a smile.

"I imagine this will be the last time I repaper the
bathroom in this lifetime. I want to be sure I get a
good-quality paper."

Tessa busied herself returning sample books to the
shelf. She didn't want to appear as if she were eaves-
dropping on the Steele sisters' discussion. It was surprising, and a little alarming, how interested she was
becoming in the lives of the people she waited on.
Was this an occupational hazard of living in a small
town?

Or perhaps it was because you saw these same people every day, and over time learned to care about
them in a way you never could in a city.

"Let's sleep on it," Ruth suggested in the same no-
nonsense tone she'd used before.

Rachel pushed back her chair. "I suppose you're
right. After all, I'll be looking at that paper every
morning for the rest of my days."

"Take the sample book with you," Caleb offered,
giving Tessa a sharp look. She should have suggested
that herself, but she'd been too lost in thought. She
sighed. Another point against her. "Prop it up against
the side of the tub and see how it looks on the wall.
You might find it's not what you want at all. Or it just
might be perfect."

"An excellent suggestion, Caleb. Yes. That's exactly what I'll do."

"I'll carry it out to the car for you," Tessa said, leaning forward to pick up the heavy book. Her belly brushed against the table and the baby did a somersault. She sucked in her breath on a little "Oh" of surprise. She wondered if she would ever get used to the feeling of another human being moving around inside her.

"No, you might hurt yourself," Rachel warned. "The baby could get the cord wrapped around its neck." It was the only reference either sister had made to her pregnancy.

"Rachel, that's an old wives' tale," Ruth scolded.

"I'll carry it," Caleb said, taking the book from Tessa before she could protest that she was pregnant, not incapacitated.

"We'll have it back tomorrow," Ruth promised.

"I'll need more time than that to decide," Rachel said.

"You take as long as you like," Caleb urged, settling the argument.

"Yes, yes. I'll do just that," Rachel agreed. "Goodbye, Ms. Masterson. It was nice meeting you."

Rachel was all smiles again. Her blue eyes sparkled with quiet satisfaction, and Tessa rethought her first impression that Ruth made all the decisions for the two. Rachel might not be as outspoken as her sister, but Tessa had the feeling that sooner or later, the flowery striped paper would find its way onto Rachel's bathroom wall if that was what she wanted.

"You handled that very well," said a voice from

behind Tessa as she turned to replace the sample books on the shelves.

She looked over her shoulder to see who had spoken. Another elderly lady was standing by the display of paint-chip cards. "Rachel and Ruth can take hours just to decide what to have for lunch."

Tessa tried not to smile at the blunt assessment of the sisters' personalities. "I really wouldn't know. I only met them a few minutes ago."

"Trust me. We've been friends for over sixty years. My name's Margaret Leatherman, by the way. And you're Tessa?" she asked, looking pointedly at the name tag on Tessa's royal-blue Sterling Hardware vest.

"Tessa Masterson."

"I'll bet Tessa's short for Teresa, isn't it."

Tessa laughed. "Yes, it is. But no one calls me that."

"Then I won't, either. But you may call me Maggie."

"Thank you, Maggie. Can I help you with something?"

"I need paint for my kitchen. But unlike Rachel Steele, I know exactly the shade of green I want. The trouble is, so far I haven't found a paint chip to match."

"If you have a picture or even a piece of fabric that color, we can match it on our computer," Tessa offered.

Maggie looked interested. She was tall and heavyset with salt-and-pepper hair pulled into a bun on top of her head. She was wearing jeans and running shoes and a rust-colored sweater open over a T-shirt that said Genuine Antique Person in big red letters. "One of the ladies at the Altar Society meeting told me you could do that. Seems hard to believe, but with computers these days, I suppose anything's possible. Here." She fished in a big canvas bag slung over her shoulder and pulled out an old knitted baby sweater in a soft shade of apple-green. "This is exactly the color I want. I knitted this for my oldest son when he was born. He'll be forty-nine next week, so please take care of it."

"I'll be very careful," Tessa promised. She had so few things for her baby, only some sleepers and little T-shirts that fastened between the legs, which she'd acquired in the first flush of her pregnancy—when she thought Brian would be as happy as she was. She had nothing at all handmade with loving care like the apple-green sweater. "Is there anything else you want to look for while I run the match for you?"

"No. I'll just hang around and watch you, and ask nosy questions about how a California girl like you came to end up in Riverbend."

"I got here because I have a deficient sense of direction and almost ran out of gas," Tessa said, slightly taken aback by the old lady's directness.

"We're a long way from the interstate."

"I know." Tessa smiled. "If I may have the sweater, I'll get started."

"You're not brushing me off that easily, young lady. I have ways of finding things out." The broad smile on Maggie's face, and the twinkle in her eyes took the rudeness from the words.

"Aunt Maggie, what are you doing here today?" Mitch came down the wide aisle that bisected the sales floor. He'd evidently come from the lumberyard. The scent of fresh-cut wood clung to his clothes, and sawdust flecked his dark hair. Tessa found herself wanting to reach out and brush it away, and tightened her grip on the baby sweater to keep from doing just that. Maggie Leatherman felt no such reluctance. She reached up and brushed the sawdust away with the ease of long familiarity.

"I've finally found the color I want to paint my kitchen, and Tessa says she can match the shade exactly on your computer."

"She can. Want to watch, or do you want to come have lunch with me? I'm just heading off to the Sunnyside for a sandwich."

"I could eat a bite. But I insist that Tessa come with us."

"Oh, no. I couldn't possibly." She didn't want to be seen eating with Mitch Sterling. She was almost certain there was enough gossip about his impetuous hire swirling around Riverbend as it was.

"Sure you can. I'm buying," Maggie insisted.

"There's no use arguing with Aunt Maggie, Tessa."

"The special today is pot roast and apple pie. I called the restaurant and asked before I left the farm."

"The Sunnyside serves the best pot roast in the county," Mitch told her. "How can you turn that down?"

"I can't," Tessa said, giving in because she was

hungry and almost as starved for company as for food. "I'd be happy to join you for lunch."

THE SMELL OF POT ROAST and gravy hit Mitch with almost tangible force as he held open the door of the café so that Maggie and Tessa could enter first. His stomach growled so loudly he was afraid the two women would hear it. He'd missed breakfast because Sam had been playing a video game until the last possible minute and then couldn't find his homework paper. Belle had treed a squirrel, or so she thought, and had to be dragged back into the house and put in the basement because she was covered with mud.

Caleb had been cranky and short-tempered over the muddy paw prints on the kitchen floor, and by the time Mitch had deposited Sam at school, he'd been ten minutes late opening the store. Two pickup trucks with their impatient drivers had been waiting in the parking lot when he got there. All in all it was one of those days that Mitch wished he'd joined the French Foreign Legion right out of high school.

But letting his curious aunt Maggie maneuver Tessa into having lunch with them might be the beginning of an upturn in the day. Tessa had kept to herself all week. She seldom left the boathouse when she wasn't working, and he suspected she was catching up on her sleep. The fatigue lines that had bracketed her mouth and eyes had disappeared. She looked a little less haunted, too. The shadows that darkened those blue eyes from cornflower to twilight were fading.

Mitch had kept his distance. She was as wary as a doe in hunting season, and he didn't want to scare her off. But deep down inside, he had to admit he was hoping he could find a way to keep her in Riverbend.

Having lunch with Aunt Maggie as chaperon wasn't the ideal first step, but it was the best shot he was going to get.

"Mitch, got a booth empty over here," Lucy Garvey called from across the crowded room. Mitch headed in that direction, acknowledging a friendly wave from Evie Mazerik, Aaron's mother, perched on a stool at her usual spot behind the cash register.

"What can I get for you?" the waitress asked after they'd seated themselves, Tessa and Maggie on one side of the high-backed booth, Mitch on the other. Tessa hadn't made a fuss about sitting in the booth, the way Kara used to when she was pregnant. She maneuvered her way carefully across the seat, being careful not to bump her rounded belly on the table, and smiled as Maggie thumped down beside her.

"Still have a couple of orders of the special left, if you want some, but you'll have to make up your mind right away—I can't guarantee how long it will last," Lucy informed them, order pad at the ready. Lucy was the sister of his best friend, Charlie Callahan, and Mitch had known her all his life.

"Sounds good to me," Mitch said. "Aunt Maggie, what about you?"

"I'll have the special, too. And don't be stingy with the gravy."

"Gotcha."

"And you, ma'am?" Lucy's voice was suddenly more formal. It was her waitress voice, reserved for the few tourists and out-of-towners who found their way to the Sunnyside.

"I'll have a salad, please. French dressing on the side. And a big glass of milk."

"You can bring her the milk," Maggie said imperiously, "and the salad, too, if she wants it. But add another special to the order."

"No, really—"

Maggie Leatherman hadn't taken no for an answer for as long as Mitch could remember. She wasn't about to start now. "You're eating for two. And you look as if it's been a while since you had a good meal. I'd cook you one myself, but after forty-nine years of cooking for Will and my boys, I'm retired from the kitchen, unless the spirit moves me."

Tessa looked at Mitch, a little frown line between her eyebrows. He shrugged and tried to put her at ease. Maggie was even nosier than his granddad when she put her mind to it, but she didn't have a mean bone in her body. "Aunt Maggie's been bossing people around since she was a sergeant in the WACs in World War II. Just sit back and enjoy the meal."

"Longer than that. I helped raise six brothers and sisters. All younger than me. All still living, thank the Lord."

"Okay." Tessa spread her hands in surrender and gave Mitch that little half smile that sent a thrill of electricity along his nerve ends, as if he'd touched a bare wire. She looked up at Lucy and smiled a little more broadly. "So I guess I'm going to have the special, too."

"It comes with dessert. Apple pie. A la mode is fifty cents extra."

"We want the works," Maggie responded.

"You got it." Lucy hurried off to take orders at another table.

"Now we can talk." Maggie settled back against the cushion. "I haven't seen you since Will and the boys started taking off beans, Mitch. Seems I do nothing but haul soybeans to the elevator these days. How's business?"

"Can't complain, Aunt Maggie," Mitch said, giving the ritual response as he stirred cream into the cup of coffee Lucy had poured. In a small town it didn't pay to brag too much in front of customers, just as it wasn't good form to complain when times weren't so good. "Got the plans for the new greenhouse from the contractor yesterday. It's going to be a real beauty."

"A new greenhouse?" Maggie repeated. "Your granddad hasn't said anything about it." She sipped on the diet cola Lucy placed in front of her, along with Tessa's glass of milk and a basket of dinner rolls and a jar of strawberry jam.

Lucy rolled her eyes. "He's doing it just to get more of my hard-earned tip money. As if I don't spend enough at your place buying plants for my garden as it is."

The greenhouse was a Victorian design, glass and cedar. It would be a showplace on the east side of the building. He'd seen one like it at a hardware show last year in Chicago. Their spring and summer vegetable and bedding-plant business had outgrown the plastic and metal greenhouses they'd used in the past. The only landscaper in town had retired two years before, and that was a niche they could fill, too. Caleb hadn't been too keen on the idea at first, but he'd come around once he'd seen the plans and the estimated increase in revenue.

"I want to get it framed and under roof before the weather turns bad. Then the guys can work on the inside when it gets slow this winter." Tessa had been tearing her dinner roll into pieces while he talked. She stopped and raised her eyes to his. Her expression was assessing and easy to read. When the weather got bad and business slowed down at Home-Mart, they just laid people off. But that wasn't the Sterling way. It wasn't the Riverbend way. Here you kept employees on the payroll regardless.

Mitch stopped talking. What made him think Tessa was interested in his long-term plans for the business, or his life? She'd made it clear she wasn't going to be in town more than a few weeks. Her future didn't include a man with a hearing-impaired son and cantankerous grandfather, a guy who planted pumpkins among the marigolds in front of his business to give away to kids at Halloween and who worked at the concession stand for high-school football games.

The silence stretched out for a moment or two before Maggie turned to Tessa with a new subject. "Mitch's father was my godson. Celia, Mitch's grandmother, always wanted a big family, but she and Caleb were only blessed with Dale. And Dale and his wife, Charlotte, God rest their souls, they only had Mitch here. Not like me and Will. We raised five boys," she said with pride. "And eleven grandchildren."

"How wonderful for you," Tessa said, her smile making the words more than just polite.

"They're a trial sometimes. But I love them all. Mitch's grandmother and I were best friends from the time we were five and went to the one-room school together."

"A one-room school?"

Lucy returned and set three plates of steaming pot roast and gravy before them. Maggie answered Tessa's question as they busied themselves with napkins and salt and pepper shakers. "Each section hereabouts had their own one-room school in those days. We rode one of the plow horses when the weather was bad and walked when it was good. Later my dad got me an old Model-A Ford when I was old enough to go to high school here in town. You didn't need to be six-teen to get a license in those days if you lived on a farm. And girls learned to drive just like boys. What good times we had!"

Maggie was looking off into the distance, remembering times and places that were well-worn memories years before Mitch was even born. She looked a little sad, and he knew it was because she still missed her girlhood friend, though his grandmother had been in her grave these ten years past.

"I'd love to hear all about your days growing up on a farm and your service during the war," Tessa said, her fork poised over a roasted potato swimming in rich beef gravy.

"Someday when the farming's done, I'll come into town and we'll have lunch and I'll tell you all about it," Maggie promised. "Why, I've got as many stories as Laura Ingalls Wilder. Wish someone would make a TV show out of them and make me a bushel of money.'' She laughed. ''That's not likely to happen, so I guess I'll keep on doing a little day trading in cattle futures. Who knows? I might strike it rich like the president's wife, and me and Will can retire to Florida and bake our old bones in the sun. Now, let's eat before the food gets cold.''

''THANK YOU for keeping Maggie from asking me about…things,'' Tessa said as she and Mitch crossed the parking lot to the store. They'd dropped the ''genuine antique person'' off at the grain elevator. Tessa had marveled at the old lady's agility and expertise as she fired up the huge green tractor and drove out onto the street, pulling a tandem of empty grain wagons behind her, promising to pick up her paint when she came through with the next load later in the afternoon.

''It's just a reprieve, you know,'' Mitch warned Tessa as they approached the hardware store. If Aunt Maggie's determined to find out your life history, she'll do it.'' The parking lot was half-full. Caleb and Bill Webber were probably knee-deep in customers, but Mitch lingered outside with Tessa, enjoying the slight warmth of the October sun.

''I have a feeling the same could be said about Ruth and Rachel Steele.''

He fixed his steady brown eyes on Tessa. ''Riverbend is a small place. You're a stranger. And fair game for some. Not Ruth and Rachel, or Aunt Maggie, no matter how nosy she comes across. But there are others a lot less charitable and goodhearted and just as curious. Don't let yourself think for a moment there aren't.''

Over the past few days she'd become increasingly convinced that Riverbend was the kind of idyllic small town she'd been searching for in her heart. Mitch must have read that longing in her eyes or her voice. She hadn't thought she was so transparent, but apparently to this man she was.

A tractor and wagons rumbled by on the way to the elevator down the street. The dry earthy scent of the grain they carried wafted by on the breeze. Mitch stopped walking as they reached the shadow of the hardware store. From around back she could hear the insistent beep, beep, beep of a tow motor as it backed up with a load of lumber.

''I don't want to see you hurt, Tessa.'' He was warning her off, perhaps from more than the hurt that small-town gossips could inflict, Unlike Brian, unlike the men her mother had unwisely fallen for, Mitch was an honorable man. A small-town knight in shining armor, riding to her rescue in the front seat of a police cruiser.

But rescued damsels in distress sometimes fell in love with their knights.

In fairy tales. Not in real life.

And this knight in shining armor had enough problems of his own, without taking on hers.

*God, I haven't let him see I have feelings for him, have I?* she thought in sudden panic. No. She wasn't guilty of that because she hadn't let herself think about Mitch Sterling as anything but a boss since the morning she'd set foot in the store. It was a promise she'd try very hard not to break, for her baby's sake, as much as her own.

She felt the baby move inside her, almost as though she, too, could hear the sound of Mitch's low deep voice. "Don't worry. I won't be staying around long enough to get hurt."

## CHAPTER SIX

TESSA HAD DECIDED to teach herself to knit. She'd never held a pair of knitting needles in her life, but holding Maggie Leatherman's baby sweater in her hands that day at the hardware store had triggered a longing inside her. A longing to create something to welcome her baby into the world.

The vague desire had coalesced into purpose when she'd come across the Stitch in Time Shoppe, around the corner from Killian's department store. Most of the interior of the long narrow shop was taken up with needlepoint kits and row upon row of fabrics in prints and solids. Beautiful quilts hung from the walls and could be seen in various stages of completion in frames at the back of the store. But as interesting as the combinations of color and pattern were to Tessa, it was the honeycomb of shelves along the far wall that drew her. They were filled with skein after skein of knitting yarn. All the colors of the earth and sky, pastels and primaries, thick and thin, soft and heavy. And toward the end of the display a section of pinks and blues, pale greens and downy duck yellows.

Yarn for baby things. It beckoned her to hold it in her hands and fashion it into something soft and warm for her baby.

The fantasy brought a smile to her lips and her heart.

The reality brought a frown and an urge to throw everything into the river.

"Knit three, purl two." She sat on the worn leather sofa, her feet drawn up under her, and practiced the stitches the apple-cheeked lady who ran the shop had taught her.

"You don't want to tackle anything too hard for your first project," she'd explained. "Here's a nice little sweater, no set-in sleeves, no buttonholes to work. Believe me, there's nothing more discouraging than taking on a project that's beyond your skill level. It just plain turns you off."

So Tessa had bought the yarn and needles, the pattern book and stitch markers, and she'd spent the whole first evening casting on stitches. The next day she'd gone back for another lesson, then come home to knit row after row. She was getting pretty good at that. Purling was okay, but not as much fun as knitting. Now she had to put the stitches all together and come up with a sweater.

She pulled her lip between her teeth and concentrated on getting the lower edge, the ribbing, just so. No stitch too loose. No stitch too tight. And, heaven help her, none dropped at the end of the row.

The boathouse didn't have a TV, so she was already becoming familiar with the programming on the local radio station. In the evening WRBN played a mixture of classic rock and pop country tunes—if there wasn't a sporting event being broadcast from one county venue or another. And that was a *big* if. All the area teams got their chance to be on the radio. And all the area merchants bought commercial time.

It had surprised Tessa at first when she'd heard Mitch's voice telling listeners they could shop at Sterling Hardware and Building Supply with satisfaction, and be confident that they would get the best value for their dollar that he could provide. After all, his family had been doing business in the same location for more than seventy years. He sounded relaxed and at ease, as though he were talking to you over the counter at the hardware and not in a studio on the second floor of the Steele Building on Main Street.

No gags, no gimmicks. A message as straightforward as the man himself.

Tessa was fast coming to realize that she could learn just about anything she wanted to know about life in Riverbend if she listened to WRBN.

The announcers were more like the town criers of old than disc jockeys. Not only did they read advertising copy and give weather updates, they read the obituaries every morning at eight-twenty-five, the humane shelter report at nine-fifteen—listing the lost and found and adoptable animals—followed by the lunch menu at the seniors' center. And at ten o'clock the so-called "stork report." The circle of life in a small town. Old folks dying and new citizens making their appearance at the Riverbend Community Health Center. Even out-of-town births, phoned into the station by proud grandparents, were announced.

No one would care enough about her baby being born to make such an effort.

"We're all alone in this big world, little one," she whispered.

The slow sad music on the radio and the sound of rain dripping from the eaves had turned her mood melancholy. Tessa let her knitting rest in her lap and stared out into the darkness beyond the window. Every day that passed made her more and more reluctant to leave. She wasn't looking forward to her baby being born in a big impersonal hospital in a city where she knew no one but her sister, instead of in Riverbend, where she at least knew that one of the doctors was Mitch's friend, and the mayor's daughter was a nurse.

A silly way to feel, since she hadn't actually met those women, but it made no difference to her heart. No difference at all.

A scratching at the door was followed by a short sharp bark and a snuffling whine. It was Belle, Sam's dog, begging to be let inside. It wasn't the first time Belle had come visiting. But it was the first time Tessa was tempted to let her in.

"Hey, doggy, did you slip your leash?" she asked, opening the door. The night smelled of rain and smoke from Mitch's fireplace, and wet dog. Tessa wrinkled her nose, reconsidering her invitation. She'd opened the door only a crack, but it was enough for the big yellow dog to get her head through. And once Belle had her head through, the rest of her soon followed.

"Uh-oh," Tessa said, taking a step back, a little startled at the Lab's strength and determination. "I bet you're not supposed to be in here, right?"

Belle looked up at her, tongue lolling, a doggy grin

on her face proclaiming her pleasure at having made a successful entry into forbidden territory.

"You'd better go back outside right now," Tessa said, hesitating to reach out and grab Belle by her collar. "Will you take a bite out of my arm if I try that?" she wondered aloud.

Belle looked hurt at the suggestion that she would bite anyone. She sighed and rolled over to have her belly scratched. "All right—I'm sorry." Tessa laughed as she knelt with the aid of her hand on the back of one of the kitchen chairs. "I apologize. Of course you'd never bite anyone. There, girl. Does that feel good?"

The Lab sighed and wriggled closer, all seventy-five pounds of her, knocking her head against Tessa's belly. Tessa stood up, a little breathless. "Enough of that. If you want your ears scratched, come over to the couch like a good guest."

Belle surged to her feet and ambled across the room, looking back over her shoulder to make sure Tessa was following her. A knock sounded, then Sam's head appeared around the door, his wheat-colored hair darkened with raindrops.

"Hi," he said. "Have you seen— Belle!"

Tessa said, "Come in."

Sam hesitated a moment, then sidled into the room. "She ran away," he said slowly and with obvious care so Tessa could understand. "I've been looking for her all over the neighborhood."

"She's only been here a couple of minutes. I imagine she didn't want to be scolded for running away."

"Gramps makes her stay in the basement when she

gets muddy.'' Sam stomped across the floor in his oversize running shoes and grabbed Belle's collar and pulled. Belle pulled back. She and Sam weighed about the same, but she had the advantage of digging in with four feet, not just two.

"Why don't you both stay a minute," Tessa invited, facing Sam head-on so he could read her lips. "I promised Belle a good ear scratching."

"We shouldn't. Gramps doesn't know where I went. He's watching TV." By that Tessa surmised he meant Caleb was napping in front of the television and Sam hadn't bothered to wake him when he went looking for Belle.

"Where's your father?" The hardware closed at seven on weeknights. It was now a few minutes before eight.

"He's at a meeting."

Tessa remembered the town council was meeting tonight—she'd heard it on the radio. She glanced at the clock. She had no idea how long small-town council meetings might last. "Is your homework done?" she asked, still scratching Belle behind her ears. The dog's head was a comforting weight on her knee, Sam's presence a welcome change from her usual solitary evening.

"All but my vocabulary words." *Vocabulary* was scarcely recognizable, but being around Sam the past week had made her more familiar with his speech patterns, and she made an educated guess.

"Vocabulary," she repeated, emphasizing the combination of vowels and consonants that seemed the most difficult for him, the way she had seen Mitch do.

"Whatever," Sam said, giving her a sly grin that made him look like an angel whose halo was just a little tarnished.

"Okay, no word practice here," Tessa said. She'd been put neatly in her place, but she didn't mind. After all, what right did she have to act as an authority figure to Mitch's son? None at all. Sam knew that, even if she had forgotten for a moment.

"What are you doing?" Sam asked, pointing to her knitting.

"I'm trying to knit a sweater for my baby. It's much harder than I thought."

Sam looked at the inch of painstaking knitting with a skeptical eye. "Is that what you do when you don't have TV or the Internet?"

Tessa laughed. "Yes, it is."

Sam rested his elbows on the back of the sofa and dropped his chin into his hands. "Granddad Caleb didn't have a TV until he was as old as my dad," Sam said, talking so quickly Tessa could scarcely catch the words. He was a great kid, but he wasn't above testing her. He wanted to see if she'd do it again, attempt to assert her grown-up authority. He was going to see how much slack she'd cut him. She'd spent enough time with her sister's kids to read the signs.

Or was it because she was going to have a baby herself? Some kind of hormonal sharpening of her instincts, maybe? It didn't matter how she knew. It only mattered that she did.

"I'm sorry, Sam, I can't understand you," she said gently, but firmly. Her tone of voice couldn't register with Sam, she knew, but her body language and expression would. "If you don't speak more slowly and clearly, I'm going to have to ask you to write it down." She got up from her seat and went over to the kitchen drawer, where she'd found a couple of decks of cards and a writing tablet and pencil, testimony to the fact that the boathouse must have been the scene of many a Friday-night card game in its day.

She might not have any authority to correct Sam, but she had a duty. It was in his best interest to speak as clearly as possible. She wasn't doing him a favor by letting him get lazy with his words. Tessa held her breath, wondering how Sam would react to her ultimatum.

A spark of anger and humiliation flared in his blue eyes. "You're not my boss," he said very plainly.

"I know."

"I don't have to do what you say." He grabbed Belle by the collar and stalked toward the door. Or attempted to. It was hard to stalk when you were dragging your own weight in reluctant dog. "Damn it, Belle, come on."

Tessa didn't scold him for the mild curse. She'd played the heavy enough for one night. She was actually shaking a little. How did parents do it every day?

She wondered if she'd be any good at this parenting thing. She started forward to tap Sam on the shoulder and call him back.

Sam was two feet from the door when someone else knocked.

"Come in," she said.

Sam stopped in his tracks. Tessa didn't know if he

could hear the sharp tattoo of knuckles on wood, or if he could see a figure through the thin cotton curtain that screened the glass in the upper half of the door.

Her third unexpected visitor was Caleb, raindrops darkening the shoulders of his jacket and the red baseball cap he wore. ''There you are, boy. What are you doing out here?''

''Belle got loose. She came here,'' Sam said, indicating the whining dog by his side. Belle obviously wasn't ready to end her visit, even if Sam was.

''You know she's not supposed to run loose, Sam.''

''She got out of her kennel again.''

''I didn't know. Perhaps I shouldn't have let her in.'' Tessa said. ''I was going to bring her over to the house—''

''Shouldn't be your place to be bringing the dog home,'' Caleb said, still unsmiling. He removed his baseball cap with old-fashioned courtesy and held it between his gnarled hands. ''But I do thank you. She means a lot to the boy, and she's going to get hit by a car sure as shooting if she keeps running loose.''

''I enjoyed having her,'' Tessa assured him. ''She's a good dog. Won't you sit down?'' she invited. She wasn't at all comfortable around Mitch's grandfather, but it was so nice to have the little apartment filled with voices. A dog lying on the rug would be a comforting sight. All she needed was a fireplace to make it perfect.

''We should be getting back to the house.''

''I...I baked brownies. They're just from a mix, but I could use someone to help me eat them. I'm watching my weight, you know.'' She smiled, hoping to coax one from Caleb in return.

He didn't smile, but he didn't refuse her invitation. ''Thank you,'' he said formally. ''I'd be pleased to have a brownie.''

''Sam? Do you like brownies.'' The boy hesitated. Tessa realized he was waiting for her to tell Caleb of his rudeness. He was watching her intently, eyes narrowed. She smiled at him, too, ignoring the opportunity to report his misdemeanor. Chocolate was the best peace offering she could think of. ''They're double-chocolate walnut.''

Sam nodded, then grinned. The anger and humiliation she'd glimpsed in his eyes a few moments before was gone. ''Yes,'' he said clearly. ''I'd like one. Do you have milk?''

He was a bright and inquisitive child. It must be horribly frustrating to have such trouble communicating even the simplest requests. But she'd be doing him no favor in letting him misbehave, either. She smiled, showing him she agreed to a truce. ''Brownies and milk coming up. Make yourselves comfortable, won't you?''

She bustled about taking chipped and mismatched plates and glasses from the metal cupboard. She didn't have napkins, but paper towels would do. She'd picked a few last-of-the-season daisies from alongside the boathouse and put them in a small vase on the table. Sam took the glasses to the table and poured milk from the Shirley Temple pitcher Tessa had found pushed to the back of the highest shelf.

''I hope you don't mind me using this,'' she said to

Caleb as he pulled out a chair. "I found it in the cupboard. It really shouldn't be out here. I assume it's quite valuable."

Caleb picked up the small dark blue pitcher and studied the smiling face of the curly-headed little girl. "I have no idea where this came from. We haven't used this place for years. Maybe the people who bought the house from me and my wife left it behind."

"Mitch told me you sold the house when he was a boy." Tessa hadn't been inside Mitch's house. She wondered what it was like. High ceilings, she supposed, and dark old woodwork. Or had it been remodeled to a high-tech gloss? It would be a shame if it had.

"Me and Celia—that's my late wife—we wanted something smaller. She had trouble with arthritis in her knees. We had a nice little rambler over in the new addition. But Mitch loved this house. It went on the market right after Sam was born. He scraped up every penny he could beg, borrow or steal to get it. I'm kinda glad he did now that there's only me and him and the boy left."

It was the longest, most personal speech Caleb had ever made to her. Tessa searched for the right response. Sam was eating his brownie, oblivious to what the grown-ups at the table were discussing.

"Mitch is very conscious of his roots," she said.

Caleb considered her words. She was afraid for a moment that he would lash out and say that she didn't know a damn thing about how his grandson felt, but he surprised her. "More so than I ever was," he said at last. "Maybe it was growing up trying to make ends meet all through the depression. Then going into the army right out of high school. I'd never been out of Sycamore County until I went overseas on my eighteenth birthday. I wasn't even twenty when we marched into Berlin. Made me a little less sentimental, maybe. Or just glad to be alive. I wanted to move on with my life. Celia wasn't from around these parts. She didn't even like the place. Anyway, that old house across the driveway didn't mean near as much to me then as it does now. I'm glad Mitch brought it back into the family.''

Tessa stared down at her untouched brownie. ''The Sterling house,'' she said very quietly. There had never been a Masterson house. Just a series of shabby apartments and run-down duplexes. Even the condo she'd shared with Brian hadn't felt like a home—although she knew in her heart that it should have.

''That's what it's called around town. Always been the Sterling house, no matter who was living here.'' Caleb took a bite of his brownie, then looked at Sam. He tapped his finger on the tabletop. Sam looked up. ''You got homework, boy?''

''It's done,'' Sam said, not quite meeting the old man's gaze.

Caleb tapped his finger again. ''Vocabulary words?''

Sam made a face. ''No.''

''You need to be working on them.''

''Dad's going to help me when he gets home.'' Sam lifted his plate. ''Could I have another brownie, please?''

Tessa laughed, pleased, even though she knew there

was almost nothing a ten-year-old boy wouldn't ask to have seconds of. "Certainly you may." A thought struck her. Perhaps Mitch didn't allow Sam to have seconds of dessert. A great many parents limited their children's intake of sugar and fat. She looked at Caleb. "Is it all right if he has another brownie?"

"That'd be fine. Can't say I blame the boy for asking."

"Would you like another?"

"I would, but I'll pass. I have to watch my sugar intake these days."

She nodded.

It was quiet in the little room for a while, except for the sound of Belle's snores, the clink of Sam's fork against the china plate and the faint music from the radio. The song ended and a series of commercials began. One of them was Mitch talking about the store's big fall sale.

Belle woke up and padded over to the radio, then stood facing it, head cocked comically. Tessa listened, too, and so did Caleb. Even Sam stopped eating, although Tessa suspected with the volume so low he was only reacting to their responses, and not his father's voice.

"Mitch does a fair job with those commercials. I admit I didn't think it was a good use of money. Still don't, as far as the business it brings in. But the goodwill in town—well, they're worth their weight in gold that way."

Tessa suspected the ladies in town didn't mind listening to Mitch's sexy voice over the airwaves, either. The thought, and the flush of heat that surged through her veins, startled her. The baby, too. Tiny fists and feet sprang to action inside her. She folded her hands on the table and took a deep steadying breath.

When she looked up again, Caleb was watching her, his wise old eyes narrowed to slits. Tessa felt the flush that had heated her skin climb into her cheeks. She stood up and took her plate to the sink, keeping her back to him. "Can I get you anything else?" she asked.

"Nothing more."

She came back and sat down.

Sam finished his brownie. "It was good," he said. He put his plate and empty glass in the sink, then went back to the couch and put his arms around Belle's neck.

"Have you decided yet when you're leaving town?" Caleb asked bluntly.

"I...no. Not precisely. I have an appointment at the clinic the day after tomorrow. I'll probably decide then."

"You'll want to be settled with your sister before the baby comes."

"Yes."

"You've been a real help at the store."

"Thank you. The job has been a godsend to me. I owe Mitch a great deal for hiring me on faith the way he did."

"Mitch has a good heart. Sometimes it gets in the way of his head." Caleb had been following the outline of the red flowers that dotted the vinyl tablecloth with his fingertip. Now he looked up, pinning Tessa with his gaze. "Mitch doesn't always make the right choices when he thinks with his heart. But once he's committed, he sticks, come hell or high water. It's easy to get hurt that way. I don't want to see him go through that again.'' He was warning her away. She couldn't blame him. She was a woman alone. Pregnant. Almost penniless. Caleb had every right to be worried that she would take advantage of his grandson.

''I haven't always made the right choices, either,'' she said, not looking away, although she wanted to, desperately. She could feel tears pricking her eyelids, and she was determined not to cry. ''I let my heart do the thinking once too often myself.'' She laid her hand on her stomach, under the table, where Caleb couldn't see. ''So from now on I'm determined to go it alone. Just me and my baby. Working for you and Mitch will give me a little more security when I leave here. That's why I want to stay in Riverbend as long as possible.'' She stood up. Caleb followed suit, still watching her, but his eyes had softened a little, or perhaps she'd only imagined it. ''But you have my word that's the only reason I'm still here.''

# CHAPTER SEVEN

MITCH STOOD at the end of the dock and let tendrils of mist eddy around him. He took a deep breath. The air was heavy with the smell of the river and the wet earth behind him, and over it all the tang of burning leaves. Off in the distance the roar of a combine came to him as a faint growl. A farmer working late, staying ahead of the weather. The harvest was nearly complete, the grain stored. Midway through another season, and winter not far away. He loved these still, quiet nights with the first real bite of autumn chill in the air.

Rocking back on his heels, he looked up at the sky. The clouds were breaking up, chased off by a freshening breeze. Tomorrow was supposed to be cool and clear. The rest of the week the same. He was going to have to bring the dock in soon, or the water would be too cold to get into without hip waders.

Charlie Callahan would probably help, if he gave him a call. That is, if he wasn't off somewhere with Beth planning their wedding. It was still four months away, but you'd think it was scheduled for day after tomorrow. It was going to be bigger and more elaborate than their first, because it was damned well going to be their last, according to Charlie and Beth. He smiled as he turned to head back up the steep flight of stairs that lined the bank alongside the boathouse.

Charlie and Beth were sure making up for all the years they'd been apart. You almost never saw one of them without the other these days, and Mitch was glad of it. He'd always thought they were meant for each other. But maybe for old times' sake he could coax them apart long enough to get the dock put away for the winter. Especially if it meant giving Charlie a chance to escape from picking out wedding music or deciding between chicken cordon bleu and roast beef for the reception menu.

Mitch took his time climbing the steps. He wasn't in any hurry to get back inside. What did he have to look forward to? Caleb and Sam were already in bed. That left the late news, maybe Letterman. He was too wound up to sleep. It had been one of those days.

Most of the time he enjoyed his job on the town council. But not tonight. Not when half-a-dozen irate citizens came to make complaints about barking dogs and uneven sidewalks and motor homes parked on the back alley right-of-way. All of them had to be given their say, on top of the council's regular agenda. After a session like that, he wished he'd never let the mayor, Barb Baden, talk him into running for town council. It was just too damned tedious for words.

But one by one they'd solved the complaints, or at least defused most of the controversies, and by the time the meeting was adjourned, the warring factions were at least speaking to each other again. Maybe none of the members of the Riverbend council would qualify for the Nobel Peace prize, but they were keeping the place ticking along. And that was what mattered.

"Hell, I love this town," he said, grinning as he topped the riverbank.

"Who's there?" Tessa called out.

Mitch rounded the corner of the boathouse to see her standing beside her little red car, draped in that ridiculous big sweater he'd seen her in the first day she'd come to town. He supposed a sweater like that was all the rage in California, but it looked to him as if it had been made from one of his grandmother's old bedspreads.

"It's me," he said. "I was just down on the dock getting a breath of fresh air."

"Hi, Mitch," she said. It was too dark to see her smile, but he felt the current from it, anyway. "I came out to see if I'd locked the car and I heard your voice." She looked past him into the darkness.

"You know, you don't have to lock your car. We don't have much crime around these parts."

"Everything I own's in the trunk of this car," she said. "I wouldn't have been able to sleep a wink if I hadn't come out to check the locks."

"You haven't done that lately," he said.

"Done what?" she asked, tilting her head a little to one side.

"Remind me that you're not staying around town any longer than you have to." God, maybe he was getting senile before his time. He should never have spoken those words aloud.

"Mitch—"

"I know. You're heading for your sister's as soon as her kids get over the chicken pox."

"I called her this evening. She sounds like she's got her hands full now that both of them have come down with it, but there's nothing I can do to help. Her doctor said I should stay away at least another week since her husband's not sure he ever had them, either."

"It's okay, Tessa. I told you I'm happy to have you stay on here as long as you like."

"I know that. It's just…"

"What, Tessa?"

She squared her shoulders. "Nothing. I'm just getting antsy being in limbo this way."

"Yeah, I know what you mean." He was in limbo, too, about his feelings for her. He shoved his hands in his pockets. "It's getting late. I should let you go back inside."

She made no move toward the cottage. He waited, too.

"What were you doing down on the dock?" she asked after a handful of heartbeats.

"Just watching the mist on the river and the stars come out."

She looked up, and he let his eyes linger on the curve of her throat. His hands itched to reach out and touch her to see if her skin felt as soft as the mist rising off the river. "They're so bright here. I watched them whenever I was driving at night. You never seem to see them in Southern California."

He held out his hand before he could stop himself. "Come with me. I'll show you Hoosier stars."

She hesitated so long he thought she'd say no. "I'd

like that," she said at last. He folded his hand around her much smaller one and led the way down the steps to the dock. She walked lightly, but carefully, her body angled slightly to compensate for the burden she carried.

"I should have brought a flashlight," he said when she stumbled over an uneven plank.

Her laugh was light and clear, echoing off the bank and out over the water like little bells. "It's all right. I'd probably float if I tumbled in. I feel like I swallowed a balloon sometimes."

"Better a balloon than a watermelon. Isn't that the old cliché?"

"I suppose it is." She crossed her arms under her breasts, hugging herself. "But when I think of my baby, it makes my heart soar—like a balloon."

He wanted to tell her how brave that made her sound. She'd confessed she was nearly penniless, homeless for all intents and purposes, with family and friends a thousand miles away, but still the thought of bringing a child into the world made her heart soar.

He couldn't remember Kara ever expressing such a thought when she was carrying Sam—at least not to him.

"Have you picked out a name for the baby yet?" he asked.

She shook her head. He could see her profile in the light reflected off the river. "No. I guess I've been waiting to discuss names with my sister."

"We named Sam after his mother's father."

"My dad took off and left us when I was five. And I don't think I'll name the baby Brian."

"Is Brian the father's name?"

She turned to look at him, and her features were lost in shadow. "Yes," she said, and there was no hint of emotion in her voice. "Brian Delaney."

"Brian's a good strong name."

"He's a strong man. A baseball player. Centerfielder for the Angels." She paused as if waiting for an acknowledgment.

The name didn't ring a bell. "I don't follow the West Coast teams much," he said by way of apology.

"He's only been with the club since August."

"You met him in Albany?" *What in hell am I doing asking questions about her lover?*

"He went to high school with my brother-in-law. We met at a New Year's Eve party."

"And it was love at first sight?" A professional baseball player. Just what he needed in a rival.

"Yes. Or at least I thought it was." She grew silent.

"But the can't-eat-can't-sleep-can't-wait-to-see-him-again feeling didn't last." That was the way it had been for him and Kara. He had a hunch he hadn't been able to keep the bitterness out of his voice when she looked over at him and shook her head.

"Love isn't a match for wanting to make the big leagues."

"The Angels didn't make the playoffs, did they? Is he still in California?" *I must be a glutton for punishment. How else to explain the words that just left my mouth?*

"He's in Honduras playing winter ball."

"I see." Mitch didn't know what else to say. He'd brought this conversation on himself.

"I wish I had." She curled her hands around the railing. "Brian's a nice guy. Fun to be with, easygoing. Or at least that's the way he seemed at first. He's a decent utility infielder. He played Triple-A ball for twelve years but never got his big break. Then the Angels' centerfielder got hurt and they called Brian up. I was thrilled for him. At least at first." Her voice faded almost to a whisper. "Until I realized that staying in the majors was the most important thing in his life. That's when it hit me I didn't know him at all. As it turned out, the baby and I came second to his dream. A very distant second."

"He left you alone and pregnant?"

"After I refused to go with him. Was I wrong?" she asked suddenly. "Was I just selfish and cowardly not to want to have my baby in a faraway Third World country?"

He chose his words carefully. He wanted to tell her she was right to ditch the selfish jerk, but he held his tongue. "I think your fears were normal. Bringing a child into the world is a risk and a responsibility that shouldn't be taken lightly."

"I cried my eyes out for three days. When I stopped crying, I realized I didn't feel the same way about Brian as I had before. From then on it was going to be just the two of us. Me and my daughter. That's when I packed up and headed east."

Mitch chuckled softly. "You sound very certain the baby is a girl. Do you know for sure?"

She shook her head. "I know in my heart."

"Did you make an appointment at the hospital yet?" He wasn't sorry to move the conversation in a different direction. He had to deliberately uncurl his hands from the fists they'd molded themselves into. If he ever came face-to-face with Tessa's lover, he'd be hard put not to punch out his lights.

"Yes. Day after tomorrow. With Dr. Stevens, the one you said was a friend."

"Yes." He rested his arms on the railing of the dock he'd installed two years before. "She's a good doctor."

"I appreciate your help finding her. And thanks for letting me vent about Brian," she added softly.

"No problem."

She leaned back and looked at the sky. "The stars are getting brighter every minute." Whatever joy she felt in her pregnancy must be blunted by her precarious situation, Mitch thought. She probably didn't want to dwell on the subject any more tonight, not with hours of lonely darkness to be gotten through before the sun came up. He'd been there himself, sleepless with worry over Sam's future, more nights than he cared to remember.

"There's the Big Dipper." He pointed to the familiar constellation. "It's easy to see tonight."

"There's the handle. And that must be the North Star, so the Little Dipper—" she followed the outline of the constellation with her finger "—is right there."

He laughed at the triumphant lilt in her voice. "And there's Orion's Belt."

"And the rest of him." She made a sweeping gesture with her hand, graceful and utterly feminine. His lower body tightened unexpectedly, and his breath came quick and hard for a moment. He wanted her.

Here and now, under the blanket of stars with the river running silently beneath their feet.

"For someone who hasn't seen the stars in ages, you're pretty good at spotting them," he said when he could trust his voice again.

"I took a course in astronomy one semester. It rained for days on end, and we did most of our star-gazing in the university planetarium, but I loved it. I aced the course."

"I imagine you ace most anything you set out to do."

"No," she said. "Some things I've failed miserably at." Again she was silent, no longer looking at the stars. Mitch put his foot on the lower railing and followed the path of her gaze, watching the reflections of stars in the dark water. "What was it like growing up in this town?" she asked after a long moment.

"It was good," he answered without hesitation.

"Tell me about it." There was a wistfulness in her voice he imagined she didn't want him to hear.

It was cold enough now that he could see his breath when he exhaled. He shouldn't keep her out here too much longer. She wasn't dressed to stand in the cold. "We played in the river in the summer. Fishing, swimming, water skiing. We played on the river ice in the winter—when we weren't going out for one sport or another in school. There was a gang of us who hung out together. Nick Harrison was one. Charlie Callahan, too."

"The contractor? I've met him at the store," she said, turning her back on the river, leaning against the railing, once again looking up at the stars.

"And his ex-wife, soon-to-be new wife again, Beth Pennington. Actually she was more an honorary member. Her brother, Ed, was the real River Rat. Beth's a physician's assistant. She works with Dr. Bennett. He's Lily Mazerik's dad. You've met Lily at the store, too, haven't you?" She nodded. "She's married to Aaron Mazerik. He's the basketball coach. Tom Baines was one of us, too, when he was here in the summer."

"Tom Baines the reporter?"

"The Pulitzer-Prize-winning reporter," Mitch supplied.

"I had no idea he lived in Riverbend."

"He doesn't, not officially yet. But I've got the feeling he's going to be spending more time in town. He's been seeing a lot of Lynn Kendall. She's the minister of the Riverbend Community Church. He's Rachel and Ruth Steele's nephew, by the way. Bloodlines are important in this neck of the woods."

"Was there anyone else?" She'd picked up on something in his voice that he hadn't realized was there.

"Just me and one other—Tom's cousin and Aaron's half brother, Jacob Steele."

"Jacob doesn't live in Riverbend any longer, I take it."

"He left town shortly after college. He hasn't been back since. Not even when his father, Abraham, died suddenly last spring. Not even his aunts know where's he's gone or what he's doing."

"I wonder if something happened to drive him away?"

"Damned if I know," Mitch admitted. "But it gets better. Abraham left a bunch of us bequests in his will. He left the old homeplace to Tom, and it brought him back to town from halfway around the world. He left Reverend Lynn money for her youth center. He left Beth and Charlie each half interest in a houseboat, and after years apart they've reconciled. There was money for Aaron Mazerik, too, although the old man never acknowledged him as his son while he lived."

"Those are most of the River Rats," she said. "What did he leave you?"

"Not me. He left Sam a fair-size sum of money."

"Sam? Why, because of his hearing-impairment?"

"It could be. No one knows for sure." He and Caleb and Rachel and Ruth had looked at Abraham's bequest to Sam from every angle. But none of them had come up with a reason, and Abraham hadn't chosen to enlighten them in his will. "Granddad claims it's because he saved Abe's life once when they were kids and he fell through the ice. But Abraham never admitted the incident happened in the first place. And even if it had, why leave Sam twenty-seven thousand dollars?"

"Wow!"

Mitch couldn't help but smile at the note of wonder in her old-fashioned exclamation. "It does take the edge off coming up with his college tuition," he agreed. "I've already invested most of it. In eight years it will be a tidy sum."

"It is now," she said emphatically. "I guess it doesn't matter why he did it. But if I were in your place, I'd want to know why he chose Sam."

"That would be nice, but it's not likely we'll ever learn the reason. Abraham Steele was a strange bird."

"It's like a story."

"Or a soap opera?"

"You're going to tell me once again that Riverbend isn't what it seems on the surface, aren't you?"

"I just don't want you to think everything here is perfect. It isn't. Abe Steele left money to Sam and Lynn's church and a houseboat to Charlie and Beth that brought them back together. But he had a son he never acknowledged, even when the boy was on the road to a bad end. Something must have happened between him and Jacob that was so serious Jacob turned his back on friends and family and has never set foot in this town again."

She turned sideways to face him. From this angle he couldn't see the gentle roundness of her belly, only the curve of her hip and the swell of her breast. He sucked in his breath as another wave of longing and sexual desire came out of nowhere. "You're telling me it's just like anyplace else. There are small people here, as well as generous ones. There are mean and angry people. Maybe even violent ones. There are probably as many unhappy marriages as happy ones. Am I right?"

"You're right." His voice sounded harsh even to himself.

"I'm sorry. I shouldn't have said that. I sounded as if I was prying. I don't mean to."

"You're not prying. I've been divorced for almost four years. You get over it."

"Do you?" She sounded as if she wanted to believe

him, but couldn't, because she knew he didn't believe the words himself.

"Look, it's getting cold and late. I don't want you showing up at the clinic with pneumonia. Let's go in."

She didn't say any more as they climbed. They stopped outside the door to the boathouse. "Thank you for showing me the stars."

"It was my pleasure." Before he could stop himself, he lifted his hand and brushed a stray wisp of honey-blond hair from her cheek. He lowered his head, bringing their mouths within inches of each other.

Tessa's eyelids fluttered shut, but then snapped open again. She took a quick step backward. "I think I'd better go inside. It's getting cold and this sweater isn't all that warm."

The surge of desire through his veins hadn't lessened. He still wanted to touch his lips to hers, feel the warmth of her skin beneath his fingers. He wanted to lie beside her, make love to her, see the smile of contentment the baby moving inside her would bring to her face.

He must be losing his mind to be in such a state over a woman who was only passing through his life. A woman who was pregnant with another man's child. A man she'd left only weeks before. A man she was probably still in love with.

He straightened and put even more distance between them. "I'll hunt you up an old coat of my mom's," he said. Anything to stop himself from thinking of what her hair smelled like. Wildflowers and summer dew. Or remembering that the skin of her cheek felt like silk beneath his fingertips. Her mouth would be as soft and as sweet. She had been pretty that first day he saw her. Now she was beautiful. "You'll need one if you're going to be staying around for a while."

"I won't be staying that long, Mitch," she said softly, but with finality.

She was warning him off, but he couldn't just walk away. "You'll be here long enough to come to the pumpkin party next week."

"Pumpkin party?" Her hand was on the doorknob, but she paused to look back over her shoulder at him. She was lovely in the moonlight, all gold and silver and big luminous eyes.

"It's at the store. I'll be putting up the posters tomorrow. A couple of days before Halloween the kids from around town come and carve jack-o'-lanterns. They bring their own, or we provide them for the ones who might not be able to afford a good big one. The little ones paint faces on theirs. I coerce just about everyone I know to supervise the older kids with the knives. Then later, the folks who help out come here to the house. We have a bonfire and cider and doughnuts, and Charlie Callahan makes chili over an open fire." He tried for a smile and thought he succeeded. "The party will be right in your backyard, if the weather cooperates. Don't tell me you're going to be inhospitable and lock yourself up in your little hideaway and snub my friends."

He said that deliberately to goad her into coming. She wanted friends. She wanted to belong. He could see it in her eyes. He had heard the longing in her voice. And if he was going to be foolish enough to lose his heart, then he was going to use every means he could to see that the same thing happened to her.

"When you put it like that," she said, wistfulness and reluctance tangled together in her words, "how can I refuse? I'll be there."

IT WAS GOING to be a long night. Tessa stood at the window and watched the lights go out in Mitch's house. She wasn't certain which bedroom was his, but she suspected it was the first one on the left, because it was usually the last to go dark.

She wondered if he was going to have as hard a time going to sleep as she was.

Had it affected him at all, that fleeting brush of his fingers across her cheek? That almost kiss? Lord, she'd been blindsided by the surge of soul-longing and sexual desire that had flooded over her in equal strength. Even the baby had been affected. She had felt the tiny entity within her jump, as though jolted by an electrical charge.

Or had it all been her imagination and her neediness? Had his touch meant much less? Was it merely a friendly gesture to a lonely woman on a cold autumn evening? The truth was, she wanted it to be more. The reality was that she didn't dare even dream of that happening. She had given her word to Caleb that she wanted nothing from Mitch. And she meant to keep it. She wasn't going to let her foolish emotions lead her into heartbreak again.

She couldn't be interested in Mitch Sterling romantically. She had been separated from Brian for less than a month. She was carrying his child. But the reality was that she could barely remember what he looked like. And deep in her heart she had to admit that she had known long ago that their relationship was headed for an end.

But she had stayed for the baby's sake. And finally she had left him for the baby's sake. That should be her answer. They were alone in this, the two of them. There was no room in her life for a man. There was no room for dreams of a man, even a man like Mitch, who, she was coming to believe, was everything a woman could want in a husband and father.

She was going to have to guard her emotions very carefully. Circumstances demanded that she stay in Riverbend for a few weeks longer. They would be weeks fraught with danger for her bruised and battered heart. But there was no way she was going to give in to the impulses of that unreliable organ. She wasn't going to fall in love with Mitch Sterling. She was not.

SAM LAY IN HIS BED with his hands behind his head, watching the strip of light under his door. He was waiting for his dad to come in and yell at him for being rude to Tessa.

Well, not yell at him. His dad didn't yell. He talked. He asked Sam to explain what he'd done wrong, then he'd tell him why it was wrong, and finally he'd think up some kind of punishment to make Sam remember not to do it again. When he was little, it meant taking away his video game. Now it usually meant no e-mail privileges.

He hadn't wanted to be a smart-ass to Tessa. It was

just that sometimes… He rolled over in bed, facing the wall, making his isolation complete. Sometimes it was just so frustrating to always have to slow down, form your words more carefully, talk more softly, repeat yourself so others could understand.

He didn't want to write notes, or use sign, or e-mail. He had so much he wanted to *say,* so many things he wanted to express and couldn't that he almost busted with it. He wanted to *talk* to people. Sometimes he let his frustration get in the way.

But most of the time it was okay. He liked the way his dad nodded when he agreed with something Sam said. He liked the way Granddad Caleb's nose twitched when he was trying not to laugh at one of his corny jokes.

He liked the way Tessa smiled at him—like tonight.

He just plain liked Tessa. She was funny and smart and she knew a lot about guy stuff like plumbing and electricity. She would be a great mom. He knew that.

And she liked him. Or at least he thought she did. Until tonight, when she'd acted like all the other grown-ups. *If you don't speak more slowly, I'm going to have to ask you to write it down.*

Sam rolled onto his back so he could see the door. His face burned. Not just because she hadn't been able to understand him, but because he'd been a butt-head about it. It wasn't Tessa's fault she wasn't used to hearing him talk. He had to remember that. He had to slow down around her until she got used to him.

But maybe it was already too late. He'd seen his dad go outside. He'd seen him coming back up the steps from the dock when he came out of the bathroom and looked out the window to see if it was still raining.

Tessa had been outside, too. They had talked a little and then they'd gone down the steps together. Sam just knew she was going to rat on him for being rude to her. He'd turned off the light and watched until they came back up the steps. They'd talked some more, and his dad had reached out and touched her cheek.

Maybe they hadn't been talking about him at all. Maybe they were talking about other things. Man and woman things. Touching led to kissing, and kissing led to…well, Sam wasn't exactly sure what kissing led to. But it was good if his dad and Tessa were kissing. That meant they liked each other. A lot.

A shadow appeared at the bottom of his door. Sam closed his eyes to little slits and held his breath, pretending to be asleep. He waited for his dad to come in and sit down on the side of the bed and turn on the light—a sure sign they were going to have a man-to-man talk, no matter how late it was.

But he didn't. He just came in and gave the covers a little pull so that Sam's foot was covered up. He always stuck his foot outside the covers. He didn't know why. It was like his feet had claustrophobia or something. He didn't know how to explain it. And his dad always covered him up. It was just a thing they did.

Better than a good-night kiss. He was way too old for that.

Sam saw his dad's lips move and knew he was whispering good-night. He left the room and closed the door, leaving Sam in darkness except for the glow from his oversize clock face.

So maybe Tessa hadn't said anything about how he'd talked back to her. Maybe she'd really meant it when her smile had told him she understood.

He closed his eyes and breathed a sigh of relief. He was going to be the best kid in Riverbend, and if Tessa fell in love with his dad...well, she'd have to fall in love with him, too.

# CHAPTER EIGHT

"You're a healthy young woman and you're going to have a healthy big baby."

Tessa was more relieved than she wanted to admit by the doctor's words. She had done everything she could to eat well and get enough rest since she'd left California, but it wasn't easy. She would never forgive herself if leaving Brian and striking out on her own had caused harm to the baby.

She finished buttoning her top with fingers that weren't quite steady, as she watched Dr. Annie Stevens make notations on a computer screen attached to the wall of the small examination room. She'd been pleasantly surprised at the up-to-date look and feel of Riverbend's hospital. The facility was new, three stories high, built of redbrick with what seemed like acres of mirrored windows. The inside was as high-tech and sleek as the outside.

"You don't think I should have another ultrasound?" She tried not to let anxiety shade her voice. But the doctor raised her eyes and regarded her with an assessing look over the rims of her half glasses.

"If you were staying in Riverbend for the delivery, I'd say yes. But since you say you'll only be in town a couple more weeks, and I have your previous ultrasound results here—'' she indicated the folder of medical reports Tessa had brought with her from California ''—there's no clinical reason to repeat the procedure. Unless you've changed your mind and want to know the sex of the child.''

Tessa shook her head. ''I can wait.''

''It won't change the outcome.'' When she smiled, the doctor's rather severe expression lightened and she looked much younger and prettier.

''The cost is also a factor,'' Tessa said candidly. ''I don't have health insurance.''

Annie Stevens's serious expression returned, but was softened by the understanding in her dark eyes. ''Cost wouldn't have been a consideration if I thought you needed the procedure. I'm not totally in thrall to the HMOs yet.'' Her smile was rueful. ''But as I said, you're healthy and the baby's healthy. You don't smoke, you don't use alcohol, and you're watching your intake of sugar and caffeine.''

''Coffee's the hardest to stay away from,'' Tessa confessed.

Dr. Stevens laughed. ''I know. When I was nursing my daughter, I used to dream about going to Starbucks nearly every night.''

Tessa smiled as she slid down off the exam table. She liked Dr. Stevens. She wished she *could* be the one to deliver her baby.

A ripple of longing skittered through her veins and settled in her heart, but she immediately squelched it. She was not going to think about staying in Indiana. She had made herself that promise two nights ago under the stars. She intended to keep it.

"We won't know about your blood tests until to-morrow, but they're strictly routine, and I don't fore-see any problems with your blood sugar or kidney function. Your blood pressure's a little high, but that's probably because you're scared of me."

"Oh, no." It took Tessa a moment to realize the doctor was joking. She stammered an explanation, feeling a little foolish. "I don't like going to the doctor all that much, if you want to know the truth."

"Most people don't. I'm terrible about it myself." Dr. Stevens gave her a surprisingly mischievous grin, shut down the computer screen and motioned toward the door, all business again. "Your doctor in Califor-nia pegged your due date as December fifteenth. I agree. But with babies you can never tell. Especially the first one. I'd like you to be settled with your sister by Thanksgiving. Do you think that's possible?"

Thanksgiving was less than a month away. "Set-tled" meant more than on her way to Albany. It meant living there. Her time in Riverbend was coming to an end. "Yes...yes, I think so. Even if my brother-in-law does get the chicken pox, he should be over it by then."

"I agree." Dr. Stevens led the way down a hall lined on both sides with closed doors. Her office was in the specialists' wing of the hospital. Obviously the citizens of Riverbend could have all but the most se-rious of medical procedures performed in their own hometown.

"My sister's on the lookout for a doctor in Al-bany," Tessa said. So far Callie hadn't found an obstetrician willing to take her on such short notice, and with no health insurance.

"A friend of mine from medical school has a practice in Albany."

Tessa wondered if her ears were playing tricks on her. It seemed too good to be true.

"He's a cardiologist."

"Oh." Her disappointment was hard to hide.

Annie Stevens put her chart down on the high counter that separated the receptionist's desk from the waiting room. She laid her hand over Tessa's. "I'll give him a call tonight and ask him to forward me the name of a good women's clinic. I know there are some in the area. They treat patients on a sliding scale. It won't be fancy. Not many bells and whistles, but they'll deliver your baby safely and take care of you both after."

"Thank you, Dr. Stevens. I'm very grateful that you'd go to so much trouble."

"I'm glad I can be of help. Mike only moved to Albany a year or so ago. Before that he was in Georgia. I don't know another living soul in New York State. Jackie, will you see that Ms. Masterson gets a copy of all her lab work and my notes. She'll be needing them for her doctor in New York." She handed Tessa's chart to a heavyset, pleasant-faced nurse behind the counter. Mayor Baden's daughter, according to Maggie Leatherman. Tessa had met the small, round-figured mayor at the Sunnyside Café a couple of days earlier. The resemblance between mother and daughter was marked.

"I'll get right to it. You can pick them up tomorrow

if you want,'' Jackie said to Tessa. The phone started ringing and she spoke with her hand on the receiver. ''Or I can mail them to you. You're staying in Mitch Sterling's boathouse, aren't you?''

Tessa was already getting used to everyone knowing who she was and where she was staying. ''I'll pick them up.'' She didn't doubt for a moment that Mitch's mailman would deliver the package, but she didn't want to start getting mail at the boathouse. That would be just one more detail to make it feel like home, instead of the temporary refuge that it was.

''MITCH?''

He was helping Bill Webber load two-by-fours into the back of Will Leatherman's pickup, and he didn't hear her call his name. Tessa took a moment to watch him. She'd caught herself doing that more and more lately. He was a good-looking man, athletic and graceful in a totally masculine way. The movements of his body were natural and unstudied. Brian moved that way, too. But he worked out for hours in the gym to keep himself in top shape. It was an obsession with him. The muscles that flexed across Mitch's arms and shoulders and beneath the fabric of his blue chambray shirt were put there by hard work.

She crossed her arms beneath her breasts and squeezed, trying to squelch the image of those muscled arms wrapped around her, those strong thighs pressed against her legs. That firm mouth on her lips. Images that had begun to invade her waking hours, as well as her dreams.

Bill Webber looked up from his chore and saw her

waiting. He said something to Mitch that Tessa couldn't hear over the pickup engine and the roar of the tow motor. Mitch turned and gave her a wave that indicated he'd be with her in a minute.

She went back into the store to wait for him. If she stayed outside, she'd want to keep watching him, and she was proving to be too weak to avoid temptation. She didn't know how it had happened, this growing infatuation, but it had. And now she had to deal with it. Her life was a shambles. She was only a few hundred dollars from being destitute and homeless, yet her heart wasn't listening to reason. She was dangerously close to falling in love with her boss.

*Falling in love. Love at first sight. Impetuous. Foolhardy.* Something like that had happened with Brian, and look where it had gotten her. She couldn't trust her heart or her emotions, so she intended to ignore them.

She turned blindly to straighten a display of stovepipe joints that were housed on one of the nearby shelves just as Mitch walked up. He slapped his work gloves on his thigh to loosen the sawdust clinging to them, then pushed them into the back pocket of his snug-fitting jeans. Taking a deep breath, she cleared her mind of thoughts of making love to Mitch, thoughts that refused to be banished without a fight. "I was looking for a gallon of dark base to mix for a customer," she said, "and noticed it was dated three years ago. The whole department needs to be inventoried. I'd like to get started on it right away."

"I agree that section needs some work, but you're not going to do it."

Tessa met his dark gaze head-on. She had never been one to ignore a challenge. "Why not?"

"I don't like the idea of you lifting all that weight. A gallon of paint runs eight or nine pounds."

"I'm carrying more than that around all the time," she said, patting her stomach.

Mitch's face turned beet-red. "I mean, I..." He shut his mouth and shook his head. "No. Someone else can do it."

"Mitch, you're not paying me to stand around straightening wallpaper sample books until Rachel Steele or your aunt Maggie comes in to buy something."

"Come to think of it, I don't want you rearranging those big sample books on the top shelf, either," he said.

Before she could defend herself on that score, he asked another question. "What did Annie Stevens have to say this morning? Is everything okay with you?"

"I'm fine," she said, seeing an opening and taking it. "No restrictions on what I can do. That includes moving paint cans and wallpaper-sample books."

One corner of his mouth turned up in the devastatingly sexy grin that made her knees go weak. She'd scored a point, but he wasn't about to give in. She could see it in his eyes. "Maybe there are no medical restrictions, but there definitely are employer restrictions."

"Mitch, you're being unreasonable."

"It's unnatural for employees to ask for extra assignments," he said.

"It's unnatural for bosses to refuse the offer of an employee to take on an extra job." She put her hands on her hips. She enjoyed sparring with him. Her relationship with Brian had been too intense, too volatile, to allow much room for banter like this.

Their sex life had been the same way. Brian was so focused on performance, on the mechanics of love-making that sometimes Tessa had felt more like she was in a training film than in bed with the man she loved. Somehow she didn't think making love with Mitch would leave time for her mind to wander as it often had with Brian.

He grinned. "You're right. That's one situation they don't teach you how to deal with in bosses' school."

She laughed and he laughed with her. "Then I'll get started right away."

She should have kept her mouth shut.

His smile faded, replaced by a look that reminded her he was Caleb's grandson and every bit as stubborn. His tone and his attitude turned serious. "I said no. And I meant no. Tessa, you can't afford to take the slightest risk—"

"Dad!"

Sam hurtled himself down the main aisle, his blond head swinging from side to side as he searched for his father. The afternoon had gone so quickly Tessa hadn't realized it was time for school to be out.

"Here I am, Sam," Mitch called, stepping away from the shelves where they'd been standing so Sam could see him.

"We'll discuss this later," Tessa said, not ready to give up. She was determined to earn the salary Mitch was paying her. Every cent. There was no reason on earth she couldn't rearrange paint cans. "I'm pregnant, not an invalid."

"The subject is closed," Mitch said over his shoulder.

"Dad. Can I buy a weight-lifting set? One of those real neat ones with a bench and everything?"

"What brought this on?" Mitch asked, hunkering down to eye level with his son.

"I know I could make the Mini-Rivermen basketball team if I lift weights before tryouts. Me and Tyler figured it out."

"There's only a couple of weeks left until tryouts. I don't think—"

"I want one," Sam said, eyes narrowed and hands balled into fists. "I want one right now. I don't want to wait. I'm going to the bank and get my money and buy one."

"No you are not," Mitch said firmly. He reached out and put his hands on Sam's shoulders. "Weight-lifting equipment is too expensive to buy without doing some research—"

"It'll be too late if we wait. You never let me have anything. You don't want me to be on the team."

"That's not true," Mitch said.

Sam jerked away. He swung his arm and sent the piles of stovepipe joints crashing to the floor. Tessa jumped back as they scattered at her feet with a deafening clatter. Even Sam heard it. He flinched. His eyes flew to her face. She saw anger and humiliation, and something more, a need and a desire to belong. And deep in her heart a lonely little girl who had never truly belonged, either, felt those same hurts.

There were so many things Sam couldn't do. Playing basketball didn't need to be one of them.

"Samuel, apologize to Tessa for that behavior."

"No." Sam folded his arms over his chest and closed his eyes. His face was red with both anger and embarrassment.

Tessa's heart squeezed. Other children would put their hands over their ears if they wanted to block words they didn't want to hear. Sam closed his eyes.

Mitch tapped Sam on the shoulder. "Sam, open your eyes and listen to me."

"Mom would let me have it," Sam said, his eyes still closed.

Mitch's shoulders sagged. He dropped his head for a moment, but when he spoke again his voice was firm and steady, even though Sam couldn't hear it. Tessa's heart ached for both of them, the isolated little boy and the man who was trying so hard to raise him.

Mitch angled his face close to his son's. "Sam," he said loudly enough for his son to hear.

Sam opened his eyes. "Mom would let me have it," he said again. There was no mistaking the longing in his words, and Tessa found herself actively disliking a woman she'd never met. A woman who was selfish enough to leave her husband and child without looking back.

"Maybe she would," Mitch agreed. "But we've discussed this before. Your money from Mr. Steele is not to be spent on just anything that comes along."

"I know." Sam's lower lip stuck out in a mutinous pout.

"It's invested. We'll have to pay a penalty to take it out of the bank."

"How much?"

"As much as your weight bench would cost. Probably a lot more."

"I still want it." He signed the words for emphasis.

"You can put it on your Christmas list."

"Christmas is too late. I want it now."

"We can't always have what we want, Sam. Now, apologize to Tessa for shoving those stovepipes off the shelf. You could have hurt her."

"I won't." Sam broke free and bolted for the door.

"Samuel, come back here."

"No, no, no," he repeated, running faster.

Mitch stood up and took a step after him. "Wait." Tessa put a hand on his arm and felt the corded muscles tight with tension. "Maybe you should both cool down a minute."

"He can't be allowed to throw tantrums like that. He's too old."

"He's only ten."

"Life isn't going to be easy for him. He has to understand—"

"When you're ten waiting until Christmas seems like forever," she reminded him gently.

Mitch sighed. "Maybe I was too quick to say no. But you realize that even if I bought him a weight bench, he'd be bored with it in a week. And it isn't going to help him make the team."

"I'm sure he'll realize that on his own—if you give him a chance to think about it."

Mitch raked his hand through his hair. "You're probably right. He's just so fixated on this tryout. He's a remarkably levelheaded kid most of the time. But making the starting lineup is his dream."

Linda Christman's voice came over the loud-speaker. "Mitch, come to the office please. The tool salesman is here to see you."

"Damn. I forgot he was coming."

"Go ahead and talk to him. I'll keep an eye on Sam." The top half of the big double doors leading to the lumberyard were wire-mesh-reinforced glass. Tessa could see Sam sitting on the picnic table where the employees ate lunch in nice weather, and where those who smoked were banished no matter what the weather.

"He's going to apologize."

Tessa nodded her head. "But don't force him. I...I want him to like me."

"Tessa, that's not—"

"I know it's not good parenting. I'm not talking as a parent. Yet. Let's just say I know how it feels to be ten and an outsider. Something I imagine you never experienced—you and your River Rat friends."

"Mitch, you have a call on line two." Linda's voice sounded through the store once more.

He looked over his shoulder toward the office level, then back at Sam. "Okay. I won't talk to him again until we've both cooled off."

"Thanks." She'd already said too much. She should

never have let him know that Sam's friendship was important to her.

Tessa pushed open the heavy metal doors and went outside into the chill of the October afternoon. She walked over and stood directly in front of Sam. He had found the basketball Bill Webber and some of the other employees used to shoot hoops on their lunch hour. Head bowed, he was sitting on the picnic table, feet spread on the seat, bouncing the ball between his knees. He ignored her. She put her hand out and stopped the ball. He looked up at her, his face still mutinous and wary. "Want to shoot some hoops?" she asked.

"You're going to have a baby."

"I can still shoot hoops."

He looked at her stomach. "You can run like that?" he asked after a moment.

Tessa laughed. She couldn't help it. "Well, not very far or very fast. But I can still play H-O-R-S-E." It had been years since she'd played the old schoolyard game of assigning letters to missed shots, but she'd been pretty good at it.

She took the ball from Sam's hands and began to dribble in place. It was a little awkward, but she managed, even when the baby decided it was time to kick.

"Are you going to yell at me for what I did in there?"

She shook her head. "No. I'm not your mother."

"My mom left us."

"So did my dad."

"He did?"

"When I was five. I don't remember him."

"My mom sent me a picture of her and her new dog last summer." Mitch said his ex-wife hadn't seen Sam in more than a year, but she had time to have her picture taken with a dog. "My dad's pretty cool. Most of the time." Sam scratched a line in the dust that coated the blacktop paving. He looked up at her. "You didn't rat on me the other night, either."

"I try not to rat on my friends," Tessa said.

"I'm sorry I was a butt-head in there."

"It's not me you have to apologize to." She had told Mitch it was important to her that Sam like her. It was. But she also realized it was important for him to learn to control his emotions and his frustration with his handicap.

"My dad never listens to what I want."

"Buying a weight-training bench is a big investment. You need to think it over."

"I want one. And I have the money old Mr. Steele left me."

"The money is for college."

"What if I don't go to college?"

She didn't have an answer for that one. Tessa decided to change the subject. She offered him the basketball. "You go first," she said.

Sam took the ball and dribbled a little, set his feet and shot. His technique was pretty good, but his throw was short.

"*H,*" he said, his face turning beet-red when Tessa sank her first shot.

He threw himself into his next attempt and the ball hit the backboard six inches above the basket. "Damn," he said, and stalked over to the picnic table.

Tessa pretended not to hear him, set her feet, and her second shot *swished* through the net without touching the rim. "Your turn," she said, offering Sam the ball.

"You win. I don't want to play."

"Is that what you're going to tell the coach when he wants to put you in the game?"

Sam gave her a dark stare. "He won't put me in the game. I'll only get to play with the losers and the nerds. I wouldn't if I had a weight-lifting bench."

"Yes, you would," Tessa said. She was going where she'd never been before. She'd never tried to reason with, or discipline, a child Sam's age. "Not because you don't have a bench, but because you're a quitter."

"I am not." His shoulders came back.

Her throat contracted painfully. Of course he wasn't a quitter. He tried hard at everything he did. She felt like the meanest woman in the world, but she had a point to make. She held out the basketball. "Prove it."

He took the ball and dribbled for a long moment, then he moved down the court and under the basket, heaving in a layup that rolled around the rim and slipped off the edge. He took the rebound and set himself for a second shot. This one hit the backboard just right and dropped in. "There," he said, breathing a little heavily. "I am not a quitter."

Tessa nodded. "Of course you're not. You just proved that. That's not a bad layup by the way. You just need a little more height and a little more muscle behind the shot."

"I need a weight bench," Sam said, sensing victory and snatching at it.

Tessa hid a smile. "You may be right. But I don't think you're going to talk your father into one before tryouts."

"He's too damned stubborn."

"I bet you don't use that word around him."

Sam colored to the tips of his ears. "I'm sorry. Sometimes I forget."

"I won't tell." It was Tessa's turn. She missed her shot, but not by much.

"*H,*" Sam said.

"I think I know a way you could get some weight training in and help me out, too," she said with deliberate casualness. Sam might not be able to hear the inflection in her voice, but he was very good at reading body language.

Sam turned to face her head-on, an indication his interest was piqued.

"I want to inventory the paint supply in the store, but your dad doesn't think I should be lifting those cans. I could use your help moving them around."

"That's not lifting weights," Sam sneered. Disappointment darkened his blue eyes.

"Oh, yes it is. It's like lifting eight-pound weights."

"Eight-pound weights? How heavy is that?"

Tessa laughed. "As heavy as a can of paint."

Sam looked as if he was going to take offense for a moment, then he laughed, too.

"I could try it," he said, obviously not wanting to give in too easily.

"If your dad sees you're serious…" Tessa let her words trail off and took another shot. She missed.

"Okay. I get it. You don't have to try and trick me into doing it like I was a little kid." Sam caught the ball on the rebound and put it back in the storage basket beside the picnic table where it was kept.

Tessa just nodded, not wanting to press her luck.

"I'll help you with the paint cans. I'm going to have to do some kind of punishment for mouthing off at Dad and knocking those pieces of pipe on the floor, anyway. Maybe if I do this, he won't ground my e-mail," he suggested hopefully. "I just started getting stuff from this kid in Ireland that Pastor Lynn's boyfriend hooked me up with."

"Maybe," Tessa said.

Sam slung his book bag over his shoulder. "Yeah. When pigs fly."

It was such an old-fashioned grown-up expression—probably gleaned from Caleb—that Tessa had to hide another smile. Sam really was a great kid. She would miss him when she left town.

As always, the strength of the longing to stay right where she was caught her unawares. She might be building a relationship with Sam, but by necessity it would be a short-lived one. It was unwise, and unfair to take it any farther than it had already gone.

If she had been smart, she would have gone back to her work and let Mitch handle the aftermath of his confrontation with his son. But she wasn't smart when she thought with her heart, instead of her brain. Instinctively she put her hand on her swollen stomach, felt the fluttering movements as the baby settled back to sleep. She made terrible mistakes when she let her emotions get the better of her. This time it had turned out okay. But she couldn't take the chance on being that lucky a second time.

Sam wasn't her child. She had no real place in his life.

"You'll try and see your dad's side of it, okay?" she said as she reached for the handle of one of the big double doors.

Sam got there first and pulled it open, stepping sideways so she could enter first. "Yeah," he said. "I'll try. But I really want a weight bench."

"Then tell him so. In a nice way."

"He'll say no."

"Then we'll move paint cans every day until you look like Arnold Schwarzenegger."

Sam laughed. "I don't think there's that much paint in the whole world."

MITCH HADN'T EXPECTED to see Sam laughing again for a long time. But he was. He was also putting the scattered stovepipe joints back on the shelf and evidently having a good time doing it.

Somehow Tessa had defused the situation and coaxed Sam into a better mood. It had been difficult enough being mother and father to his son for the past four years; Mitch knew it would be even harder raising a volatile teenager alone. Today had been just a small ripple on the water compared to the battle of wills he'd face in the next few years.

He didn't want to raise Sam alone. He needed a female partner. But until Tessa had walked into his life, he hadn't actually focused those longings on any one woman.

Now he couldn't keep her out of his thoughts day or night.

"How is everything going?" he asked, coming up on them while Sam's back was turned.

"Fine." She smiled at him and the force of it hit him right in the gut the way it always did. "Sam wants to apologize." She touched Sam's hand and motioned that Mitch had arrived. Sam turned to face him, but he wasn't smiling any longer.

"I'm glad to see you're putting the shelves back to rights," Mitch said because he didn't know where else to start.

"I'm sorry, Dad." Sam was holding a big silver-colored elbow joint so tightly his knuckles were white. "I acted like a real butt-head."

"Lashing out the way you did doesn't solve problems."

"I know. I'm cleaning up the mess I made. You can ground my e-mail if you want, but I'm still going to help Tessa with the paint."

"I'll have to think about your e-mail privileges." Sam couldn't be allowed to think he could get out of this without some consequences. "What's this about helping Tessa with the paint?" Mitch looked over at Tessa. Her cheeks were pink and she didn't meet his eye.

"I'm going to move all the heavy paint cans," Sam said. "She says it will be like lifting weights. Is she right, Dad?"

"Close enough."

"You'll see. By the time we're done, I'll have big muscles. I'll be Arnold Schwarzenegger.'' Sam struck a bodybuilder's pose and Mitch grinned. He reached out and ruffled Sam's hair.

"If you look like Arnold by this time next week, we'll patent the paint-can bodybuilding method and make enough money that you can buy yourself a whole gym."

"It's a deal," Sam said confidently, as if he could do just that.

"I'll practice shots with you every day for an hour after school."

"You can get off work for that long?"

"We'll do it here, but I promise I won't come back inside the store unless it's a real emergency. And I'll ask Aaron Mazerik if there's any way he can free up some time at the school weight room for you little guys."

"Cool. But don't worry—I'm not going to be little for long," Sam vowed.

Mitch knew that better than Sam, and it was bitter-sweet knowledge. He'd always wanted a big family, lots of kids. Now it looked as if Sam would be an only child, just as he had been. "You're growing up way too fast. I guess we can skip the e-mail grounding this time—if you do a real good job for Tessa."

"I'll do the best job you've ever seen."

He gave the stovepipe such an enthusiastic boost back onto the shelf that two more fell off the other end.

"Oops," he said. "See? I'm stronger already." He jogged down the row of shelving.

Mitch took advantage of his absence. "Thanks, Tessa. I was about to come down too hard on him until you stepped in."

"Sometimes an outsider can see that more easily." She wasn't smiling any longer. Her eyes had darkened with some emotion he couldn't read.

"I suppose that's true."

"I needed the practice." The brittleness in her voice surprised him.

"Tessa, you're going to be a good mother." He wasn't just saying that. He could see many qualities in her that Kara had lacked. She was dependable, steady, caring of others. She was grounded in reality, the here and now. Not very sexy attributes, but she still made the blood boil in his veins.

"I don't have any choice." Her hands had balled into fists at her sides. He saw her deliberately relax them, then shove them into the pockets of her sweater. She stood a little taller, and the look in her eyes became a shade more determined. "I'm in this all alone now."

"Tessa..." He closed his mouth and set his jaw. What had he been about to say? *You don't have to raise this baby alone. Marry me and I'll be the best father I know how to be.*

My God, what had come over him? He couldn't be thinking of proposing marriage to her. They'd only known each other a couple of weeks. They'd never had a real date. They'd never kissed. They'd never made love.

But he was falling in love with her. He suspected he had been since the moment they'd first met.

And Tessa didn't believe in love at first sight. She might not have told him in so many words, but he knew. And heaven help him, he had no business believing in it, either. He'd never looked at another woman once he'd set his heart on Kara, and their marriage had been a dismal failure. What made him think he'd do better a second time if he acted on those bolt-from-the-blue kind of feelings?

*Because Tessa isn't Kara, and I'm not nineteen anymore.*

"Yes? Was there something else you wanted to say?" She tilted her head a little, looking up at him.

"Nothing," he said, breaking the contact of those blue, blue eyes with an effort that was almost physical. "Nothing at all."

## CHAPTER NINE

HER BABY'S SWEATER was coming along nicely. Tessa looked down at the pieces of the little garment she'd knitted so diligently. It might not be county-fair-blue-ribbon quality, but every stitch had been done with love.

Tomorrow she would go back to the shop next to Killian's and have the proprietor, whose name she now knew was Marcie Captor, show her how to put it all together. Then maybe she'd tackle a hat and booties to match. She had some yarn left. If she bought another skein, it would probably be enough.

And she had the time to learn the more complicated stitches it would take to finish the ensemble. Tessa smiled to herself, looking out over the river as the setting sun gilded the orange, red and brown leaves on the trees lining the bank with a blaze of gold light. Her brother-in-law had chicken pox. She wasn't going to have to leave Riverbend for at least another week.

She tightened her lips until the smile was wiped away. She shouldn't be this happy about another delay in getting to Albany. But she was. Her little nest egg was growing, and she was comfortable in the boat-house apartment. Tiny as it was, it was hers—for the time being. She could even close her eyes and picture a crib at the foot of her bed, the mobile of brightly colored circus animals she'd seen in Killian's baby department circling around as it lulled her infant to sleep.

Forbidden dreams.

She shouldn't let herself revel in the sudden lift in her spirits whenever she looked out over the river, or greeted Evie Mazerik and Lucy Garvey when she stepped into the Sunnyside Café. Or, be relieved that she would have another prenatal visit with Dr. Stevens and not some anonymous nurse practitioner in an Albany clinic.

Riverbend wasn't her home. She had to stop thinking of it that way. She picked up the tiny sweater, put it in a plastic bag and set it on the chair beside the sofa. Her job at the hardware was only a means to an end—an independent life for her and her baby in a city nearly a thousand miles away from the flat Indiana cornfields that encircled the town like rows of golden sentinels.

She had to stop thinking about things like what the subject of Reverend Lynn's sermon would be that day when she heard church bells ring out on Sunday mornings. She'd met the young minister when she came into the hardware to look at carpet samples, and found her friendly and easy to talk to.

Her mother had partied too hard on most Saturday nights to have any inclination to get up on Sunday mornings and spend an hour in church. But when Tessa was settled in Albany, she intended to find a church for her and her baby to attend. A church with a young, forward-thinking minister like Lynn Kendall.

And she would pick a neighborhood with good schools. Even if she never fulfilled her own dreams of finishing her degree and teaching, her child was going to have the best education she could provide.

A truck pulled into Mitch's driveway and came to a halt in front of the boathouse. Tessa glanced at the sunflower-shaped clock she'd bought at a flea market and hung on a nail above the sink. It must be Charlie Callahan arriving to start the chili. He was going to cook it over an open fire in a big iron kettle on the riverbank.

She looked out the window and saw Charlie kneeling beside the fire pit. He had the same rangy build, the same broad shoulders and narrow hips as Mitch, the same laugh lines around his nose and mouth. She had no trouble at all imagining the two of them playing in mud puddles after a thunderstorm when they were little, hunting squirrels in the woods outside town with their fathers, anchoring the basketball team in high school, consoling each other when their marriages went bad.

Tessa grabbed her sweater and reminded herself sternly that Charlie Callahan had reconciled with his ex-wife. And Mitch's love life was none of her business. Too many times lately she'd found herself imagining what it would be like to be his wife, fantasizing that the baby she carried was his and would be born into a family full of shared values and love.

Another forbidden dream.

"Hi, Charlie," she said as she walked to her car. It was time to get back to the hardware for the party.

"Hi, Tessa." He stood up and brushed crushed

leaves from the knees of his jeans. He was wearing a green chambray shirt and a canvas jacket with a dark brown corduroy collar, which enhanced his rugged good looks. "Are you off to help with the pumpkin carving?"

"Wouldn't miss it for the world."

"Hang on a minute until I get this fire started, and I'll drive you over to the store."

"You don't have to do that," she said.

"I'm going to swing by there and pick up some folding chairs, anyway. It'll save you having to find a parking space when you get back here tonight. The driveway will be full." He was watching the kindling and crumpled newspaper he'd placed under the tepee-shaped pile of logs as it caught fire and sent licks of yellow flames curling up between the split wood. "There it goes. Have a seat in my truck. I'll holler at Caleb and tell him I'm leaving. He'll keep an eye on the fire until I get back."

"Whose idea was it to put candles in the trees?" she asked.

He shrugged and looked up at the mason jars with votive candles inside them hanging by heavy strings tied around their mouths. They'd been placed in the lower branches of the maples that shared the backyard with the huge old oak. The heavy glass jars swung to and fro in the gentle breeze, casting a flickering play of light and shadow across the yard. "Mitch's mom, I guess. She always used to hang them out here for trick-or-treat night when we were kids. We sorta kept up the tradition when Mitch started the après-carving party a few years back."

"I like them," Tessa said. She liked the tradition, too. There had never been any traditions in the Masterson family. She would have to make some of her own—for her and her child, just as Callie was doing for her girls.

Flames were licking at the larger pieces of wood now. Caleb came out with a folding lawn chair and sat down close to the fire. "Looks like it's going to stay lit," he said, holding his hands out to the warmth.

Charlie nodded, satisfied with his handiwork, and motioned toward his truck. "I'll be back ASAP. Let me give you a hand up." His hand was warm and strong and rough, like Mitch's. A workingman's hand. She stepped onto the high step of his truck and wriggled her way onto the seat. It was a cool night, and she stuck her hands in the pockets of her coat, a raspberry-colored all-weather coat with a heavy zippered lining that had belonged to Mitch's mother. She'd barely worn it, he said, and he'd just never gotten rid of it after she died. It was several sizes larger than Tessa usually wore, but she needed the extra material to cover her growing belly. She'd found an ivory scarf and matching gloves at Killian's. Callie would probably have an extra pair of boots lying around, so she'd be ready to face an upstate New York winter when she finally got to Albany without dipping into her savings.

Tessa wondered what winter was like in Riverbend. Did it snow a lot? Or was it barren and bleak most of the time? Did kids skate on the river ice? Or was it never safe enough for that? She remembered what

Mitch had said about Abraham Steele falling through the ice many years before.

"It's a nice night for a bonfire," Charlie said as they pulled out onto River Road. "Never know if it's going to be clear or raining cats and dogs this time of year."

"No rain tonight—there's a full moon," Tessa said. She'd been watching the waxing of the big harvest moon all week. Some nights when it came up over the horizon like an enormous gold coin, it seemed almost close enough to touch.

"'Shine on, shine on harvest moon, up in the sky,'" Charlie warbled horribly off key.

Tessa laughed. "I hope you never plan to earn a living as a singer."

Charlie put his hand over his heart. "You wound me to the quick, woman. I intend to be the next Sinatra."

"Oh, dear, then please forgive me," she said, still laughing.

He grinned. "But until I get my big break I'll just keep building garden centers for Mitch and houses for the good citizens of Riverbend."

Tessa was still smiling when they pulled into the parking lot at the hardware store. It was already more than half-full, and cars were pulling in as they parked in the roped-off area around the new greenhouse. "Rank has its privileges," Charlie said. He'd bounded out of the pickup cab and rounded the hood to open Tessa's door before she could do it for herself.

"Let me give you a hand down. This thing's built a lot higher off the ground than a car."

"I noticed," she said, doing as he asked. "I like being above the crowd that way."

"Why do you think SUVs and trucks are so popular? Everyone wants to be up high where they can see what's going on."

"And not have to spend hours in stop-and-go traffic looking at a bumper sticker on an eighteen-wheeler that says, How Am I Driving?"

"That, too. Although there's not a lot of stop-and-go traffic in Riverbend except maybe after a football or basketball game on Friday night."

"Or Sunday mornings after church."

Charlie nodded. "Yeah. My sister makes her best tips when she works Sunday mornings."

"Your sister?"

"Lucy Garvey. She's a waitress at the Sunnyside Café."

"I've met her. I didn't know she was your sister." It seemed as if everyone in Riverbend was related to everyone else.

"Lucy should be here tonight. I'll introduce you properly."

"Thanks. I'd like that."

Charlie held open one of the big glass doors to the store and Tessa stepped into a scene of brightly lit confusion. Kids were everywhere, lugging pumpkins so big most of them couldn't get their arms around them.

Lynn Kendall was supervising a quartet of teenagers as they put up folding tables and spread newspapers on the floor. Part of her Meacham House crew, Tessa guessed. She'd read about the new youth center in the

*Riverbend Courier.* At another table Linda Christman, half glasses perched on her snub nose, was sorting through a stack of patterns for a dozen different jack-o'-lantern designs she'd been running off on the copier all afternoon.

Tessa saw Dr. Stevens and a towheaded little girl who was obviously her daughter searching through some of the designs Linda had already laid out, their heads bent over the patterns, looking for just the perfect one.

One day she would be doing the same thing with her daughter, getting ready to carve a Halloween jack-o'-lantern, going shopping at Killian's to find just the right costume. Except, she reminded herself for the thousandth time, she wouldn't be shopping at Killian's. She wouldn't be living in Riverbend.

"Tessa! How nice to see you here." She turned to see Kate McMann with her daughters. Kate managed the bookstore, and Tessa had met her and her precocious five-year-old twins a week or so before on her lunch hour. Steele's Books was a wonderful place, a treasure trove of new books and old. The history section took up half an entire wall, and Tessa had fallen in love with the place at first sight.

She watched as the two little girls picked out their pumpkins from the pile Mitch had brought in that afternoon, then went racing to the table to paint them. Kate, looking slightly harassed but with a smile on her face, was only a step behind with smocks to cover their clothes.

Someone tapped her on the shoulder. It was Sam.

"Hi, Tessa," he said. "Did you pick out your pumpkin yet?"

"Not yet."

"I'll find you a good one."

"I'm in charge of the little kids," Lily Mazerik said, smiling at Tessa from behind a nearby table. "We're painting our pumpkins. No sharp objects allowed."

"This is probably where I should be," Tessa confessed. "I'm not very talented with a carving knife."

"I am." Sam had been following their conversation. "I've already carved a real neat pumpkin. Want to see?"

"Sam and a couple of the older guys from Meacham House carved a few of the biggest pumpkins right after school. Mitch has them on display over in the corner." Lily motioned toward the aisle that held plumbing fixtures.

Tessa followed Sam to where Lily had indicated. Three huge pumpkins were displayed against a burlap backdrop. They were lighted from inside with small electric bulbs, she noticed, instead of candles, a safety precaution Mitch's insurance company had probably insisted on.

The designs carved into the pumpkins were intricate and detailed. Sam laid a hand proudly on one that contained an entire graveyard scene complete with a skeletal tree and the grim reaper with beckoning hand and scythe. A thumbnail moon-and-star shapes had been carved into the back of the pumpkin, and their silhouettes were reflected on the burlap behind the table where the pumpkins were sitting.

"Sam, it's great. Did you use a pattern?"

Sam shook his head in vehement denial. "I did it all on my own."

"It's wonderful. We should take a snapshot. I wonder if your dad has a camera here."

"Sure do," Mitch said, coming up behind them. "I've already taken about half-a-dozen shots." He ruffled Sam's hair. "I'm thinking about having this baby cast in bronze it's so good."

"You can't do that. It's a pumpkin. It would cook or melt or something," Sam scoffed, but he looked pleased at his father's reaction.

Tessa added her compliment to Mitch's. "I could never carve anything half so good, even with a pattern. You're very talented, Sam."

"I like to draw."

"The others were done by kids four or five years older than Sam," Mitch told her.

"Is he taking lessons?" It had been a busy day at the store. She and Mitch had barely crossed paths, and then Mitch had sent her home at two to put her feet up for a while before the carving session. She hadn't been this close to him, close enough to feel the warmth of his skin, breathe in the scent of his aftershave, all day. The pleasure it gave her made her a little weak in the knees.

"Lily's giving him lessons, but she says he needs more expert instruction. She's going to get in touch with someone from the university after the holidays."

"In the meantime…"

"In the meantime, everything's taking second place to his making the Mini-Rivermen team."

Sam had given up demanding a weight bench, but he had held Mitch to his promise of an hour's practice every day, and the paint department had been totally reorganized. Sam declared his biceps were half an inch bigger, and he was positive he would make first team.

"Tessa, could you help me with these patterns?" Linda Christman called.

"Of course. Excuse me," she said, and hurried off. Maggie Leatherman stopped her to say hello. So did the mayor and her husband, and one or two other people before she got to Linda. Friendly everyday welcomes that she stored in her heart. Sunbeam memories of this time and place.

At the pattern table, she was caught up in a swirl of children choosing their designs. After that, Ruth Steele drafted her to ladle cider into plastic cups while Rachel passed out powdered-sugar doughnuts from the bakery, Maggie kept an eagle eye on the big boys, who kept coming back for seconds and thirds. Tessa never did get around to carving a pumpkin of her own.

Before she knew it the carving session was over. The smallest children were wiped free of paint on fingers and noses and rosy cheeks. One or two nicked fingers were bandaged and tears mopped up. Several broken pumpkin stems were wired back on the lids. And when all were satisfied with their handiwork, Mitch lined up forty-seven children and their creations on and around an old flat-bed farm wagon at the side of the building. While applauding parents and grandparents watched, the photographer from the *Courier* took a roll of pictures of glowing grinning children and their glowing grinning pumpkins, ensuring a sold-out Monday edition.

After the photo session Tessa turned to go back in the store, but Beth Pennington stopped her. "Charlie's here to take me to Mitch's to help set out the food. Why don't you come with us? You look tired."

"There's a lot of mess to clean up," she said, although Beth was right. She was tired. And hungry. She had been so busy she hadn't even had time to eat a doughnut. And the salad she'd had for lunch seemed a long time ago.

"Mitch has plenty of help. The football team is due here in five minutes to police the parking lot and clean up the mess. Aaron arranged for it. Sort of a preemptive strike in case any of them get caught swiping pumpkins off front porches this week." Right on cue a van pulled into the parking lot and a dozen tall, broad-shouldered teens in red-and-white Rivermen football jerseys piled out. "See? What did I tell you?" Beth laughed.

Tessa laughed, too. "Okay. I'll get my coat."

She went into the store, grabbed her coat from the employees' lounge and headed back toward the entrance. It took her five minutes to walk the length of the store. There were friends to say goodbye to and a few last pumpkins to admire. She realized as she turned to wave a last goodbye to Kate McMann and her girls that she had begun to make friends in Riverbend. Real friends, not just acquaintances. And in return she was beginning to be treated as if she belonged.

She was beginning to *feel* as if she belonged.

And God help her, that was the last thing in the world she wanted to happen.

THE FIRE WAS DYING down. Lily and Aaron had already left. Kate had taken her girls home an hour ago. Lynn Kendall and Tom Baines had dropped by to be congratulated on their engagement, and Mitch had introduced Tessa to the world-famous journalist. Caleb had walked Maggie and Will Leatherman to their truck half an hour earlier, then gone up to bed. Sam was spending the night with Tyler Phillips. Soon he would have a few minutes alone with Tessa, Mitch thought.

Charlie and Beth were still there, but Charlie had already loaded up the chili kettle and started his truck. It was cold and still, and frost was thick on the windshield. Charlie turned up the collar of his coat, glad for its heavy warmth for the first time that season. Beth and Tessa had put away the pickles and cheese and crackers and the last of the pumpkin cookies Ruth and Rachel had sent over, and were talking quietly as they crossed the yard. There was nothing left to do but finish his beer and put out the fire.

"I had a great time tonight, Mitch," Beth said, coming up behind his lawn chair to rest both hands on his shoulders. "The pumpkin carving was great. When did you start doing that?" Beth had been living in Iowa during the years she and Charlie were divorced. She'd only come back to Riverbend that summer.

"The year before Kara left," he said. And wished he'd kept his mouth shut. It was a bad habit he'd gotten into, breaking his life into two parts. Before his divorce and after.

Beth squeezed his shoulder, a signal she understood, perhaps better than the other River Rats, what he'd gone through. "Thanks for inviting us. It was like old times tonight," she said, leaning over to give him a peck on the cheek. "River Rats reunited."

"Except for Jacob."

"Yeah." Beth straightened again. "Where is he?"

"Your guess is as good as mine."

"Do you suppose he'll ever come home?"

"He didn't come home when Abraham died. I doubt he'll put in an appearance after all these months."

"What happened with him?"

"I wish I knew."

Beth turned at the sound of heavy footsteps deliberately shuffling through the fallen leaves. Their dry woody scent lay heavy on the night air. "Ready to go home, Charlie?" she asked.

"Yep." Charlie wrapped his arms around her and nuzzled her neck. "Got a big day ahead of me tomorrow."

Mitch stood up as Tessa walked into the circle of light around the dying fire. She had a couple of blankets and an old afghan of his mother's folded over her arm. He'd brought them out for Kate's twins, Hannah and Hope, to wrap up in when they complained of the cold. She was smiling at Charlie and Beth, but the smile was pensive and didn't light her blue eyes.

"Good night, Tessa," Beth said. "Call me for lunch next week, okay?"

"I...I'll do my best. We've been very busy at the store."

If Beth heard the reluctance Mitch detected in Tessa's voice, she ignored it. "Great. I'll look forward to it. C'mon, Charlie. It's time to get you home to bed. You need your beauty sleep."

"It's not beauty sleep I need," Charlie said with a wolfish grin.

Mitch rose from his chair. "The chili was magnifico, as always, buddy."

"Yes," Tessa seconded. "It was delicious."

"I'm saving the five-alarm batch for Superbowl Sunday."

"C'mon, Charlie, I'm freezing," Beth prompted.

"Your wish is my command," he teased, and they headed off down the walk.

Tessa watched in silence as his friends drove away. Mitch put his empty beer bottle in the cooler beside his chair and picked up a bucket of water to douse the fire. "Thanks for your help tonight," he said when the silence had stretched out too long.

"I enjoyed it. I've never done anything like that before. Whatever made you think of such a thing?"

Mitch shrugged. "It just grew like Topsy. The first year it was Sam and a few friends. Then a few more. We started having it at the store a few years ago. I've been growing pumpkins out front that long, too. Any kid who doesn't have a pumpkin when he gets there can pick one out of the patch. The doughnuts and cider don't cost much, and the store gets some free publicity."

"I don't think that's why you do it."

He poured more water on the fire, let the snap and sizzle of steam hitting the hot coals delay his answer. He watched the smoke eddy into the branches and the stubbornly clinging brown leaves of the big oak that had dominated the yard ever since the house was new. She was right. He didn't do it for the free publicity. The doughnuts and cider and overtime for his employees, which Tessa wouldn't know about until she got her paycheck, cost far more than an ad in the *Courier* or airtime on WRBN.

She answered for herself. "You do it because this town means a lot to you."

"My roots are here, Tessa," he said, watching the steam rise off the darkened logs.

"And your heart."

He nodded, poking at the dying embers with a stick, moving them apart. The smell of wood smoke was strong in the frosty air, the night suddenly very dark as his eyes reacted to the loss of the firelight. "I belong here," he said simply.

"And I don't." Her words were so soft he could barely hear them, but they cut deeply into his soul with a sense of loss that was sharper than a knife.

He went to her and took the blankets from her arms, dropped them onto the seat of his chair and took both her hands in his. "You could belong here, Tessa. You're already starting to put down roots and you know it."

"No." There was real panic in her voice. He ignored it.

"You felt it tonight, maybe even before. But tonight I could see it in your eyes, I could hear it in your laughter. You're forming a connection to this place and these people.''

''Mitch, don't. I can't—'' He could see tears forming in her eyes as his vision adjusted.

''Shh, Tessa. Don't say anything. Let me do the talking.'' Tugging her with him into the dense shadow of the old oak, he leaned his back against the rough bark of the trunk and lowered his mouth to hers. ''Better yet, let's not talk at all.'' He kissed her, long and slow and thoroughly, the way he'd wanted to since almost the first day they'd met.

He angled his hips to bring her close without putting pressure on the baby. She resisted him for a moment, then molded herself against him. He untied the belt of his mother's old coat and slid his arms around her. She pressed herself closer. Her breasts were lush and full and his body responded instantly.

''God, Tessa. I knew kissing you was going to be the best thing that ever happened to me.'' He wanted to tell her so much more. That he had longed to hold her this way for days. That he wanted so much more— her body, yes, but her heart and soul, as well. But all he could do now was learn the taste and scent and feel of her. ''Kiss me back.''

Her mouth opened under his, and she kissed him back, longingly, hungrily. He bracketed her face with his hands and held her still, afraid the kiss would end too soon. She made a sound deep in her throat, and he felt her hands on his hips, holding him lightly, then more boldly as the kiss grew more intimate.

Flame erupted around him as though the fire had come back to life. The half-formed, half-denied longings of the past two weeks fused together like glass forming from sand and fire. This was the woman he was meant to be with. This was the partner he wanted to go through life with. No matter what the difficulties, no matter what obstacles she threw in his way, he would make her his.

"I love you, Tessa," he said, barely breaking the contact of their mouths to say the words.

She went very still in his arms, then laid her head against his chest. He could feel her trembling against him and turned her a little so that he could tighten his embrace without causing her distress. *God, I shouldn't have said that. Not out of the blue that way. Not so soon.* But it was the truth, and he couldn't keep it in his heart any longer.

"You can't mean that, Mitch." The night was quiet. It was late. Only the barking of a dog across the river and the slow roll of a car going by on River Road broke the silence, but still he had to tip his head to hear her words.

"I love you, Tessa," he repeated so that there could be no mistake.

She lifted her head and a stray beam of moonlight caught the sheen of tears in her eyes. "I don't believe in love at first sight."

"I do," he said, and he meant it.

"I'm pregnant," she said, pushing against his chest with her hands. He released her but caught her cold hands between his when she would have turned away.

"I noticed."

"I'm pregnant with another man's child."

"Do you still love him?"

She dropped her gaze for a moment, then lifted her eyes to his. "No, God help me. I don't love him. But I thought I did."

"And you're not in love with me." He shouldn't be pushing her this way. He should sweep her into his arms and take her to her bed in the boathouse and make love to her until she couldn't think or analyze her feelings. He wanted her to feel his love and his willingness to make a commitment to her and her child.

"I don't know. I..." She moved swiftly to free her hands from his. She took two steps away. "I have my baby's welfare to think of."

"I love children, Tessa."

She closed her eyes, not so much shutting him out as shutting herself inside. "I don't want to be hurt again."

"You won't be, Tessa. I promise you."

# CHAPTER TEN

TESSA WAS SHIVERING like the oak leaves overhead. She couldn't seem to stop. She laid her head against Mitch's chest, heard the fast steady drumming of his heart. His coat smelled of wood smoke and sawdust and apple juice. Hannah McMann had spilled a cupful of it on him when she'd run full tilt into him, giggling that she and her sister were being chased by "monsters." The monsters were Sam and his friend Tyler.

Mitch had only smiled and wiped away the stain with a paper napkin, sending Hannah on her way with a hug, and cautioning Sam and his pal not to get the little girls too excited so close to bedtime. He was a such a good man. A good father, as different from Brian—her baby's father—as night from day. She choked back a tiny sob.

*He loved her.* He had said it not once, but twice. And if he loved her, he would love her baby, too.

If he really loved her, that was, and didn't just feel obligation meshed with sexual desire.

That had to be what it was. Obligation, honor, integrity. A man like Mitch would honor those impulses, might even confuse them with love.

He felt her trembling in his arms and pulled her closer against him. "What's wrong?"

"I'm fine." She didn't sound fine and she knew it.

"It's freezing out here. Let's get you inside." She made no protest as he turned her toward the boathouse. Once inside the apartment he led her to the sofa, and when she was seated he turned up the thermostat. Almost immediately she could feel warmth return to the room. "You shouldn't let it get so cold in here," he said, his voice raspy. He didn't come back to the sofa, but remained on the far side of the room.

"I don't like to waste electricity when I'm not going to be here."

"It doesn't cost that much to heat the place. I insulated it damned good." He raked his hand through his hair and turned back to the couch. In the blink of an eye, he closed the small distance between them. "Tessa, I'm sorry. I shouldn't have said what I did out there. Just forget it."

She felt small and helpless sitting while he stood over her. For a moment she let herself wonder what it would feel like to be able to lean on him for comfort and support, not to have to take on all her dragons by herself. It was too tempting a fantasy to indulge. She stood up so that she only had to lift her head slightly to meet his gaze. "We can't just forget it."

He made a noise deep in his throat, a low feral growl. "Okay, then let's say I had one too many beers."

"I only saw you drink two the whole evening."

He pulled her back into his arms. "God, Tessa. You're not going to make this easy, are you? I know you weren't ready to hear me say I love you. But I did say it, and there's no taking it back."

"You can take it back," she said softly. "I'll understand." Tears still pricked behind her eyelids. She wanted so desperately to say she loved him, too, but her insecurities prevented the words from forming.

"It doesn't work that way." He kissed her again, hungrily, passionately, telling her even more plainly than words how much he wanted her.

Tessa felt breathless and a little dizzy. She hadn't felt particularly sexual during her pregnancy. Brian hadn't seemed to enjoy making love to her once she started to show. By then she was already growing apart from him and almost welcomed his indifference. But there was no indifference in Mitch's kiss or his embrace. He wanted her. His erection was hard and hot against her thigh. And she wanted him. At least her heart and body did, though her brain refused to surrender.

That stubborn, scared, uncertain part of her made her lift her arms and push against his chest, separating them a fraction of an inch, then a little more. "I'm not ready for this, Mitch," she said truthfully. "I can't think straight when you kiss me like that. And I don't believe you're thinking straight, either."

"Don't think, Tessa. Just feel," he said roughly, but he made no move to pull her back into his embrace.

"No." She shook her head, seeing the movement reflected in the darkness of his eyes. "That's what got me where I am today."

"Here with me," he said softly.

She took a deep breath. "Here with you. Pregnant. Unmarried. Nearly penniless. Mitch, don't you understand? I thought I loved Brian and I was terribly wrong. Now—'' She stopped abruptly and turned away, walked to the window to look out at the black ribbon of water scattered with starshine. She'd been about to say, *Here I am, falling in love with you.*

But she could not. She dared not say it aloud, because this was how she'd felt at the beginning with Brian.

Mitch came up behind her and put his arm around her, just above where the baby lay sleeping beneath her heart. ''There's nothing wrong with falling in love at first sight, Tessa.''

''There is if it doesn't last.'' Unshed tears blurred her words. ''If it wasn't really love in the first place.''

''You couldn't know it wouldn't last.''

''I don't want to go through that again.''

''Neither do I. This time it will be for keeps. I promise you.''

She twisted away from his embrace and immediately felt the chill of her aloneness. Instead of throwing herself back into his arms, she forced herself to move another step away. ''I'm not ready for any kind of commitment, Mitch. I have my baby to think about. And you have Sam. Have you considered him in all this?''

''Yes,'' he said. The light from the small lamp barely reached this end of the room. Mitch's face was in shadow, but she thought he sounded slightly less sure of himself than before.

''What if he doesn't want me?''

''He'll come to love you just as I have, Tessa.''

''Perhaps.'' She wished with all her heart she could

believe that. ''But what if I can't be the kind of mother he needs?''

''You've been great with him so far.''

''As an acquaintance. Maybe even a friend. But not as a mother.'' She couldn't bring herself to say stepmother. She would love Sam as her own if she dared.

''You're going to be a wonderful mother, Tessa.'' There was no uncertainty in his voice this time. His rock-solid conviction brought fresh tears to her eyes, but she blinked them back, just like the others.

''I need time, Mitch. And we don't have time.''

He reached out and took her hand, moving a little closer, yet still allowing her the space she both wanted and needed. ''Give me that time, Tessa, if you don't feel you can give me your heart. I can wait for you to say you love me. I can wait until you have as much faith in yourself as a woman and a wife—and mother—as I have. But I can't let you walk out of my life.''

''Mitch...'' He was going to ask her to stay in Riverbend. Oh, God, how could she deny him that when it was what she herself so wanted?

''Promise me you'll stay in town. At least until after the baby is born and you're strong enough to travel.''

''No strings attached?'' She steeled herself against the treacherous familiar longing to belong to this place and this man. The baby had been sleeping until that very moment. Now she came awake and moved strongly, adding her insistence to the clamoring of Tessa's heart.

She watched Mitch's jaw set, felt his muscles tense.

His hands squeezed hers, reflexively, painfully, and then he let her go. He nodded. "No strings attached."

Her joy was bittersweet. She would be able to stay here in her cozy little boathouse apartment. Annie Stevens would deliver her baby. She wouldn't have to impose on Callie and complicate her complicated life even more. But she would have to do it all without Mitch at her side.

"I need time, Mitch," she said, praying he would understand what she barely understood herself.

"You can have all the time you need."

She wondered how long that would be. Could she ever truly trust her heart again? How could she? With Brian she hadn't known the difference between infatuation and love. With Mitch she was very afraid she wouldn't be able to tell the difference between love and gratitude. Not on her part, but on his. Mitch was a white knight, a man of integrity, and she was the closest thing there was to a damsel in distress in Riverbend, Indiana.

Maybe his heart was as unreliable as hers. After all, he was divorced. He'd failed at love just as she had. He needed time as much as she did, even if he didn't think so now. She was going to have to be strong and unwavering for both their sakes. Because if she risked falling in love—and lost—a second time, she knew it would truly break her heart.

"YOU'RE UP MIGHTY LATE, boy." Caleb spoke from the depths of his favorite chair.

"So are you."

"Ate too much of Charlie's darned chili." His

grandfather grunted, stifling a belch. "I'm too old for that kind of spicy stuff."

The television was tuned to the weather channel, but the sound was muted. Mitch sat down on the couch and put his elbows on his knees as he watched the blue-and-green satellite image of the earth that filled the screen.

"Fire's been out for some time. You been sitting out there in the cold?"

Mitch shot his crafty grandfather a look. "You know I wasn't alone."

"You must have had something important to talk to Tessa about to have spent so much time out there alone with her." His grandfather had never been a man to mince words, but he was of an age and a generation where talking about sex wasn't so easily done. Mitch was well aware his grandfather suspected more than talking had been going on between him and Tessa, but he wouldn't come out and say so.

"I asked her to stay in Riverbend." He waited for Caleb's reaction, wondering if his grandfather would pick up on what he'd left unsaid.

"I thought you meant to give Mel Holloway's boy that job."

"I do." Mitch looked down at the floor, letting his hands dangle between his knees. Belle had padded into the room when he came in. She flopped down at his feet, looking a little lost. She'd probably want to sleep on his bed tonight since Sam was staying overnight with Tyler. He supposed he'd let her, although she was too big and heavy to be a comfortable bed partner.

"If you don't have permanent work for her, then

why'd you ask her to stay?'' Caleb said bluntly. "She's got no family here. No ties to the place." He worked the handle on his recliner, bringing it upright, then planted his feet firmly on the floor. Mitch could feel the shrewd old eyes drilling holes in the side of his head. "Moving her into the boathouse lock, stock and barrel is a mite more than Christian neighborliness."

Mitch didn't answer.

"You fallin' in love with that young woman?" Caleb asked at last.

"I am in love with her, Granddad."

Caleb snorted. "I was afraid of that."

Mitch's head came up. He looked over at his grandfather's craggy face, blue-tinged from the light of the TV screen. "I hoped no one would notice."

"I'm not just anybody. I'm your flesh and blood. I got eyes. I'm not so old that I can't see the way you look at each other."

"She's not in love with me." Mitch said it straight out, as much for his own ears as Caleb's.

"She tell you that?"

"She said she needed time to sort out her feelings."

"Well, I'll be damned."

"What's that supposed to mean?" Mitch thought about going to the kitchen and getting another beer, letting the alcohol soothe the frayed edges of his mind and body. He'd feel better now, but not at three in the morning when the alcohol wore off and he lay staring at the ceiling, unable to sleep. That had happened too many nights after Kara left for him to fall into that trap again.

"I misjudged the girl, that's all."

"What the hell are you talking about?" Mitch demanded.

Caleb didn't take offense at his exasperated words. "I mean, I owe her an apology. I figured her for a gold digger."

"Hell, Granddad. Have you been on her case behind my back?" Mitch got up from the couch and stalked to the window, where he could look out over the river and see the corner of the boathouse where Tessa's bedroom light was still shining.

"I have not. I've been my usual gracious self in her presence."

This time it was Mitch's turn to snort. "Granddad, gracious is the last thing I'd call you." He stood by the window for a few more seconds, then came back to sit down beside Caleb.

"Be that as it may, I had her figured all wrong. Why shouldn't I? A woman on her own, going to have a baby, lookin' all lost and alone. First you offer her a job, then a place to live rent free. Then you begin squiring her here and there around town. She'd be blind and not too bright not to start getting ideas about hooking up with you. You've got a soft heart, Mitch, even if you don't want me saying so. I figured she would have you all tied up in a blue ribbon by now. But she's got more grit than I gave her credit for."

"She's got grit, all right. She's a damned stubborn woman. I love her, Granddad. I'm not one of those guys with some kind of rescue complex or whatever you want to call it. I spent too many years trying to convince myself I still loved Kara when I didn't. I'm not about to make that kind of mistake again. This time it's real. And it's for keeps.'' He dragged his splayed fingers through his hair. ''At least on my side.''

''You don't know much about her, boy. She's pregnant and she didn't get that way by herself. Did she tell you anything about him? The man she left behind?''

''A little. He's a baseball player. He got a chance to play winter ball in Central America and left Tessa behind.''

''What are you going to do if he all of a sudden shows up on the doorstep?''

''I'd like to beat the hell out of him.'' Mitch leaned his head against the back of the couch and swiveled his neck to look at the old man again. ''I'd do my best to show her she and the baby were better off without him. Better off with me. How would *you* handle it?''

Caleb threw up his hands. ''Hell, I don't know. Maybe I'd pop him on the nose, too, just for my pride's sake, if nothing else.'' Caleb grinned over at him and Mitch grinned back. He and his grandfather had always been close, even before Mitch's parents had been killed.

Caleb's expression grew serious once more. ''There's Sam to think about.''

''I am thinking about Sam. I know I've said I didn't want to marry again if it meant bringing other kids into the family. Life is hard enough on Sam without taking on that kind of challenge.''

''But that was then. And now you've changed your mind.''

"I fell in love," he said simply. "And that means taking the hard with the soft. It means you find the strength in yourself to make two separate halves into a whole."

"It won't be easy. You have to convince Sam."

"I know, but I think he and Tessa are already friends and that's a good first step."

Caleb stood up slowly, favoring his arthritic knees and new hip. "Looks to me like you have to convince her, too."


"WHAT DO YOU THINK? Pretty cool, huh?" Tyler sat cross-legged on his bed, up by the pillows, and Sam was at the foot. They were looking at their pumpkins, displayed on the desk.

Tyler had made his look like Frankenstein, except he'd got in too big of a hurry and nearly cut off his head. Tessa had pushed a toothpick down the back of the monster's neck and it was holding together pretty good, just a little crooked.

"No shit," Sam replied.

His buddy's eyes got big.

"Was I too loud?" Sam twisted around to check to make sure the bedroom door was firmly shut.

"No," Ty signed.

"Did I pronounce it right?"

"Yeah." Ty eyed the closed door a little apprehensively. "But that doesn't mean you'd get a big hug for saying it. My mom'd wash both our mouths out with soap if she'd heard you."

"Guys say stuff like that."

"Not in my house, they don't.

Sam grinned a little sheepishly. "Not in my house, either." The older kids he'd hung around with at Meacham House last summer had said bad words—at least when Reverend Lynn wasn't listening. He wanted to be cool like them. But maybe this wasn't the way to go about it. His dad didn't cuss much, neither did his granddad or Coach Mazerik. Maybe it wasn't so cool.

And girls didn't like swearing. That was a fact. Not that he was interested in girls—only Tessa. But she wasn't a girl, really. She was a grown-up. Like his dad. "Girls don't like cussing." Sam spoke his thoughts out loud.

"What do you care about what girls don't like?" Ty wanted to know.

He hadn't told Ty of his idea yet. Of getting his dad and Tessa together. At first he'd thought Granddad Caleb would help, but he and Tessa hadn't hit it off too well, so Sam had given up on that idea.

But he needed someone to talk to about it. Tyler had two sisters. And a mom. And a grandma who lived in Riverbend. He might know something Sam could do that he hadn't thought of himself.

"What would you think if my dad got married again?"

Ty shrugged. "It'd be okay if it was someone you liked."

"I didn't want him to at first. I thought my mom would come back. But she's not going to." Sam worked hard to keep his voice low, make it easy for his friend to understand his words. He didn't sign. Ty knew a lot of words, but signing was hard. You put words together differently, and Ty got distracted if

Sam tried to do both. This was important. He wanted to get it right. "I want a mom. I want a baby brother or sister like you've got."

"Sisters are a pain," Ty stated with great emphasis. He had two, one older, who really was a pain, and a baby sister who was still cute and cuddly.

Sam wondered when girls got to be pains. Hope and Hannah McMann had been at the pumpkin party. They were five and pretty cute. They'd teased him and Ty all night until they chased them giggling into the circle of adults sitting around the fire. That got him and Ty yelled at, but the twins weren't pains. Not really, but he supposed someday they would be. A little brother would be best, but he would take what he could get. "I don't care. I want one. Or the other."

"Who are you going to get to marry your dad? He doesn't have a girlfriend."

Sam grinned. He remembered his dad and Tessa talking and laughing that night at the party. And how close they'd been standing that other night outside the boathouse. Close enough to kiss. "I think he does. It's Tessa."

"The lady who's living in the boathouse?"

"Yeah." Sam nodded emphatically.

"But she's going to have a baby—some other guy's baby," Ty said, his face getting kind of red.

Sam didn't want to think about how Tessa came to be having a baby. He had an idea how things worked that way, but he wasn't interested in the specifics just then. He was interested in getting Tessa and his dad together.

"She's not going to live with him. She told me so."

"So, do you think she likes your dad?"

"Yeah. And he likes her. I told you that. But..." Sam paused, not sure of his next words. They were hard to say. He'd never told anyone of that day he'd walked in on his mom and dad arguing. The day she'd said, *No more babies like Sam.*

"But what? If they like each other, maybe they'll get married on their own."

"What if she doesn't want a kid like me?"

"Huh?"

"One who's deaf."

"It's not catching, is it?" Ty looked pleased with himself for the joke.

"No. But, well, sometimes I've been a pain." Sam remembered how he'd acted that day at the store, knocking off the stovepipes and throwing a tantrum over the weight bench, like he was a little kindergartner or something. "I'm afraid she'll think I'd be like that all the time."

"Hey, man. You've got a lot on your mind. Trying to make first team. That's a lot of pressure on you."

Ty was lousy at basketball. He was taller than Sam, but big and slow. He was good at football, though. Sam's dad said he would be a great Riverman linebacker when he was in high school.

It was a big deal. Only another couple of weeks till tryouts. But Sam pushed aside thoughts of tryouts and the fluttery feeling that gave him in his stomach.

"I want to show her I like her. That I won't be a jerk like that again. That I like babies. That I'd be a good big brother." He strove to put the right inflection in his voice. *Earnest.* That had been a vocabulary word the week before. It meant he wanted people to know that he cared, that he was speaking the truth. That was how he felt. That was what he wanted Ty to know. And Tessa, too.

"All that?" Ty looked puzzled. He reached up and scratched his head until his red hair stood on end. Then he stuck out his lower lip and scrunched up his eyes, looking as if he was thinking hard. "You should give her a present," he said at last.

Sam punched his friend's shoulder playfully. "I thought of that, dork. What *kind* of present?"

"Oh." Ty was silent a moment, then he brightened. "Girls like flowers and candy."

"I don't have much money." Well, he had money. Old Mr. Steele had left him a lot of money, but he couldn't spend it. Ty knew that.

"Bummer. And anyway, how would that show you like little kids?" Ty paused. "You could draw her a picture. You're real good at that."

"Yeah." Inspiration struck Sam like a lightbulb turning on in his head. "Or I could make her a really excellent jack-o'-lantern. She thought the one I made at the store tonight was really great."

"But it's scary." Ty looked over at the ominous grim reaper and the cemetery outlined by the flickering candle behind it. "You shouldn't scare a lady who's going to have a baby. My mom told me that when she was going to have Kimberly and she caught us up on that tree branch getting ready to jump in the river."

"Yeah, I remember." His dad hadn't been too happy to hear what they'd been up to, either, even though Granddad told him his dad had jumped from the same tree branch when he was ten.

"So jack-o'-lanterns are out." Ty propped his elbows on his knees and put his chin in his hands. "Bummer."

"Scary jack-o'-lanterns are out. But I have an idea for a not-so-scary one." Sam hopped off the bed, rummaged through Ty's book bag and pulled out a notebook. He grabbed a pencil off the desk by his pumpkin and started sketching. The idea had come to him in another flash of inspiration. He really did like to draw, he thought as his design took shape. But he didn't have time, not until after basketball season, anyway.

Ty climbed off the bed and came to look over his shoulder. "Wow!" he said after a moment. "That's great. Want to make one like that for me to give my mom?"

Sam shook his head. "Nope. There's only going to be one." He looked at what he'd drawn. It was a teddy bear, sitting down, holding a pumpkin. And on the pumpkin he'd drawn tiny eyes, nose and mouth. A big, happy, smiling mouth. He'd have to find a really sharp knife to do the eyes and nose, but his dad would help him if he asked. He'd carve the moon and stars on the back like he'd done for his scary one, but this time they wouldn't make it scary, just cute.

And then he'd put it out in front of the boathouse for Tessa to find Halloween night when she came home from work. He would sign it at the bottom with his initials just like Lily had taught him. She'd see the cuddly little bear holding his smiling pumpkin and know it was from him.

She'd know he really liked her.

She'd know he liked little kids.

And if he was lucky, it would make it easier for her to fall in love with his dad.

# CHAPTER ELEVEN

"HELLO, TESSA."

"Good afternoon, Rachel." Tessa smiled as the old lady sailed into the store like someone half her age. She stepped out from behind the main counter, where she'd been tracking the whereabouts of a wayward shipment of electrical components on the computer, to greet her. "How may I help you?"

"I've come to look at the new wallpaper book you just got. Caleb told me about it when he stopped by the bookstore. I can't believe I've still not found the right paper for my bathroom." The pink-flowered pattern had been deemed too large and busy when viewed from the edge of Rachel's tub.

"It's right over here." She led the way to the L-shaped alcove where the wallpaper sample books and the big old library table were situated. "I'll get it for you."

"Thank you. I do so want to find just the right paper. If I don't choose soon, Miriam will be too busy with other jobs to hang it before Christmas." Rachel sat down to wait. She was dressed in a powder-blue jogging suit today, with embroidered pink roses on the jacket.

"You look very springlike for such a blustery fall

day," Tessa told her, setting the big sample book in front of her. The store was quiet, only a few customers wandering the aisles. Mitch was out in the yard dealing with a delivery of lumber, and Caleb was in the employee lounge taking a break, so Tessa could devote herself to Rachel's quest for the perfect bathroom wallpaper.

"It's been so dreary these last few days. Ever since Mitch's pumpkin carving. But at least it's not supposed to rain. Or worse yet, snow." Rachel smiled and opened the book. "It's Halloween, and tonight all the trick-or-treaters will be out. I do so love the little ones in their costumes." She looked at Tessa over the rims of her glasses. "I understand you will be staying on in Riverbend longer than you'd originally planned."

Tessa had been about to comment on how enjoyable she found small children in costumes, too. The change of subject caught her off guard. "I—"

"I can't tell you how happy I am to hear the news. We need young people like you moving into the community."

"Thank you. I'm happy to be here. But I don't know how long I can stay..."

"Of course, dear. You have your baby to think of, too. Mitch is a very good employer, but I don't see you working in a hardware store all your life."

"You don't?" Tessa was intrigued, despite the mention of Mitch. They hadn't spent any time alone together since the night of the pumpkin-carving party. He'd honored her request for time and space almost too well. She missed having lunch with him. She missed his smile, though he hadn't smiled much at all since that night. She was aware that it was her fault. And that she could bring that wonderful warm and sexy smile back by telling him what was in her heart. What she knew to be the truth.

But she couldn't overcome her own doubts about her ability to love, wholly and forever, and so she stayed silent.

"I do not," Rachel said emphatically. "Not that there's anything wrong with an honest day's work done for a fair day's pay. But I've watched you in the bookstore, and you always make a beeline for the history section. Is that where your interests lie?"

Tessa placed her hands flat on the table. The wood was cool to the touch, gleaming with polish. She liked Rachel. She'd never known her grandmothers, either of them, and she doubted they were anything like Rachel Steele. But in a perfect world they would have been. "Yes, it is. I've almost got my degree. I...I wanted to teach. But for the time being I've put that dream aside. Making a home and as good a life as possible for my baby is what's important to me now."

Rachel folded her hands on the book. They looked small and frail resting on the vibrantly colored paisley print on the page. "You can tell me to mind my own business if you wish, but I'm going to ask you this question, anyway. What about your baby's father? Isn't he going to face up to his responsibility and provide for your child?"

"He's in Central America playing baseball," Tessa said.

"I see." Rachel's pink lips firmed into a straight

disapproving line. "He left you to go play a boy's game. A real Peter Pan complex, eh?"

Tessa looked down at her reflection in the table's surface to keep from smiling at Rachel's apparent indignation on her behalf. The urge to smile faded as she remembered how badly Brian's desertion hurt. "He's a very talented athlete." She wondered why she felt compelled to defend him.

"I know I was raised to think differently, but you're better off without a man like that in your life. Not that I don't think a baby doesn't need a father. But just because God gave a man the means to reproduce doesn't mean he should exercise them."

This time Tessa did smile, in fact, she laughed out loud. "I wish I'd known you when I first met Brian. I might not have fallen so hard or so fast."

"Swept you off your feet, did he?"

"Yes, he did."

"Well, it happens to the best of us," Rachel said cryptically. "Now. Let's forget about men who aren't worthy and talk about babies."

"I thought you wanted to look for wallpaper."

"That was just my excuse to come and see if Caleb was telling me the truth about your staying in town, or if he was beginning to go senile."

"He was telling the truth," Tessa said guardedly. She'd caught Caleb watching her when she was talking to Mitch about things around the store. She suspected Mitch had told the old man he loved her. He and his grandfather were close, and she doubted they kept many secrets from each other, but Caleb hadn't confronted her with his knowledge.

She wondered how he felt.

And Sam.

How would the boy react to the prospect of a step-mother and a new baby in his life, if she suddenly threw caution to the winds and told Mitch she loved him, too?

"Do you have everything you need for the baby?" Rachel was still talking.

Tessa made herself pay attention. "Actually, no. I have very little. I...I thought I would be using my sister's baby things."

Rachel thumped the forgotten wallpaper book with the tip of her finger. "That's exactly what I told Ruth and Kate. I bet she was planning on using her sister's baby bed and high chair, I said. She can't have those big things stashed in the trunk of her little red car. Oh, and speaking of cars. You must have a car seat. It's the law."

"Yes, I know. I guess I'll have to start looking for all those things."

"No you don't."

"I'm sorry?"

Rachel was beaming. "No you don't have to start looking for all those things. We have them for you. Or at least Kate does. A baby bed. A high chair. A car seat. Well, to be accurate she has two of everything, but you aren't having twins, are you?" she asked, looking hopeful.

Tessa shook her head.

"That's too bad. Ruthie and I are always on the lookout for more twins to welcome into the world." She laughed, and Tessa managed a smile, too. A bewildered one, she was certain, and Rachel's next words confirmed it. "I'd better get to the point. We want to have a little party for you, Tessa. Ruth and Kate and me. A baby shower. Very small and friendly. We thought of asking Beth Pennington and Maggie Leatherman. Lily Mazerik and Reverend Lynn."

"Oh, no. I—"

"Of course you can. That's what friends are for. A week from today. Is that okay? For lunch. At the bookstore."

"But you barely know me."

"We like you. Some friendships are formed more quickly than others. When you're as old as I am, you'll learn to relish them and not question the gift." Rachel stood up. "I'll look through this book another day. I have some shopping to do." She gave Tessa one last sparkling look. "Do you know if the baby is a girl or a boy? It does make it so much easier to shop."

"No. Not really."

"But you have your suspicions."

Tessa nodded. "I think it's a girl."

"But if it's a boy, you'll be just as pleased." Her laughter trilled across the table. "It's not as if you can change the outcome at this stage of the game, anyway. I'll get back to you with the details of the shower." She waved a cheery goodbye and left the building as regally as she'd entered.

Caleb came over to stand beside her. He was limping a little, she'd noticed. The damp weather must be bothering his hip. "She didn't spend much time looking at wallpaper books," he observed, watching as Rachel passed the big plate-glass window at the front of the store. He continued watching as she climbed into her car and drove away. "She really came to quiz you about staying in Riverbend, didn't she?"

"Yes." Tessa didn't volunteer any more. Caleb hadn't been as openly hostile as he had the first week she'd worked at the hardware, but neither had he gone out of his way to be friendly.

"From the shell-shocked look on your face she did more than that."

"She and her sister and Kate McMann want to have a baby shower for me."

"That's nice of them."

"Yes, it is. I'm still practically a stranger."

"One of the good things about small towns is if you treat people with kindness and fairness, they'll pretty much do the same for you." He cleared his throat. "That's as good an opening as I'll make for myself to say I'm sorry for my behavior toward you when you first got here."

"Mr. Sterling, that's not necessary."

"The apology is necessary. The 'Mr. Sterling' isn't." He straightened his shoulders and folded his arms behind his back, then looked around to make sure they were alone in that part of the store. "I know about Mitch's feelings for you. I also know you asked him to keep his distance."

"I didn't mean it that way. Not that I don't want to be around him—"

Caleb grinned and held up his hand. She'd rushed to Mitch's defense when he didn't need it, and this wasn't lost on his grandfather. "I've got eyes in my head. I've seen the way you look at him when you think no one's paying attention.''

Tessa could feel her face grow warm. ''I hoped it wasn't that obvious.''

''It's not. I'm looking out for his welfare. And, well…'' The tips of his ears grew red and he rubbed his palm over his white hair.

''I'm an unmarried woman with a baby to raise, you thought, and Mitch would make a great catch.''

''Well, yes. I can't deny that was my original impression.''

''A natural one, considering the circumstances.'' Tessa smiled ruefully.

''But I've changed my mind. I just wanted to let you know that.''

''I don't want Mitch to be hurt, but I'm not ready to make a commitment to anyone or anything but my baby right now.'' Yet she wanted to so badly she could feel it beating inside her as strongly as her baby's heartbeat, as strongly as her own.

''That's as it should be. You and the little one will be snug as bugs in a rug in the boathouse this winter.''

''I really ought to be paying rent.'' It had been on her mind lately. She couldn't turn away from Mitch as she had and remain at the boathouse as his guest.

''That's for you and Mitch to work out.'' Caleb was no longer actively hostile, it was true, but he was still wary of her. And well he should be, if the uncertainty of her feelings was as easy for him to read as her initial attraction to his grandson had been. ''That's all I've got to say.'' He gave her a quick nod of dismissal and limped away.

Tessa closed the wallpaper book and was about to lift it onto the shelf, then left it where it was. It would attract more attention on the tabletop. It really was a wonderful book of patterns. She'd looked through it first thing that morning.

If the boathouse was going to be her home, she'd seen a border of egrets and herons, stalking their prey along a riverbank, that would look great in her tiny utilitarian bathroom. Paired with a new shower curtain in blues and green, and some thick soft towels, and a throw rug to take the chill off the tile floor—

She pulled herself up short. She was staying in town, but she wouldn't stay at the boathouse. She'd almost made up her mind about that before her talk with Caleb, but now she was certain she would have to find someplace else to live. She couldn't tell Mitch she needed time and space and then stay so close by that she could see his every coming and going. When he turned out his bedroom light at night. When he got up in the morning. She didn't want to leave the little apartment any more than she wanted to leave River-bend, but it wasn't fair to either of them if she stayed.

She needed time. And Mitch had promised her that. But she needed some distance, too.

''Tessa.'' His voice interrupted her thoughts. She looked up from the cover of the wallpaper book she'd been staring at but not seeing.

''Yes?''

He was wearing heavy work boots, and she should

have heard him coming from several aisles away, but she hadn't. Now that he was standing in front of her, he filled her senses. The scent of his aftershave, the breadth of his shoulders, the warmth of his skin radiating from him.

"Would you get me the printouts of the last order we got from Midwest Distributing? We're sending back a couple dozen defective roof joists, and I need the purchase-order number for them."

"Of course. It'll only take me a moment." He could have called her from the yard on the intercom, but he hadn't. He'd come back inside to do it. It was the first time since the pumpkin party that he'd sought her out for any reason. And his nearness had thrown her so off balance she could scarcely think.

He followed her to the counter but stayed on the customer side as she fed the information he needed into the computer. "Are you ready for trick or treat tonight?" he asked her. She avoided his eyes, fixing her gaze on the computer screen as they waited for the file to download the purchase order to the printer.

Her head jerked up. She was immediately lost in the gold-flecked brown eyes, drowning in their depths. "Excuse me, what did you say?" He was watching her too closely. She could barely breathe.

"Trick or treat. Are you ready for Halloween? If you don't want to pass out candy, just leave the porch light off in the boathouse."

"Not on your life." She took a step back, away from the temptation of his nearness. "I bought two bags of candy. Sam said that would be enough. He said that since your house is almost the last one on River Road, some children don't come that far.''

''Sam should know. He's an expert. Although I think this is the last year he'll be going door to door. Some of the other boys his age are already saying they're too old.''

''But he's only ten.''

''He'll be eleven in January.''

The printer began its work with a series of beeps and gurgles. It was an older model, a little slow, a little noisy. Mitch fell silent, perhaps contemplating how fast time went by. Or was he looking into a future that stretched out too long to spend it alone, as she so often did?

''Here you are,'' she said, just to break the tension she could feel building between them as the seconds ticked by. She handed him the printout. ''Anything else you need?''

''Yes,'' he said. ''But you're not ready to give it to me.'' He turned on his heel and walked away.

''Mitch,'' she called after him.

He lifted his hand in a wave and kept on walking.

MITCH PULLED ON the knee-high black boots and stood up. The boots were stiff and pinched his feet. They'd been sitting in an upstairs closet since *last* Halloween. He probably should have tried them on earlier, to break them in a little, but he'd been busy at the store right up until six, when he left Bill Webber to hold down the fort for the last hour. He checked the mirror above the fireplace to make sure his eye patch was straight, then gave a tug to the sleeves of his flowing white shirt and reached for the long black cape that completed the pirate outfit.

"I'm heading out, Granddad," he called, stomping into the kitchen. Trick or treat started in about ten minutes, and he needed to get to his post on the corner of Main and River Road. The Chamber of Commerce recruited members to act as safety patrols for the two hours the town reserved on Halloween night for trick-or-treaters, and this year was no exception.

As usual, he and Charlie Callahan had paired up for duty. Charlie dressed as a country bumpkin, in coveralls and an old straw hat his dad had thrown out twenty years earlier. After two hours of making sure a couple of hundred kids on a sugar buzz didn't dart out into traffic or trip over lawn gnomes, they usually stopped by the Riverman Lounge for a beer. But probably not this year. Charlie and Beth were picking out wedding invitations tonight, and he'd told Mitch on the phone two hours earlier that his life was in jeopardy if he missed showing up. So Mitch would be on his own.

But where he really wanted to be was with Tessa— the one place or person in Riverbend that was off-limits.

"I'm ready, too," Caleb said, hefting a big metal washpan he kept on a hook in the pantry. "I hope we get rid of most of this. It's too big a temptation to have lying around in the cupboard." He looked down at the assorted bite-size candy bars that almost filled the big pan.

"It's a nice night, so I imagine we'll get our share of kids." A breeze had come up in the afternoon and blown most of the clouds away. The evening promised to be clear and still.

Mitch pushed the button that activated Sam's pager. A minute later his son came stomping down the stairs. He was dressed like a hunter, in some old canvas pants of Mitch's, with a safety orange hat and vest and his BB gun slung over his shoulder. He'd blackened the lower half of his face to resemble a three-day growth of beard, and carried a khaki knapsack to hold his booty.

Sam was caught between childhood and growing up. He wanted to trick-or-treat, but he didn't want to seem like a little kid doing it. Mitch caught his grand-dad's eye and kept his smile from reaching his lips. Caleb looked down at his pan of sweets just in time to mask his own amusement. When he lifted his head, his face was perfectly serious.

"Good-looking outfit, boy. Made sure the gun's not loaded, right?"

"Thanks," Sam said, beaming. He showed Caleb the gun. "Not a BB in it."

"Good. Safety first with guns."

"Yes, sir."

"Ready to go?" Mitch asked. "Want to walk as far as the corner with me?"

"I have something to do first," Sam said. He slapped his knapsack on the kitchen table and hurried out to the back porch. When he came back, he was holding a big pumpkin carefully in both hands. "What do you think?'' he asked, turning the pumpkin so that the carved side was facing Mitch and his granddad.

"It's great," Mitch said, marveling at the detail on the teddy bear and the grinning jack-o'-lantern he held between his legs.

"Did you have a pattern for that?" Caleb asked.

Sam watched him form the words, then grinned more broadly. "Nope. I did it myself. It's for Tessa. Do you think she'll like it?"

"I think she'll like it a lot."

"I'd better get it over there. Want to come along, Dad?"

"Uh, no. But I'll wait for you, if you want to come with me."

"Ty's mom is dropping him off here."

"Then I'd better be going. You guys stay in the neighborhood and take your pager, okay?" He held Sam's attention with two knuckles under his chin. "And watch for cars."

"Okay." Sam pivoted carefully and headed for the boathouse.

Mitch watched him go, then looked back across the kitchen at his grandfather. "The boy's smitten," Caleb said, shaking his head. He narrowed his faded brown eyes in Mitch's direction. "He's near as moonstruck over her as you are."

"I'm not moonstruck."

"You could have fooled me. You make up any lost ground with her the past couple of days?"

Mitch shook his head. "I don't have time to talk about it. I'm late."

"Don't give her so much lead she slips the leash and runs off," Caleb advised as the doorbell rang. "Here they come," he said. "I'd better get out on the porch or they'll have the doorbell worn out."

Caleb shrugged into his jacket. Mitch grabbed his stuffed parrot off the kitchen table, stuck it on his shoulder and opened the door to the first wave of ghosts and goblins. Or Ninja warriors and Star Wars characters, as it turned out.

"Avast, ye hearties," he bellowed as he swirled his cape over his shoulder. "Ye'd best be gettin' out of me way, or it'll be the plank for ye."

The kids looked at him and giggled, then held out the glow-in-the dark goblin sacks they'd been handing out all week at the grocery store, for Caleb to fill with candy.

Mitch headed down the sidewalk toward the street. In the distance he saw Tessa and Sam lighting her pumpkin on a little table outside the boathouse. She was still wearing the silky blue tunic with the high neck and slim darker blue leggings she'd had on at the store. He'd wanted to tell her she was the sexiest pregnant woman he'd ever seen, but he'd clenched his teeth against those words and a torrent of others.

Was he doing the right thing staying away, giving her space to work out her problems and her feelings for him? *God, I sound like one of those New Age radio psychologists,* Mitch thought disgustedly.

What if Caleb was right? What if he gave her so much space she decided she could live just fine without him?

He listened to the echo of his heavy black boots as he tromped down the street. If he been born three hundred years ago, he wouldn't be having this conversation with himself. He'd have swept her up into his arms and carried her off to the nearest preacher and then to his bed.

"Damn it, I love you, Tessa," he muttered. "And I'll love the baby you're carrying like my own. I just hope I can figure out what I have to do to convince you of that before it's too late."

# CHAPTER TWELVE

FROM THE CORNER of her eye Tessa watched Mitch walk down the street into the deepening twilight. He was dressed as a pirate, and he looked as dark and dangerous as the real thing, despite the stuffed parrot perched on his shoulder.

A Halloween reincarnation of Captain Blood.

And if he had been the real thing, a sword-wielding buccaneer of old, would he have marched up to her in his swirling black cape and high black boots, swept her into his arms and carried her off to his galleon? Would he kiss her senseless and pay no heed whatsoever to her half-formed pleas for time to sort out the questions in her heart as he made her his?

She almost wished those times were still in style. It was hard being your own woman, responsible for yourself every minute of every day. Strong and independent and needing no one to make your life whole. To believe that was to deny the most basic element of humanity, of man and woman together. A life partnership.

"There." Sam stepped back and blew out the match he'd used to light the candle in her jack-o'-lantern. "What do you think?"

She looked at the big orange pumpkin and clapped

her hands with delight. "Sam, it's wonderful. Thank you. I could never have made such a marvelous jack-o'-lantern even with a pattern. I wish I had a camera. I'd take a picture of it."

A camera was something else she would need, so that she would have pictures of her baby from the moment she was born.

"I'll bring over Dad's camera after trick or treat and take a picture for you," Sam offered. "I'm good at taking pictures."

"Well, you're certainly good at carving pumpkins." She reached over and gave him a quick hard hug. "Thanks again."

Sam stiffened for a moment, then wrapped his arms around her and hugged her back. "Wow!" He jumped away so fast he almost tripped in his too-big hunting boots, his eyes focused on her bulging stomach. "Did the baby just kick me?"

Tessa smiled, keeping the laughter she felt bubbling up in her throat from breaking forth. Sam's ears were red and so were his cheeks above the black makeup he'd smeared on his face. "Yes, I think she did."

"Awesome! That was something. I've never felt an unborn baby move before."

"Would you like to feel her again? She's still doing somersaults." She pressed her hand on her stomach to reposition a tiny heel or elbow that was prodding her beneath her ribs. She didn't know how Sam would react to her invitation. He was at that awkward age between child and adolescent. Touching a pregnant woman's stomach could be the grossest thing imaginable to him, for all she knew.

"Well?" Sam looked around to make sure no one was watching. Caleb was busy on the back porch with a trio of little trick-or-treaters. Mitch was gone, already out of sight down the street. Sam appeared undecided, but he was still looking at her stomach. "I don't want to hurt you or anything."

Tessa reached out and placed Sam's hand lightly on her stomach. "That's a knee," she said. "I think. Or maybe an elbow."

"Mega-awesome!" The wonder in Sam's eyes sent a rush of emotion flooding through her. It was love, she had no doubt, mother love, almost as strong as what she felt for the tiny being growing inside her. "She really is doing somersaults. Does it hurt?"

Tessa shook her head. "But sometimes it almost takes my breath away."

Sam wiggled his eyebrows. "I'll bet." He tilted his head, absorbing the sensation. "You called it a she. Is the baby a girl?"

"I don't know for sure," Tessa informed him. "But I think so."

"You can find out, you know. There's a test. We talked about it last year in fourth grade when my teacher was going to have a baby. It was a girl. That's what she wanted." He made a face. "We all wanted it to be a boy." *We,* Tessa inferred, meant all the boys in Sam's class.

"I don't care if it's a boy or girl. I just want a happy healthy baby."

Sam's expression sobered. He dropped his hand. "I always wanted a brother or sister, but one day I heard my mom tell my dad she didn't want any more babies.'' There was little change in the inflection of Sam's words, but Tessa didn't need to hear the pain behind them to know it was there. And just as fresh and hurtful as the day the words were uttered.

What kind of woman had Mitch's ex-wife been? An even poorer example of motherhood than her own careless and selfish parent, who at least had tried to do the best she could for Callie and Tessa? Surely, even with all her self-doubts, she would be a thousand times better mother than the woman who bore Sam— and left him behind.

She tilted Sam's chin with the tip of her finger, so that he could see every word she said. "You can spend all the time here you want. You can be my baby's honorary big brother for as long as I stay in Riverbend.''

Sam nodded. He was clutching his old canvas knapsack between both hands. He was still a little boy on his way to trick-or-treat, but at the same time very near to leaving boyhood behind. "I'll be the best honorary big brother in the world,'' he said so carefully and so plainly that Tessa's heart did another little flip-flop in her chest.

*I love Sam.*

*And I'm falling in love with his father and it's time to stop pretending to myself I'm not.*

All she needed now was the courage to tell Mitch so.

"Trick or treat!"

Tessa looked over Sam's shoulder at her first official trick-or-treaters. Miniature versions of Dorothy and the Scarecrow came pelting up the driveway, followed more sedately by a slender young woman in jeans and a windbreaker. Sam turned when he saw that there was someone behind them.

"Hope and Hannah," he told her unnecessarily. "Pretty good costumes. I bet Ms. McMann made them. She sews a lot."

The twins' costumes were very good. Hope's blond hair was braided and tied off with blue ribbons that matched her gingham pinafore. She carried a small old-fashioned basket with a little stuffed dog peeking out of one side. And on her feet were ruby slippers that sparkled even in the fitful light of the single bulb above the boathouse door. Not even her miniature Rivermen letter jacket, necessary against the late October chill, could detract from the resemblance to Dorothy and Toto.

And Hannah, hopping along at her side, was the picture of the hapless Scarecrow, right down to her floppy hat and the straw sticking out of her jacket and pant legs. Hannah wasn't wearing a jacket, but Tessa suspected she had a warm sweater or sweatshirt underneath her costume. Kate McMann was too conscientious a mother to let her daughters catch a chill if she could help it.

"You guys look great," Tessa said, stepping inside the cottage to get the chipped pottery bowl from the table that held her treats. "One for you."

"Thank you," Hope said immediately.

"Your ruby slippers look very real."

"Thank you," came the polite reply again. "My mom made them."

"They're perfect. How did she get them so

sparkly?'' Tessa smiled at Kate, who had caught up with her daughters, but it was Hope who answered.

''It's material from the store. My mom glued it on my last year's Christmas shoes.''

''Thank heaven for spray adhesive.'' Kate chuckled. ''It makes me look like a genius. Hi, Tessa.''

''Hello, Kate.''

''They pinch,'' Hannah said with a smirk. ''They're too small. That's the only reason Mom did that to them.''

''I told you you could be Dorothy, too, if you wanted, Hannah. You chose to be the Scarecrow.''

''I'm not wearing sissy dresses and shoes that pinch my feet. Trick or treat,'' Hannah demanded, holding up her plastic pumpkin.

Hastily Tessa dropped the candy inside. Hannah looked into her container, scrutinizing Tessa's offering. Apparently the sweet-and-sour wrapped candies that Tessa had chosen at the store after much deliberation passed muster. ''Thank you,'' she said, smiling her impish smile.

''C'mon, Mom,'' Hope urged, tugging on Kate's sleeve. ''We've got to keep going. There's only two hours to trick-or-treat everywhere.''

Tessa wanted to thank Kate for offering to host the baby shower Rachel had invited her to that morning, but the children weren't inclined to stand around while the grown-ups chatted.

Sam had been watching the scene in stoic silence. Either he knew the twins well enough to guess what they wanted, or he'd been able to follow their rapid-fire speech more closely than Tessa would have guessed. "I'll take them over to Granddad Caleb to get their treat," he offered.

"Thank you, Sam," Kate said. "What do you say to Sam, Hannah?"

"Thank you, and hurry up, let's go."

"Thank you, Sam." Hope faced him head-on as she spoke and held out her free hand.

Sam took her small hand in his. "C'mon, Hannah. Take Hope's hand."

"We're only going across the driveway," Hannah said, dancing away backward, but she, too, remembered to face Sam as she spoke.

"You're a brat, Hannah McMann," Sam said.

"So are you." Hannah stuck out her tongue, but slowed down and fell into step with the others after Kate reminded her that she could just as well stay by her side and miss Caleb's treat altogether.

"They're adorable," Tessa said, resting the bowl of candy on her stomach. The baby had quieted. Gone back to sleep, perhaps? Or was she listening to the rise and fall of children's voices, their laughter and giggles? How much *did* babies absorb from the outside stimuli that filtered into their protected and watery world? Those were the kinds of questions she wished she could ask someone. Kate was almost her age, and she had been pregnant. But she didn't know her well enough yet to get so personal.

Maybe she would have the chance, since she was going to stay in Riverbend.

"What a great jack-o'-lantern," Kate said, leaning forward to get a better look.

"Sam made it for me."

"He did?" Kate smiled. "He must've taken a real shine to you."

"I'm happy he thinks well enough of me to do this. We've had a couple of dust-ups since I've been living here."

"The weight-equipment brouhaha?" Kate asked, stuffing her hands in the pockets of her windbreaker. She was blond and slight and made the jeans and sweatshirt she wore underneath the jacket look far classier than they had a right to. "Mitch told me about it."

"Yes. Although it all turned out okay."

"Sam's a pretty grounded kid even with his disability. He's got Mitch to thank for that. Sam's mother opted out of his life quite a while ago."

"Mitch told me."

"He's a great guy," Kate said, swiveling on the ball of her foot to check out the twins and Sam. Tessa followed her gaze and saw that a trio of Ninja warriors were heading off the porch in their direction. "He's a good friend. And he's got a smile that's to die for."

Tessa only nodded.

Kate looked over her shoulder. Her expression was quizzical. "Mitch really is just a friend, in case you might have heard otherwise."

She hadn't and she was glad. She didn't like to think there were other women in Riverbend with her kind of feelings for Mitch. "I...I don't think it's any of my business."

"In a town this size it's everyone's business. A lot of people thought we'd be good together. Two single parents, lived here all our lives, businesses to run—

you know the drill. Well, on our third date Mitch said, 'Let's go to the zoo.' And I blurted out, 'Oh, the girls would love it.' I was horrified. Mitch just laughed and said he must have been thinking the same thing about Sam, or he wouldn't have come up with the suggestion. To make a long story short, we took all three of them to the zoo the next weekend, and that was our last date. But we've been great friends ever since.''

Kate McMann was a successful businesswoman, a respected citizen. She smiled often and laughed a lot when Tessa visited the store. She'd been neither beaten down nor discouraged by her lot in life. *I could do worse for a friend and a role model,* Tessa thought to herself. *A lot worse.* ''Doesn't it scare you sometimes being a single mother?'' she asked.

''It scares the life out of me whenever I let myself think about it. It will you, too. But you'll do fine. I can tell.'' Hope and Hannah came racing back, Sam right behind them.

''I'm not so sure,'' Tessa said, hugging her crockery bowl.

''Trust me.'' Kate smiled. The twins made a beeline for their mother's side. They hugged her close and thrust their containers forward for her to inspect. Kate rolled her eyes and nodded her approval at the generosity of Caleb's treat. The twins began to drag her in the direction of the sidewalk, eager to be on their way. The Ninja warriors came bounding up. From the other direction a pint-size football player in full Colts regalia and a green Teletubby were coming up the drive, with their mother in tow. ''Call me if you want to talk, or if you have any questions about being pregnant. I loved being pregnant.'' Her voice had a smile in it, but the smile didn't reach her eyes, and Tessa wondered what the details of loving and losing in Kate's past were.

"I'd like that," Tessa said truthfully.

"I'm in the book." Kate let the twins drag her off.

"There's Ty." Sam spotted his friend at the curb and took off with a wave.

Tessa gave the green Teletubby and the football player and the Ninja warriors their treats, but her mind was elsewhere. She supposed she ought to see about having a telephone installed. It might be some time before she could find another place to live.

She would talk to Mitch about it the next time she saw him.

Her heart gave a thump and so did the baby inside her. She'd made up her mind. How could such a life-altering decision come so closely on the heels of such a mundane one as getting a telephone installed? She loved Mitch, and that was all there was to it. She would tell him so the first chance she got.

TESSA EMPTIED the last of her candies into the bowl. She glanced at her sunflower clock above the sink. Fifteen minutes until eight. Trick or treat was almost over. She was going to make it. She'd even have a couple of rolls of candies left.

Someone knocked on the door. She picked up her bowl and swung it open.

"Trick or treat," the dark-haired pirate with a patch over one eye demanded.

He was born to wear a black cape, high black boots

and a rakish eye patch. He looked every inch the swashbuckling pirate of a woman's most private fantasies—even with the ridiculous stuffed parrot sitting lopsidedly on his shoulder. She had so much to say to him. But where to start? At the beginning, she thought wildly, and opened the door wider. "Mitch. Hello."

"I saw your porch light still on," he said, making no move to come into her little apartment, "So I thought I'd stop by and see how your night went."

"It was fun. I had almost a hundred trick-or-treaters. I lost count somewhere around eighty-five when a whole flock of ghosts and goblins showed up at once." She held out the bowl she'd been clutching so tightly her fingers were numb. "I'm almost out of candy. But there's enough left for you."

"No, thanks. I've had my fill. My old second-grade teacher still makes popcorn balls. She insisted Charlie and I have one. They're great, but I think I'm going to have to make an appointment with Dr. Baylor tomorrow." Dr. Baylor was one of the dentists that practiced in an office across the square from the courthouse. "I think I cracked a tooth." Mitch grimaced and lifted his hand to rub his chin. He had a shadow of beard at this time of day and she couldn't help but wonder what it would feel like rasping against her cheek.

"Would you like to come in for a minute?" She had to stop thinking that way. She needed to stay focused. She wasn't just going to fall into his arms, let him make glorious and passionate love to her, and then hope he would talk about important things later. That was the way it had been with Brian. And when they got to the important things, the life choices, everything had fallen apart.

His wonderful sexy smile disappeared. A muscle jumped in the hard line of his jaw. "Should I come in, Tessa? Or do you want me to go on my way?"

"I want you to come inside," she said, holding the bowl with one hand, beckoning him forward with the other.

He stepped over the threshold and closed the door behind him. After unhooking the parrot from his shoulder, he laid it on her kitchen table. He still wore the eye patch and a red bandanna tied over his dark hair. The illusion of being alone with some long-ago buccaneer was even stronger. When he untied the cords of the black cape and dragged it off his shoulders, she had to force herself to breathe.

His shirt was white, open at the throat and revealing a V of dark hair that made her fingers itch to touch it. The sleeves were long and full and fell in ruffles over his hands. His shoulders filled the doorway. She took another step backward. "How can you see with that patch over your eye?"

"Not very well," he admitted. He pulled it off, and the red bandanna, too. A lock of hair fell forward. Tessa plunked the almost empty bowl back down on the table, but held on to the rim with both hands to keep from reaching out to brush his hair back.

"Tessa?" He still wasn't smiling.

"Sam's pumpkin. Did you see it? Of course you did. Isn't it great? And wasn't it sweet of him to carve it for me?"

"He's a great kid."

"Yes. And wasn't it a great night for trick or treat,"

she said, dragging air into her lungs. The baby shifted inside her, reacting to the rush of adrenaline that coursed through her veins as Mitch's heat and the scent of his skin invaded her senses. Her fantasies of pirate ravishment returned full force. "The moon is gorgeous."

"Would you like to walk down to the dock for a few minutes?" he asked. "It will be your last chance to see the moon over the river from there. Charlie's going to help me take the dock out this weekend."

"I...I'd love to." Tonight there were moonbeams and starshine, ghosts and goblins about, and she had the flesh-and-blood reincarnation of Errol Flynn standing right beside her. And she loved him.

He took her hand. His palm was warm and slightly rough against her skin. She shivered with desire as he helped her into her coat, and blamed it on the cold air from the open door. They walked outside and down the steps to the dock, their footsteps echoing over the river. Mist hung low above the water, and off in the distance a dog barked. Faintly, from inside Mitch's house, she could hear Belle take up the challenge, then stop abruptly, silenced, no doubt, by Caleb's command.

The moon had begun to wane, but it was still beautiful. She rested her palms on the railing of the deck. They had stood like this once before, when she'd first come to Riverbend. And if she was brave enough to tell Mitch what was in her heart, it wouldn't be the last. There would be a lifetime of nights for them to stand here this way, side by side, watching the moon rise over the sleeping fields and the slowly flowing river.

She turned her head slightly so she could watch Mitch as he looked out over the river. His profile was as strong and clean as the moonlight that silhouetted him. She remembered the feel of his mouth on hers, the solidity of his chest against her breasts, the warmth of his arms around her.

Tessa opened her mouth to speak, but no words came. It was harder than she'd thought. With Brian the words had come so easily. "I love you," she'd told him many times. And then she found she didn't love him at all.

"Mitch?" She wished he would turn to her and take her in his arms and never let go. If he held her close to his heart so that she could feel the steady reassuring beat of it, she could find the courage of her conviction and tell him she loved him.

"Yes, Tessa?" He turned but made no move to take her in his arms. She had asked him not to, and he wouldn't until she gave him a sign.

That she could do. Even if the words were slow to work their way past the knot of emotion that clogged her throat, she could tell him without words.

Reaching up on tiptoe, she bracketed his face with her hands. He tilted his head down to hers, rested his arms lightly on her shoulders. Then, as their lips met, he slid his hands down her arms to her waist and touched her stomach. Touched her where he had never touched her before, where the child was growing within her. The baby moved. The earth moved, and she opened her mouth to speak.

"Hey, hello down there." A tall figure appeared at the top of the steps, backlighted by the security lights from the park across the creek.

"What the hell?" Mitch growled. He dropped his hands and moved to block her from sight. It was a protective, completely male action. But she didn't need protection. It wasn't a stranger's voice. At least not to her.

"Oh, God," Tessa whispered. "It can't be."

"Who are you and what do you want?" Mitch called back up the steps.

"My name's Brian Delaney." The figure came forward down the steps into a beam of moonlight that illuminated his rugged handsome face. "I'm looking for Tessa Masterson. I was told she lived in the cottage up there. I thought I heard her voice."

*Brian here in Riverbend. Not now when I've made up my mind to stay with Mitch!*

Mitch turned his head to look at her. "Your baby's father?"

She nodded, mute, unable to confirm the words aloud. He waited for her response. She wanted to turn and dive into the river and swim away, but she couldn't. She squared her shoulders and stood a little straighter. "I'm here, Brian."

"The old guy at the house was right, then. He said you might be down here." Brian descended the final two steps. "When Callie told me you'd ended up in some one-horse town in Indiana, I didn't believe her."

Tessa found her voice. "Well, now you can see it's true. Why are you here, Brian?" she asked, afraid she already knew the answer.

His voice softened, dropped to a low persuasive growl. "I've come to take you home with me."

## CHAPTER THIRTEEN

*I'VE COME TO TAKE you home.*

How often had she longed to hear him say those words? But not now. Not at this time, in this place. Not with Mitch listening.

Brian took her in his arms.

She felt the jut of his hipbones against her belly, the solidness of muscle and sinew in his arms. The baby moved restlessly. "God, I've missed you." He pulled her close, rested his chin on top of her head, but made no attempt to kiss her, for which she was grateful. She didn't know how she would have reacted. His jacket was leather, old and soft. She used to snuggle into its heavy folds when it turned cool in the late innings of a game. That all seemed a lifetime ago.

"Who are you?" Brian demanded of Mitch.

Tessa stepped away from Brian's embrace. His arms tightened around her for a heartbeat, but he let her go without a struggle. "Brian, this is Mitch Sterling. He's my employer and my friend."

"Yeah, you two looked real friendly when I was coming down the steps."

"Do you want him here?" Mitch asked quietly.

Brian turned so that Mitch was blocked from her

view. "Tessa, I'm here to ask you to come back to California with me. I want us to be a family."

There had been a time when those words would have made her the happiest woman in the world. Tonight they only confused her. Brian's shoulders blotted out the moonlight. She took a step sideways to move out of his shadow and to give herself some time. She stumbled in the darkness.

Mitch moved swiftly, but Brian was nearer. He scooped her close. "Are you okay? There's nothing wrong with the baby? This guy hasn't been working you too hard, has he?"

She resented the last question and let him know it. "I'm fine, Brian."

He smiled, and even in the darkness she could feel some of its power. "I'm glad." He held up his hand as though to forestall a blow. "And I should have known you would be." He held out his hand to Mitch. "Sorry, buddy, that last remark was out of line. It's just that I've spent the last three days tracking her down. I didn't know what kind of situation she might have gotten herself into."

"No problem." Mitch returned the handshake, but his voice was colder than the mist rising off the river.

Tessa felt something twist and crack inside her. Her serenity. Her certainty that she was making the right choice by following her heart and her dreams into Mitch's world. But the cold hard reality was that her baby's father was standing in front of her, and everything she had been certain of just moments before had shifted like sand beneath her feet. "Brian and I do have a lot to talk about."

"You understand, right?" Brian said. "We kinda want to be alone."

"Of course."

"I...I'll see you at work tomorrow," Tessa said. It was a plea.

Mitch only nodded and turned back to the river.

Brian urged her up the steps. She was out of breath by the time they reached the top. "Your friend down there sounded like he wanted me for lunch," Brian remarked as they neared the boathouse door.

"You startled us."

"Yeah. I suppose I did." He let it go at that. He stared down at her belly. "You've blossomed."

"I'm almost eight months pregnant."

"I know. I'm the guy who got you that way, remember?" he said with what sounded almost like wonder in his voice. He reached out a hand as if to touch her stomach, but Tessa shied away. Brian drew his hand back and looked at her with a furrow between his dark brows. She felt ashamed of her action and hurried to open the door. He was her baby's father. If anyone had a right to touch her there, it was Brian.

"Come in," she said. She stopped dead at the sight of his duffel sitting on her kitchen table.

"The door was open, so I unloaded my stuff." He was the only man she knew who could sound sheepish and sexy at the same time. The trait was one of his most appealing. "You shouldn't leave it unlocked like that."

"This is Indiana, Brian, not L.A. No one locks their door in Riverbend if they're only going outside to watch the moonlight on the river."

"Is that what you call it here in the boonies? Watching the moonlight on the river?"

She whirled on him. "That's enough. I told you, Mitch is my friend. He's also my landlord and my boss."

"Oh, so that's the way it is."

"Brian." The room spun around her for a moment. She grabbed the back of a kitchen chair for support.

He was beside her in a heartbeat. "I'm sorry. I promised myself I wouldn't act like a jealous jackass, but here I go already. You're sure you're okay?" He took her in his arms and she let her head rest against his shoulder for a moment until the room stopped spinning. He wasn't quite as tall as Mitch. She didn't fit as comfortably in his arms. *Stop that,* she ordered herself. *Stop comparing them.*

She moved to the sink and ran a glass of water with trembling fingers. As she took a sip her throat closed, making it hard to swallow, so she poured the rest down the drain. "I'm just tired." It was the truth. But she was also heartsick and growing more confused and uncertain by the moment.

"Callie said she thought you were working too many hours."

"I'm fine," she repeated.

"You should be taking it easy. Lying on the beach or something. There're some great beaches in Honduras." Brian was a very determined man. When he wanted something, he went after it with both hands, and for the time being, at least, he obviously wanted her—and their baby—back. She was too vulnerable at this point to give him any advantage.

"I don't want to lie on the beach."

"How did you end up in this burg, anyway?" he asked, crossing the room with restless strides to peer behind the curtain into her bedroom alcove.

"I got detoured off the highway by an accident. I got lost and nearly ran out of gas. The chief of police and Mitch Sterling came across me parked by the side of the road reading a map. They guided me into town." She sank into one of the kitchen chairs. Her head was pounding, and she rubbed the back of her neck, trying to ease the pain.

"So what did they do? Confiscate your car keys? Why did you stay on?"

"It was a beautiful day. The river was lovely to watch. The leaves were turning. Mitch offered me a job and I needed the money."

He stiffened. "I left you money in our bank account. It hasn't been touched."

She lifted her chin. "I don't want your money, Brian." Brian made what most people would call a good living playing baseball, but he also spent almost every cent he earned. He was always in debt. She was a little surprised he hadn't already spent the money she'd left behind.

He stopped his restless pacing. "Not even for the baby?"

"We're doing fine on our own."

"I've been half out of my mind worrying about you."

"Is that why you left the team and came after me?"

He smiled but didn't meet her eyes. "Of course."

"Brian, don't lie to me." She folded her hands on

the cheery yellow place mats and tablecloth she'd bought on sale at Killian's just the day before, and waited for him to answer.

"I came after you because I was worried about you. And I hurt my shoulder." The smile was gone. His eyes, the same blue as the Indiana autumn sky, were bleak.

"Oh, Brian, I'm sorry. Is it bad?"

"I saw the team doctor in L.A. just before I flew out here. He thinks it's going to be okay. He recommended therapy. That's why I have to get back to the Coast ASAP. If everything works out right, I'll be ready to play again by the first of the year. You'll have had the baby. We'll spend the winter somewhere warm and tropical. How does that sound?" He planted both hands on the table and leaned toward her. "God, I've missed you. Every night and every day I was gone." He rounded the table in a single step, took her hands in his and drew her to her feet. "I want a chance to be a father to my kid. I want a chance for us to get back together. I don't want us to be apart a minute longer."

For a moment Tessa let herself believe he meant every word he said. And he did mean them. For as long as it took him to say them.

She pulled her hands gently from his grip. "It's not going to be that easy, Brian. You chose baseball over our child and me. That's not what a good father does. I can't forget that. I won't forget that."

His eyes narrowed. For a moment there was a darkness in them she'd never seen before, then he smiled again and the moment of imagined vulnerability passed. "Okay. I didn't think it would be that easy. But I am here. Doesn't that mean something?"

"Yes. It means you think you want a family now. But I won't fall that easily a second time."

He lifted her hands and kissed her knuckles one by one. "Are you sure, Tessa? We were always really good together. We never fought in bed."

"We never talked in bed, either."

He dropped her hand as if her skin had suddenly burned his fingers. "Talk in bed?" He sounded genuinely astonished.

Talking about anything but baseball was an alien concept to Brian. She might have smiled if her head didn't hurt so badly. There was a tight dull pain across the small of her back, too. She pressed her hands to the spot and arched her spine to ease the tension. "We have a lot to talk about."

"Okay, if that's what it takes for you to believe me, we can talk till the cows come home." His jaw tightened, his lips thinned. It was the way he looked when he was facing a pitcher who had his number, and he was behind in the count. "Where do you want to start?"

"Not tonight, Brian," she said gently. "I have a full day tomorrow. You have to go."

"Go? Go where? I figured I'd stay here." His gaze shifted to his duffel on the floor beside the table, then back to her face. "I can bunk down on the couch."

She wondered what Caleb and Sam would think when they got up in the morning and saw a strange car parked beside hers in the driveway. She wouldn't let herself imagine what Mitch would think, or she'd break down completely. "There's a nice hotel on Main Street. It's reasonable. And there are a couple of motels out by the highway."

"I thought I'd stay here with you."

"That won't do."

"Why?" A hint of male challenge sparked in his eyes. "Are you afraid your pirate friend out there won't like it? What was with that getup, anyway?"

"It's Halloween. Mitch was part of the town safety patrol for trick or treat."

"A real pillar of the community, eh?"

"Yes, he is."

"Okay, okay, don't get up on your high horse. I'm sorry for that crack. It won't happen again." He held up his hands in surrender. "But don't make me go. We belong together. You know that." His voice was the low sexy growl she'd always found hard to resist.

Tessa stiffened her resolve. "You can't just walk back into my life as if nothing's happened."

He folded his arms across his chest. "Yeah, you're right. There's a hotel, you say?"

"On Main Street near the river." She was surprised he gave in so quickly. He really was trying.

"I'll get a room there. I'll call you— Hell, I forgot. No phone. I'll be back in the morning."

"I have a doctor's appointment, then I'm going to work."

"I'll go there. Where is the place? Not that it'll be hard to find. Hell, Main Street's only three blocks long."

Tessa ignored the slight against Riverbend. "I'd rather you didn't."

He opened his mouth to say something, but thought better of it. A muscle jumped in his jaw. "Fine. Whatever you want. What time do you get off?"

"Six. I told you I'm going in late."

"I'll be here to pick you up. We'll go to dinner. What's the best joint in town?"

"The Grill at the country club, I suppose. I've never been there."

"This wide-spot-in-the-road has a country club?"

"Yes."

"I'll be damned." He grinned and she couldn't help herself. She smiled back. "Maybe I'll play a round tomorrow. See how my shoulder feels. If I don't freeze doing it. They have some great courses in Honduras. And you never have to worry about frostbite." He flipped up the collar of his jacket and leaned toward her again, inviting a kiss. Tessa opened the door.

"Good night, Brian."

The rush of cold air on his back and legs seemed to cool his ardor. "I'll see you tomorrow, but you remember this. I want you and I want our baby. I'm not leaving this town without you."

MITCH GRABBED the crowbar and attacked the stubborn spike that was keeping him from freeing the last section of dock.

"Hey there, buddy, watch out or you're going to send this whole section down the river with me still on it," Charlie complained. They were standing waist-deep in cold river water, and Mitch's chest-high waders had a leak in them. His left leg was soaking wet and numb to the knee.

"Sorry." He gave the spike one last jerk and it slid free of the wet heavy wood. He pulled it the rest of the way out with the claw end of his hammer. "One, two, three...lift."

With a grunt Charlie heaved his end of the section free of the pilings, and together they maneuvered it onto the bank. Without another word they turned back to manhandle the last two support posts out of the soft muddy bottom.

With a technique that had earned him a berth at the state track-and-field championship in high school, Charlie sent the six-foot cedar posts sailing like javelins toward the ones they'd already removed. "That's it for another year," he said, sloshing toward the bank.

"I'll stack 'em and tarp 'em later," Mitch said. Charlie was a great friend, but Mitch just wasn't in the mood for company today. He hadn't been in the mood for much of anything but feeling sorry for himself since Tessa's boyfriend had shown up Halloween night.

Brian Delaney. Center fielder for the Angels. Someone at the Riverman Lounge had even seen him play in a late-season game.

Not many people in town suspected he'd made a fool of himself over Tessa Masterson, but that didn't make him feel any better. He fired the crowbar onto the pile of dock sections. It landed with a metallic clatter that echoed back and forth across the river, splitting the Sunday silence.

"Jeez, you're in one hell of a mood this afternoon," Charlie grumbled. "Want to get it off your chest?"

"Nope," Mitch said pointedly. He wasn't ready to

talk about Tessa with anyone. Even Charlie, who'd been there for him through his divorce from Kara.

Charlie sloshed his way onto the bank and headed for the built-in bench near the steps where he'd left his shoes. "Man. I bet the water's down to fifty degrees. I think my gonads are atrophied. Why the hell did we leave the dock in so late this year, anyway? It's not like we did any fishing or anything."

"Too many other things on the agenda." Like falling in love with a woman who was carrying another man's child.

"Yeah. It's been one hell of a summer," Charlie grumbled, but he was smiling.

And why shouldn't he? Mitch thought enviously. He'd reunited with the only woman he'd ever loved. Not many people got a second chance at love. His own sorry situation ought to be ample proof of that.

Except, just what was his situation? He certainly hadn't confronted Tessa with it this past week. In fact, he'd done his level best to avoid her. And succeeded pretty well, considering they saw each other every day.

Mitch looked out over the river. It was a gorgeous day. Breezy and warm for November, but the weather was about to turn cold. Winter was setting in. At least, that was what Caleb had been predicting for the past three or four days.

"Want me to hang these waders in the boathouse?" Charlie asked. He hooked his thumb in the direction of the lower half of the building. Mitch followed the gesture with his eyes, but studiously avoided raising his gaze above the level of the open doors to Tessa's windows.

"I'll do it. I've got to lock her up, anyway." He'd taken the boats out weeks ago—the runabout they used for waterskiing and the rowboat Caleb and Sam used for fishing on summer evenings.

Charlie handed over the heavy waders and started up the steps. "It's probably halftime. I'll check with Caleb and see how the Colts are doing."

"I'm right behind you." Mitch sloshed over to the shed, hung Charlie's waders on a peg and shut the heavy wooden doors. The whole building would need staining next summer, he decided, determined not to think about Tessa so close above him. Maybe he'd let Sam and a couple of his buddies do it for extra money. It would be a good project to keep three eleven-year-olds busy for a week.

They'd have to be careful not to disturb the baby, though.

He slammed his fist against the door. "Hell. She'll be long gone by next summer." Now he was talking to himself. That was enough of that.

He grabbed his shoes and climbed the steps, still wearing the leaky waders. They were going into the trash. He'd have to sneak them by his granddad, though. Growing up during the Great Depression had made a lasting impression on the old man. He never let Mitch throw anything away if he got to it first. He'd have to make sure he stashed them out of sight somewhere until the next garbage pickup.

He got to the top of the steps and rounded the boathouse. Tessa's car was in its usual spot, but the boathouse looked deserted. She was off with Delaney somewhere again. He ground his teeth and kept on walking, trailing water from his waders.

Charlie was waiting for him by the back door, leaning against the house, soaking up the weak November sun. Once winter set in, they wouldn't see the sun for days, sometimes weeks. Lake Michigan was a hundred miles away, but it still had a strong effect on the weather. A car pulled into the driveway. Mitch turned to see who it was, despite not wanting to confront Tessa and her lover. But it wasn't Delaney's high-end rental. It was Ethan Staver in one of the town's silver-gray patrol cars.

Ethan got out of the car and strode toward them. Charlie straightened from his slouch against the side of the house and moved forward to meet the policeman. He held out his hand. "Nice day, Chief," he said.

"Sure is. Probably one of the last we'll have this year."

"What's up, Ethan?" Mitch asked.

"Just on my way out to Kate McMann's place to do a little follow-up on the accident."

"What accident?"

"You haven't heard?"

"Some kid driving like a bat out of hell, stereo going full blast, nearly ran down Kate's twins when they chased a kite out onto the road."

"My God," Charlie said.

"Are the girls all right?" Mitch asked. His heart thudded heavily in his chest. The twins were Kate's life. If anything happened to either one of them, he didn't know how she would go on.

"They're fine. Can't say as much for the guy who pulled them out of the way. Banged up his leg pretty good. He's still out at Kate's place."

Mitch wasn't sure he liked the sound of that.

"Who's the guy?" Charlie asked.

"Name of Lawrence. Some businessman from Chicago, I guess, out to see a little of the countryside." The air was growing colder, and Charlie stuck his hands in the pockets of his jeans. Mitch's left leg still felt like a chunk of ice. Ethan was in his shirtsleeves and didn't seem to notice the cold at all.

"I'll give Kate a call later," Mitch said. "Make sure she and the girls are okay."

"Thought you might want to do that." The chief turned on his heel and climbed back in the squad car just as Brian Delaney's rental pulled into the driveway. Ethan gave Delaney the once-over, raised a hand in greeting to Tessa and pulled out onto the street.

Tessa got out of the car and walked toward them. She moved more slowly these days, more deliberately, as though her burden had shifted. She still wasn't very big, not in the way some women ballooned in their ninth month. She was just nicely rounded. Nicely pregnant.

Mitch curled his hands into fists as he remembered the firmness of her belly beneath his fingers. Relived again in his imagination the movement of her child beneath his fingertips. He'd felt a connection to the little one, just as he had with Sam the first time he'd felt him move inside Kara. But Tessa's baby wasn't his. Tessa's baby belonged to the tall golden-haired man following a few steps behind her as she crossed the driveway.

"Hi, Charlie," she said with that sunbeams-and-summer days smile that haunted his dreams.

"Hi, Tessa. Going to introduce me to your...friend there?" Charlie's hesitation on the word was so slight Mitch thought he was the only one who noticed. But he wasn't. Tessa's eyebrows drew together in a quick frown. Her smile faltered for a moment, then returned full force.

"Of course. Charlie Callahan, this is Brian Delaney." She didn't add, *the father of my child.* She didn't have to. Everyone in town already knew.

"Glad to meet you." Charlie held out his hand.

"Same here. Nice little town you got here." Delaney rocked back on his heels and gave Mitch's waders and threadbare flannel shirt the once-over. He was wearing a great old leather flight jacket that looked as if it was a true World War II original and had cost a mint. This was the same guy Tessa had described as undependable, the one she wasn't going to ask for child support, wearing a five-hundred-dollar jacket and driving a luxury rental car that cost him a hundred bucks a day to park in Mitch's driveway. And then there was his room at the River View Hotel.

That was one expense Mitch didn't begrudge the man. He wouldn't have closed his eyes all week if he'd had to think about Brian Delaney sleeping in Tessa's bed.

"Thanks. We like it."

Delaney waited expectantly, as if hoping Charlie would say something more. Like, *Aren't you the guy who plays for the Angels?* But Charlie kept his mouth shut. And Mitch was glad.

"Why was Ethan Staver here, Mitch?" Tessa asked quietly. "Is something wrong at the store?" She'd lifted her hand as though to lay it on his forearm, but then let it drop back to her side.

"Seems some damned kid in a souped-up truck nearly ran Kate McMann's twins down this morning."

"Oh, no." Tessa turned white and swayed a little on her feet. Delaney was at her side in the blink of an eye, but Mitch got there first.

"Are you okay?" he asked as she rested her head against his shoulder for just a moment.

"I'm fine," she said, pulling herself upright. "A little dizzy. It's just…the thought… You're sure Hope and Hannah are okay?"

"Ethan says they're fine."

"I'll give Kate a call." The phone line had been installed Friday. Delaney had offered to pay for it, but Mitch had had the satisfaction of turning his offer down flat. He didn't take any comfort in Tessa's wanting a telephone, though. While it could mean she wasn't going to leave town with the guy, it could also mean Delaney was planning to stick around for the winter, too, for all Mitch knew.

"Hey, Dad! The Colts just scored." Sam came bounding out the back door and down the steps to where they were standing.

Mitch wasn't fooled for a moment. Sam wasn't even a Colts fan. His team was the Denver Broncos. But he wanted to meet Brian Delaney.

Mitch put his hands on Sam's shoulders and turned

him enough for Sam to read his lips. "Brian Delaney, this is my son, Sam. He wanted to meet you."

Sam held out his hand. "Hello. I've seen you play on TV." The words came out too loud and in a rush.

Delaney's grin hardened, as though he was keeping it in place with an effort. He frowned and said, "Uh? Sure?" It was apparent he hadn't understood a word Sam said. "Hi, kid."

Sam's face turned red with embarrassment, but he held his ground. "I saw you play on TV," he repeated slowly and very, very carefully.

"I had a pretty good September," Delaney said, his grin still forced but less than it had been a minute before.

"You were good." Sam squirmed under Mitch's hands. "Could I have your autograph?" He must have been practicing with Caleb or Ty because the word came out clear and strong.

Delaney's smile turned genuine. "Yeah. Sure. Anytime." He turned to Tessa. "We'd better get you inside, sweetheart. You look like you could use a rest."

"I...of course. Sam, did you take my pumpkin away?"

"I put it in the compost pile. It was looking pretty gross."

"Thank you. I enjoyed it so much."

She looked sad, Mitch decided. Or was that only wishful thinking? Maybe she looked sad because she was going to leave Riverbend, and she was trying to think of a way to let Sam down easy.

It didn't matter. Either way he'd lost her. And he didn't know how in hell to get her back.

# CHAPTER FOURTEEN

THE WEATHER TURNED dreary and seemed as if it intended to stay that way for the rest of the winter. The wind blew, the sky wept, and Brian was like a caged animal as he paced around her tiny apartment above the boathouse. Tessa spent as much time as she could at the hardware store, but it wasn't any better there, with Mitch doing his best to avoid her.

Dr. Stevens was beginning to worry about her blood pressure and her insomnia. On her second weekly visit after Brian's unexpected arrival, Annie asked Tessa point-blank if something was troubling her that she might want to talk about, since her emotional well-being affected her pregnancy as much as her physical well-being. But Tessa said no. She appreciated Annie Stevens's concern, but she didn't know how to start talking to a stranger, even a doctor, about the life-altering choices she needed to make. And make soon.

So she found herself carried along by day-to-day events, avoiding any confrontation with Brian by going along with almost everything he said—except letting him move in with her. But she knew time was running out. Brian's shoulder was improving. He had therapy sessions with Beth Pennington every other day, and he'd talked Aaron Mazerik into letting him use the weight room at the high school in return for drilling the school baseball team on some of the basics.

He'd told her laughingly that Aaron Mazerik drove a hell of a bargain, and if he hadn't agreed, he'd have gone stir-crazy. But he was smiling when he said it, and some of their best conversations in the evenings revolved around his work with the teens. Tessa took his involvement with the kids as a sign that he really had turned over a new leaf and wasn't only paying lip service to her need to believe he could be a responsible and caring father.

But he'd been in Riverbend for more than two weeks, and with each good report from Beth he was growing more and more impatient to return to California to meet with the team doctor. Lately he'd begun to pressure Tessa to return with him.

Then suddenly it was the day of her baby shower, postponed after the near accident with Kate's little girls because Kate had been so busy with their mysterious rescuer. Thanksgiving was little more than a week away. And still she hadn't made up her mind what to do about Brian, about Mitch, about anything.

Tessa turned her attention back to the packages piled at her feet and opened another gift. Sleepers in soft pastel greens and yellows and covered with Winnie the Pooh characters. It was a few minutes after noon. Kate had closed the bookstore for the lunch hour, and they were gathered in the cozy seating area she had created at the front of the store. Beth was running late with a patient, and Lynn Kendall was on a sick call. But Lily Mazerik, Rachel and Ruth, Maggie Leatherman and Linda Christman had joined Tessa and Kate and her girls for fancy little sandwiches and cookies and hot spiced cider.

"Those are from my sister and me." Rachel said. "Winnie the Pooh was one of our favorite childhood stories. Was it yours, too, Tessa?"

"I like the Pooh stories very much. And the sleepers are great. Thank you both." She'd never had anyone read to her, but it'd be different for her baby. They would discover all those wonderful childhood stories together. And Brian wanted the chance to be a real father, to give their child memories of bedtime stories and walks in the park and visits to the zoo.

Mitch, too, had promised her all that for her child. And his heart. But blood was thicker than water. Wasn't that what she'd always been told?

She laid the sleepers on top of the receiving blankets and soft toys from Linda and Lily, then picked up the next package. It had been wrapped rather haphazardly in Peter Rabbit paper. The yellow bow was lopsided, too. Tessa opened the card. It was signed in big block letters by Hope and Hannah. Hannah danced around in front of Tessa, impatient for their gift to be opened. Hope stayed shyly at Kate's side, peering out from behind her mother as Tessa dealt with the bow and paper. It was the twins' regular day off from kindergarten classes at Riverbend Elementary, and they were spending the day with Kate at the store.

"It's bath stuff," Hannah exclaimed, unable to wait a moment longer for the wrapping to come off. "Because babies have to have a lot of baths. They puke all the time."

"Hannah, such language," Ruth scolded, shaking her head. "Say 'spit up.' It sounds better."

"It doesn't smell any better." Hannah chortled.

Hope came out from behind the couch where Kate was seated and stood at Tessa's side. "I picked out the little hooded blanket. It's to keep the baby's head warm after her bath. Do you think your baby will be bald? Mom says Hannah and I didn't have any hair at all."

"I don't know if she'll have hair or not."

Hannah wrinkled her nose. "I'm wishing real hard it will be a girl. There's too many boys in town, anyway."

"We can baby-sit her when she's bigger—and we're bigger," Hope said, smiling. "I'm going to be a very good baby-sitter."

"You can't baby-sit when you're only five," Hannah scoffed.

"I said when I was older." Hope went back to stand by Kate, her lower lip sticking out in a pout.

"I'll be happy to have you baby-sit when you're old enough," Tessa said, smiling at Hope, although inside, her heart had cracked open a little more. She wasn't going to be in Riverbend when Hope and Hannah were old enough to baby-sit.

She had almost made up her mind to return to California with Brian. She didn't love Brian anymore. That was the only thing she was certain of. But she had made a child with him. And if they tried hard enough, they could become a family, and give their baby the stability she herself had never had growing up. She would spend the rest of her life trying to make that happen.

But how could she tell her new friends this as she sat among them, accepting their congratulations and their gifts, given in anticipation that she would become one of them?

And dear God, how could she tell Mitch?

"Help yourself to the cookies and sandwiches," Kate said, making shooing motions toward the counter where the food was laid out. "I have to make a phone call."

"Checking up on that Lawrence guy, eh?" Maggie asked, her nose quivering with interest.

"I suppose so," Ruth declared, looking indignant. "He doesn't want any visitors, she says."

"We haven't even been able to thank him properly for saving our precious Hope and Hannah." Tears pooled in Rachel's eyes. "I can't bear to think what might have happened if he hadn't been stopped along the side of the road that way."

"Wasn't Lawrence your sister-in-law's maiden name?" Maggie asked. "Wasn't she Mary Lawrence before she married Abraham?"

"Why, yes, it was. Ruth and I noticed that right away. Of course, Mary wasn't from around here. And Kate says Mr. Lawrence has never been in these parts before. It's a common enough name. I don't suppose there's any connection."

"Still, it seems odd that he doesn't want to be seen or talk to anyone," Maggie said, obviously loath to give up the eyebrow-raising topic of the stranger staying at Kate's.

They all nodded as Lily Mazerik caught Tessa's eye and looked up at the ceiling. Tessa bent her head over Hope and Hannah's gift to hide her smile.

Someone knocked on the door. Heads swiveled and Maggie gave a snort. "It's your boyfriend."

"The baseball player?" Ruth peered over the top of her glasses.

"I've seen him around town, Tessa, but we've never been introduced," Rachel prompted. "He's a very good-looking man. Such thick blond hair. And those shoulders."

"I'll introduce you right now." Brian had spent some time at the Riverman Lounge and eaten some meals at the Sunnyside. And he'd met some of the parents of the kids on the school baseball team. But for the most part he'd avoided the townspeople. He'd been born and raised in New York, only moving to Albany his sophomore year in high school, and he found Riverbend as alien as she sometimes found Southern California. He'd kept to himself, and Tessa hadn't tried to persuade him otherwise.

"We'll let him in." Hannah skipped to the door with Hope only a step behind.

"Hello, ladies." Brian greeted the group with his just-for-you-alone smile. "I hope I'm not intruding."

"You're blocking my view," Maggie said, not in the least impressed with Brian's smile.

"Yes, ma'am," Brian said, and leaned back against the coffee bar.

"There's a present left." Hope pulled one more package from beneath the wrappings. "Here."

"It's from me," Maggie said as Tessa took the gift from the little girl.

"I don't know how we could have missed it," Tessa apologized. She removed the wrapping paper. Pink and white stripes with a pink ribbon.

"I don't get much chance to wrap stuff in pink," Maggie said with a sniff.

Tessa opened the lid of the Killian's box and folded back the tissue paper that covered what was inside. She recognized it right away. It was an apple-green baby sweater with embroidered pink rosebuds down the front. The one that had belonged to Maggie's oldest son when he was a baby. A tiny hat and booties lay beside it.

"Oh, Maggie. I can't accept this. It should go to your son. Or his children."

"Nonsense. My son couldn't care less about it, and he has five children. How on earth would I pick which one to give it to? Anyway, I made all the grandchildren one when they were born. I want you to have it to start a tradition of your own," she said more softly.

Tessa swallowed hard so her voice wouldn't wobble when she responded. "Thank you. I'll cherish it always."

"Don't cherish it. Use it. It'll wash. It's cotton, not wool."

Tessa smiled. "I will."

"I think we should start loading things into the trunk," Brian said. "It's stopped raining. At least for the time being."

Tessa glanced at the clock. "I should be getting back to the store."

"Me, too," Linda said, her eyes following Tessa's to the clock above the door. "Mitch will be wanting his lunch. Thanks for inviting me," she said to Rachel and Ruth, and then Kate, who'd just returned from making her phone call. "I got some good ideas for gifts for my daughter today."

"Goodbye, Linda," the women said.

Maggie levered her way off the couch and picked up a plate. "These cookies are wonderful, Kate. I don't know how you do it all. Especially with a stranger laid up in your spare room."

"He's no trouble, really. And how could I turn him away? He saved my babies' lives."

Tessa was loading gifts into Brian's arms. "I'll take these out to the car." He turned and headed quickly for the door as if he couldn't wait to get out of there, which was probably true.

"I'll be getting the baby bed and high chair down from the attic as soon as I find a minute to do it," Kate said as she knelt beside Tessa's chair to help her fold the wrapping paper.

"Please. Don't go to any trouble over it."

Kate gave Tessa's stomach an assessing look. "I don't think we should wait too much longer. When's your due date?"

"December fifteenth."

"Definitely not much time. Babies can't read calendars. They come when they please."

Tessa wondered if she was right. She'd begun to feel huge and clumsy. Her breasts were tender. She had twinges of pain in her back and contractions around her middle. All normal, Annie Stevens had assured her. But worrying nonetheless. She had to make up her mind about leaving Riverbend with Brian. And soon.

"Ready to go?" he asked, shaking raindrops from his hair as he reentered the bookstore.

"I'm ready." They'd returned Brian's rental car to the airport on Sunday. There was little reason for them to have two cars. She knew Brian took it as a sign she'd decided to return to California with him, but he didn't press her.

He was trying. Trying very hard to be the level-headed, responsible father figure she wanted him to be. She just couldn't be certain it would last.

Tessa said her goodbyes and Kate walked her to the door of the bookstore. "Are you okay?" she asked, as Tessa fumbled with her umbrella.

"I'm fine."

Kate folded her arms under her breasts. "You don't look fine. Forgive me for saying so, but you look like a woman with a lot on her mind."

Tessa managed a smile. More than ever she wished she could confide in this strong and focused woman. Kate had been through it all. Pregnancy, child birth. Raising her daughters without a man in her life.

What did she think about Hope and Hannah not having a father figure as they were growing up? Did she regret leaving her husband?

Would she have regretted staying with him even more?

Brian appeared in the doorway. "C'mon. It's starting to rain again." He held out his hand to usher her to the car. He looked back over his shoulder and gave

Kate one of his killer smiles. "Thanks for the party. We both appreciate it."

"Tessa's a friend. It was our pleasure. Call me," Kate said to Tessa. "Call me if you need anything at all."

"Did I hear her—what's her name, Kate?—say she had a baby bed and high chair you could borrow?"

"Yes, she did." Tessa didn't turn her head to look at him. She stared straight ahead, watching the stores on Main Street go by. Killian's had winter coats on display in the window, fake snow and child-sized mannequins having a snowball fight against a backdrop of Rockwell's famous painting of a family sitting down to Thanksgiving dinner.

She didn't think it was going to be cold enough to snow in Riverbend on Thanksgiving Day.

It certainly wouldn't be snowing in L.A.

"Does that mean you've decided to stay here?" he asked. He flexed his hands on the steering wheel. His knuckles were white from gripping it so tightly, she realized. He was worried about her decision. He did care.

She turned her head. "Kate offered me a baby bed and high chair when I thought I was going to be staying in Riverbend after the baby was born."

"And now?"

"And now I'm not," she said, and felt a sharp stab of pain deep in her heart.

"Does that mean you're going to give us...give me...another chance?" There was a tone of suppressed excitement in his voice. She knew what he was thinking. Once he had her back in California he would overcome the last of her doubts and win her back. He was ahead on the count. "I'll be a good father, Tessa."

"I know you'll try."

"When can we leave for the coast?"

"I...as soon as Mitch can spare me."

"You don't owe him anything." Brian's voice hardened slightly.

"Yes, I do. But I'll tell him Friday will be my last day."

"You won't regret this, Tessa."

But she already did.

HE'D DONE A PRETTY good job of staying out of Tessa's way all week but it looked as though his luck had run out.

"Mitch, I need to talk to you."

"How was your party?" She couldn't have been back from her baby shower more than a few minutes, but she didn't look like a woman who had just enjoyed an hour being showered with gifts and well wishes from her friends.

"I...it was wonderful. They're all so good to me."

"They like you, Tessa. They want to see you happy." He shoved his hands into the back pockets of his jeans to keep from reaching out to touch her. "We all want to see you happy."

"Mitch, I'm leaving Riverbend."

The words had a sense of finality to them that was as shattering as a bullet to the heart.

"When did you decide that?" He heard his own

voice, felt his pulse hammer in his temple and his groin, so he wasn't dead, but he might as well be.

"I don't know when I decided, exactly. I only know I have to go."

"With Delaney?"

She nodded. She was twisting her hands together in the hem of her smock. It was a rich copper-colored fleece that warmed her skin, but could do nothing to banish the misery in the depths of her eyes. "He's the father of my child."

Mitch took a step closer. There were customers all over the store today, which was probably why she'd chosen this time and place to tell him. Though he felt like it, he couldn't howl his misery to the moon or threaten to beat Delaney to within an inch of his sorry, miserable life. "He may have fathered your baby. That doesn't mean he's going to be a father."

"Don't, Mitch. I have no choice."

"You chose to leave him once before."

"I thought I was doing the right thing."

"You were doing the right thing." She put her hand to her temple. She was trembling and he could have kicked himself for badgering her this way.

"Mitch, please. Don't make this any harder for me than it has to be."

"I don't want it to be easy." God, he sounded as selfish and self-centered as he'd pegged Delaney to be. "Do you love him?"

"I don't think I know what love is. Maybe I never did." He wanted to challenge her on that score, too. But she was almost at the end of her rope, any idiot could see that, so he ground his teeth together and remained silent. "I do know the right thing for my baby is giving him a chance to know his father."

"And that means going back to a man you don't love?"

She lifted her chin and looked him straight in the eye, something she hadn't done for days. Not since Delaney blew into town. "I never questioned my mother when she told my sister and I our father didn't want us. But maybe my mother was wrong. Maybe he wanted to be a father and she wouldn't let him. I'll never know. He died three years ago. I don't want my child growing up with that question always in her heart. Brian wants to be a father. I have to give him that chance."

"He wants you," Mitch growled. He got a grip on himself before he could add the rest of what he'd started to say. *I'm not so sure he wants the baby.* How the hell did he know what Delaney really wanted? He hadn't spoken a dozen words to the man the two weeks he'd been in town.

"I have to give him the benefit of the doubt for our baby's sake."

"I don't have any doubts, Tessa. I love you. Stay here with me. I don't care how often Delaney visits the baby. I'll still love your child as though she were my own."

She pressed her fingers to his lips. "Don't, Mitch. I've made up my mind."

"Tessa. Goddamn it, I love you." He slammed his palm against a support beam, felt the sting of cold metal against his flesh. How the hell could he stop her? How the hell could he change her mind? He'd stayed in a loveless marriage for years for Sam's sake. He couldn't fault Tessa for choosing the same rocky path.

"Don't say that again, please." She looked so confused, almost ill. She started to turn away. He reached out and manacled her wrist with his hand. Her skin was like ice.

"All right, I won't." He could feel himself shutting down, just as she was. There came a point when your heart started protecting itself. He'd felt like this once before, cold and detached. It was the day Kara told him she didn't want any more babies like Sam. The day he knew for sure his marriage was finished. It wasn't fatal, this awful hollowness in the center of his soul, but he damned near wished it were.

"I...I'll stay to the end of the week. Until the Holloway boy—"

He cut her off. "No, you won't. Go home, Tessa. Try to get some rest."

"But I can't—"

"Go home, Tessa," he said gently. He couldn't be angry with her. Not when she looked as if she were at the end of her rope. "Go home. You're fired."

## CHAPTER FIFTEEN

"I DID IT!" Sam looked around to see if anyone on the street was watching him. He didn't know if he'd yelled the words out loud or only in his head. He was that excited. He'd made the Mini-Rivermen first team. The starters were all sixth-graders. Big kids. But three of the first team were fifth-graders. And he was one of them. He'd get to play in almost every game.

And if one of the other guys got hurt.

He stopped that thought right in the middle.

A team player didn't think like that. His dad had told him what to do to be a good team player, and it had worked. He hadn't tried to hog the ball. He'd passed off to the guys with the good shots. He'd kept his eye on the ball and on the other team, the way Coach Mazerik had taught him during the summer. And when he was positioned for a good shot, he hadn't been afraid to take it.

He'd remembered everything he was supposed to, and it had paid off.

He'd made it. He was one of the guys. He'd even heard the whistles most of the time, because Coach Mazerik had told his coach to make sure he used the loudest one he had.

Sam jumped straight up and pumped his fist in the

air. Even the weight of his book bag couldn't keep his feet on the ground today.

Wait until he told his dad! And Granddad Caleb!

*And Tessa.*

She'd be proud of him. He'd proved he could do what all the other kids could do. He wasn't a quitter. She'd know that now.

She would begin to see what a great kid he was, what an awesome big brother he'd be to her baby.

Except for what's-his-name. Delaney. The baseball player. The guy who must be the father of her baby. No one had told him that in so many words, but he wasn't a dummy. He could figure it out. Delaney had been hanging around for a long time now. Ever since Halloween. He didn't even have a car anymore. He was driving Tessa's. Just like he planned to stick around forever. That could be a problem. But Sam had figured he'd work on what to do about Tessa's old boyfriend later, when he had time to think and come up with a plan. Now he just wanted to tell Tessa his great news and see her smile and have her tell him she knew he could do it all along.

"SAM, HI. COME IN." She opened the door wider. She looked past him a moment at the leaden sky. There was a hint of snow in the cold wind, and the sun had vanished. Twilight was already sliding across the river, although it was barely five o'clock. Only a week until Thanksgiving. She had an appointment with Annie Stevens on Wednesday for one last checkup and to pick up her records. Then she and Brian would head for California.

"I made the team," Sam burst out, swinging around to face her as she shut the door. "I made the first team."

"Sam! How wonderful." She had forgotten all about Sam's tryouts. She'd spent the afternoon packing the most precious of her things. Brian had told her to leave them behind. They'd buy everything new to celebrate their starting over when they got to L.A. But she'd insisted, and he'd been halfheartedly helping her ever since.

"I'm seventh man. I'll get to play every game. Maybe not till the second half, but I'll get to play. And I'm going to be so good next year I'll get to be a starter!"

"Of course you will!"

"Hey, what's going on out here?" Brian came out of the bathroom and spotted Sam. "Oh, hi, kid. I thought there was a fire or something from all the noise."

"Brian." She couldn't believe he'd said such a thing in front of Sam.

Sam's face reddened. "I'm sorry. Was I talking too loud?"

"Of course not," Tessa assured him, reaching out to lift his chin a fraction of an inch with the tip of her finger. "You were celebrating. And so am I. I'm so happy for you I could shout myself. Sam made first team, Brian," she said, still keeping eye contact with Sam for a moment before looking over at Brian.

"Way to go, kid. Uh, first team for what?" Tessa turned Sam around, and after a silent prompting from her, Brian repeated the question.

"Basketball," Sam said, his face tight as he strained to make himself understood. Sam backed away a couple of steps so he could see both their faces.

"Way to go, kid." The remark was clipped and impatient. Brian didn't seem to notice the effort Sam was making.

"Sam's worked very very hard to make the team," Tessa said too brightly, in an effort to fill the silence that followed Brian's words.

"Tessa helped. We lifted weights together. Well, paint cans. But it worked."

Brian looked confused and uncomfortable.

"I'll explain later," Tessa said.

"Yeah, well. Like I said, kid, way to go." His tone dismissed Sam and his accomplishment as though it was nothing. Of course, it *was* nothing to Brian. But not to her. Or to Mitch and Caleb and all the others who cared for the little boy.

"I like baseball, too. I'm a center fielder just like you." Sam leaned forward in his eagerness to make a connection. "I'd like to talk about baseball sometime," he hurried on, rushing his words.

Brian frowned, raising one eyebrow at Tessa. "What'd he say?"

"He'd like to talk to you about baseball sometime."

"Yeah, sure, kid. We'll do that." Tessa held her breath. She hadn't told Sam she was going back to California. She hadn't told anyone except Mitch. All of a sudden she was afraid Brian would let it slip that they were leaving. She needn't have worried. He seemed bent on communicating as little as possible with Mitch's son.

"I have to go tell my granddad the news," Sam said. "I'll talk to you later, okay? Bye." He gave a little smile in Brian's direction. "See you, Tessa."

Tessa leaned over and gave him a hug, then held him by the shoulders so he could read her lips. "I'm so proud of you."

His face reddened again. "You helped me, Tessa. You told me not to be a quitter. Thanks." He reached up and gave her a quick hard hug, then jumped backward. "I didn't squash her, did I?"

"No," she said, laying her hand on her bulging stomach. "She's fine. Now, go tell Granddad Caleb your good news."

"Okay, I will." He pivoted and scooted out the door, dribbling an imaginary basketball as he went.

"Boy, I wouldn't know what to do with a kid like that." Brian's voice was a little hollow. She looked over to find him rummaging through the small refrigerator for a beer.

"What do you mean, a kid like that?"

"You know. A retard." His head and shoulders disappeared behind the door as he pulled a bottle from the lower shelf.

"Don't call him that." She grasped the back of a kitchen chair so tightly her knuckles ached. "He's hearing-impaired. He's a very smart little boy. And you hurt him with your callous remark about how loud he was talking."

The anger in her voice brought his head around. Brian straightened and looked over his shoulder. "How was I to know he wasn't slow, too?"

"He reads lips very well."

"I'm just glad our kid's not going to have anything wrong with him. I'm not good with kids like that."

"I thought you enjoyed working with the baseball team at the school."

"It's okay." His eyes narrowed slightly. He hunched his shoulders and tightened his fingers around the beer can. "But, you know...there's nothing wrong with any of them. I understand them. They're not like Sam."

*No more babies like Sam.* She leaned forward, her heart beating hard in her chest, almost suffocating her. "How do you know there won't be something wrong with our child?" She wanted to believe he was only voicing his own fears about physical imperfection. The understandable fears of an athlete who depended on the machinelike perfection of his body for his livelihood. But she was suddenly afraid it was more than that. She was afraid it was the real Brian, self-centered and selfish, the one she'd talked herself into believing didn't exist anymore.

"I don't know. I've never been around a lot of handicapped people," he said carefully, obviously feeling his way through unfamiliar territory. "I guess I'd be okay with it. I mean there are schools for kids with problems. Places where they can be happy and well looked after." He appeared wary, puzzled, as though they'd switched third-base coaches on him and he couldn't read the new signals. He shut the refrigerator door with a thud.

"If Sam were your child, you'd send him away?" They had skirted most of the big issues that remained between them, despite Tessa's insistence that they talk things through. It was as much her fault as his. She hadn't wanted to hear anything that would make her change her mind again. But now she had no choice. She had to know how he really felt.

"If that's what was best for him."

"It's what you think *would* be best."

"In some cases, yes."

"In our case?"

"I don't know. Maybe." There was a hint of challenge in his voice.

"That's not a good enough answer," she said. "Will you love our baby if there's something wrong with her? Will you promise me to keep her with us always?"

"Hey. We don't need to have this conversation. There's nothing wrong with you or the baby, right? You told me the doc says you're both doing fine."

"As far as she can tell, yes. But a problem like Sam's wouldn't show up until the baby's born. Or it could happen later. Sam didn't lose his hearing until he was almost two. What if that happens, Brian? Then what will you do?"

"I'll do the best I can, but I already told you—I'm not good with kids like that." He set the beer can on the table and stepped toward her.

"I want to hear you say it, Brian. Would you love a child like Sam?"

He looked at her for a long moment, his blue eyes narrowed and darkened with emotions she couldn't read, didn't want to understand. "Nothing I say is going to be the right answer, is it?"

She shook her head. "No." She was suddenly unutterably weary. "Nothing you can say now will make it right."

"I'm not the kind of guy to nursemaid a sick kid." He shrugged. "Hell, I don't know how good I'll be with a normal kid. I'm sorry, but you said you wanted the truth from me, and that's it."

She took a deep breath. "I've made a terrible mistake. I'm as much to blame for this as you are. I've been trying as hard as I can to make you into something you're not. A man who wants to be a husband and a father. That's not who you are, is it, Brian?"

He shook his head. "I'm not very good at pretending. You wanted the truth so here's the rest of it. I'm thirty-two years old. I'm a decent center fielder, but not a great one. I worked my ass off to get this shot at the big leagues and I'm going to take it. I've got one last chance for a couple of good years in the sun. I don't want to be tied down with kids and mortgages and that whole domestic scene. All I ever wanted is to play baseball." His voice cracked a little. "And you."

She laid her hand on her stomach. "There isn't just me anymore. There's us."

"You're not coming back to California with me, are you."

"No," she said softly.

"Are you staying here?"

She looked down at her baby gifts piled on the table to be packed. Gifts from friends. Women who knew the meaning of love and family, constancy and stability. Concepts Brian couldn't or wouldn't understand. And never would. At least never with her and their child. She'd had a chance to be part of that world, and she had let it slip away to try to force reality into a dream mold of her own making. "It wouldn't work. I'm leaving, too."

"How will I know about the baby?"

"I'll call you. You'll always be welcome to visit, Brian. You can be as much a part of her life as you want."

"If you leave here, where are you going? Your sister's?"

She had forfeited her chance for a life in Riverbend. "Yes. The way I'd planned. I want to be settled in with Callie before Thanksgiving."

MITCH TURNED OFF the ignition and sat in the pickup, looking across at the darkened apartment above the boathouse. Had she really gone? Just up and left with Delaney and not even said goodbye?

He'd stopped by the hotel to drop off flyers with the dates and times for Santa to visit the Chamber of Commerce's North Pole Village at the Courthouse square the Saturday after Thanksgiving. Denise Ball, the night clerk, had caught him looking at an autographed picture of Delaney in uniform lying on the registration desk.

"He checked out early this afternoon," she told him. "Heading back to California to finish his rehab so he can rejoin the team."

Had he taken Tessa with him? He hadn't talked to her since the day he'd told her not to come back to work. He'd told Caleb she was just too pregnant to spend so many hours on her feet. If his grandfather had seen through his excuse, he hadn't said so. Neither had Bill Webber or Linda or any of the others. Mel Holloway's boy had shown up over the weekend, and he was going to start work in the next day or two. Mitch figured with the pre-Christmas rush and a new hand to break in, he might be able to keep his mind off her for as long as five minutes at a time.

So far it hadn't worked.

He crawled out of the truck feeling a hundred years old.

He shouldn't have sent her home from the store last week. If he'd let her stay, he might have figured out what she was planning. Maybe even changed her mind. But he had no idea what magic formula to use. If telling a woman you loved her and wanted to spend the rest of your life with her wasn't enough, he didn't know what was.

He ought to go inside. Caleb and Sam were waiting. They were going to have pizza to celebrate Sam's success. All his hard work and practice had paid off. But instead, Mitch found himself at the door of the boat-house apartment.

As he noticed when he'd driven up, the place was dark, which was as much an indication as any that she had gone. Ever since Tessa had moved in, there'd been a light on in the small main room. He turned the door-knob. He'd better make sure that the water heater was turned off and the door locked. The knob turned easily and he stepped inside. She'd probably left the keys on the counter. He moved farther into the small apartment, compelled by a force he could not resist. Immediately he was enveloped by the lingering scent of her perfume. Something light and flowery and evocative of her smile.

His hand brushed fabric on the back of a chair. He could make out the lighter white rectangle of a name tag on the front. Her work smock. She'd left it behind. He stood quietly a moment, listening to the hum of the refrigerator, the ticking of the silly sunflower clock Tessa had tacked above the sink. He laid his hand on the table, touched cloth again. The tablecloth and place mats she'd bought at Killian's. Had she left those things behind, too, like her smock, because they had no place in her life with Delaney?

Headlights turned into the driveway. A car drove up to the boathouse, and parked in Tessa's usual spot. Mitch waited in the darkness, his hands balled into fists, hoping against hope it was Tessa come back to him.

Footsteps echoed on the gravel. There was no sound of a second car door opening and closing. Mitch's heart began to hammer against his ribs. The door opened. A woman's form was silhouetted against the streetlight. A Madonna figure with softly rounded belly. Cold air flowed into the room and carried with it the scent of summer flowers and rain-washed clover fields. Tessa's perfume. Tessa's scent.

The light came on. Mitch blinked against the sudden brightness. Tessa stood with her hands clutching her purse. "My God, Mitch. You scared me."

"I'm sorry," he said, feeling ten ways a fool. "I thought you'd gone with Delaney. I figured you'd left the keys inside. I came to get them and lock up."

"How did you know he was gone?"

"This is Riverbend, remember? Home of the world's fastest gossip chain." She didn't smile at his weak joke, and neither did he. "I stopped by the hotel to drop off some flyers. The clerk told me Delaney had checked out to head back to California."

"I took him to the airport to catch a plane." She set her purse on the table. "I would never have left Riverbend without saying goodbye to all of you."

"I apologize for thinking that you would."

She shook her head. "Don't apologize. I've made a mess of everything these past couple of weeks."

"If you mean trying to reconcile with Delaney, then I'm glad you screwed up. But if you're talking about us—"

She cut him short. "I don't know what I want right now, Mitch. I only know I have to leave Riverbend to find it." Her voice faltered and she fell silent.

He came around the table, wanting to take her in his arms so badly he ached with the force of it. "Why punish yourself?"

"What are you talking about?"

"Running off to live on your sister's charity. Is that what you really want?"

She shoved her hands into the pockets of his mother's old coat and faced him head-on. "I won't be a burden to her. Brian and I came to an agreement on child support. But I still have to get things straight in my own mind. I don't trust myself anymore, Mitch. Maybe it's hormones. Maybe it's the weather."

"Maybe it's because you're scared to let your heart lead the way." But what the hell could he say or do that he hadn't already said a dozen times to change her mind?

"I won't argue with you anymore. Please go. It's getting late and I'm tired. I have to call my sister and finish packing."

"When are you leaving?"

"Wednesday morning. Annie Stevens insists on another checkup before she'll release my records."

"Is anything wrong?" He couldn't stop himself from asking.

"I don't think so. My blood pressure was a little high. But all the stress—" She broke off what she'd been going to say next and tightened her lips into a straight line. "It's nothing."

"Wednesday's the day before Thanksgiving. The traffic will be bumper to bumper all the way to Albany."

"It can't be helped."

"At least stay until after the holiday."

"No." There was a note of panic in her voice that was hard to miss.

"Is Delaney coming to Albany to be with you when the baby's born?"

She lifted her chin and looked right through him. "I'm going to do this on my own."

If he hadn't believed her before, he did now. Her words hit him like a sledgehammer. Whatever she felt for him wasn't strong enough to overcome her fear of making another mistake.

"You can stay here as long as you need to."

"I'm leaving Wednesday," she said one more time, as though it was some kind of incantation. Three times the charm. "That will give me a chance to say good-bye to Kate and Ruth and Rachel. To Caleb. To Sam."

"I'll tell Sam you're leaving." Mitch spoke too harshly. She blinked at the force of his words.

"Mitch—"

"It will be better coming from me. Until then, I'd appreciate it if you don't say anything to him. He'll try to talk you into staying, and it'll just make it harder on all of us."

She bowed her head for a moment as she absorbed the full impact of his words. When she looked up at him again, her eyes were bright with unshed tears. "Of course. I understand." She was wringing her hands but didn't seem to notice. He jammed his own deep into his coat pockets to keep from taking her in his arms. "I'm sorry, Mitch. So very sorry."

"I'm sorry, too. Goodbye, Tessa." He wasn't a bas-tard. He didn't want a woman he had to bully into his arms. She looked haunted, trapped. The way Kara had looked at the end of their marriage. A marriage he'd tried too hard to save. Was he doing the same with Tessa?

She'd just sent the father of her child away. She wasn't ready to make a commitment to him or to any-one else. The time for that had passed, a small window of opportunity slammed shut on his hands. He wouldn't ask her again to stay with him. Damn it. If he could help it, he'd never say another word to her as long as he lived.

## CHAPTER SIXTEEN

IT HAD BEEN the longest damned weekend he'd ever lived through. Monday hadn't been much better. Mel Holloway's boy had shown up at the store, and while Mitch thought he'd grow into a fine manager, the week before Thanksgiving was a hell of a time to start breaking him in. To top it all off, a water line in the women's bathroom had sprung a leak sometime during the night and ruined the flooring. Tuesday hadn't turned out any better than the day before, with delays in shipments of tool sets that he wanted for a big Christmas display, and notice that the small sawmill that provided all their custom-made woodwork had burned down overnight and wouldn't be back in operation for at least three months.

He'd used the turmoil at the store to hold off telling Caleb and Sam until just a couple of hours ago that Tessa would be leaving in the morning. His grandfather had looked at him with pity and disgust written large on his face. Sam had simply refused to believe him at first. Mitch had explained about how emotional women who were going to have babies could be. He'd told the unhappy boy that she needed to be with her sister, the only family she had, at such a time.

"We could be her family," Sam said miserably. "Did you tell her that?"

"We're not her family," he'd said, knowing that was no answer at all. Sam had closed his eyes and shut out Mitch's halfhearted attempts to explain what he didn't understand himself. His son had demanded to be allowed to go to the apartment and talk to Tessa on his own. Pouring rain and a cold wind off the river was his excuse to say no. But he told Sam he could phone. Her line was busy.

Sam tried to call three more times during the evening. The line remained busy. Whether she was talking to her sister, reconciling with that bastard Delaney or just had the phone off the hook, Mitch had no idea. Sam pressed his face to the window and looked out into the rainy night. "No lights are on," he announced, looking longingly at the phone one more time.

"It's late, Sam, time for bed," Mitch said, feeling his son's anguish as sharply as his own.

"I can't believe she doesn't want to talk to me."

He had no answer for that. Finally Sam gave up and went up to his room. But not before he'd wrung a promise from Mitch to wake him early enough to say goodbye to Tessa in the morning.

"You sure made a mess of that," Caleb told him bluntly when he dropped onto the couch beside the old man's chair. Mitch ignored the gibe and stared sightlessly at the weather channel as temperature and wind conditions from a hundred cities across the country scrolled by. A huge mass of clouds covered the eastern third of the country. Mitch didn't even notice the winter-storm warning posted along the bottom.

Caleb wasn't about to be cheated of his say. "Now he's going to think Tessa's no better than his mother, sneaking off at the crack of dawn, shaking the dust of this town off her shoes and never looking back. Did she tell you she didn't want Sam to know she was leaving?"

"I told her not to tell him."

"Sometimes you're a damn fool, boy."

"Sometimes I am."

A LATE-NOVEMBER OUTBREAK of flu had Annie Stevens's waiting room packed to the rafters when Tessa arrived for her appointment. It was nearly noon before she got out of the clinic. The driving rain that had begun during the night had turned to something that more closely resembled sleet. Her last-minute packing and cleaning the small apartment had taken longer than she'd thought. She still had several boxes and sacks to load in the car, and already the afternoon had faded to twilight.

She hunched her shoulders and wrapped her coat more tightly around her. Her feet felt as if they weighed a ton each. She could barely lift them. Her fingers felt clumsy and stiff. The skin was stretched tight across her knuckles. Dr. Stevens had all but forbidden her to leave Riverbend, but when Tessa had burst into tears at the suggestion she remain until the swelling in her hands and feet went down, the doctor had relented.

But she had set conditions. Tessa was not to try to

make it all the way to Callie's in one marathon driving session, and she was to call the women's clinic for an appointment the moment she set foot in her sister's house. She'd agreed to each restriction, but had no intention of keeping at least one of them. Where would she find an empty motel room on Thanksgiving eve, the busiest travel holiday of the year? When she left Riverbend, she planned to drive nonstop to Albany.

And she wanted to leave right now. Before Mitch got home from work. Before Sam got home from school. His early-morning visit had nearly broken her heart. He'd tried to be brave and grown-up, but his lower lip had trembled and she'd seen the heartache and disappointment in his blue eyes when she confirmed what Mitch had told him. "Yes, I need to be with my sister," she'd said. "It's scary having a baby all alone."

"I would have been an awesome big brother. I even thought of a name you might like. Laura Marie. Tyler says it sounds pretty. I like how it looks."

She'd dropped into a kitchen chair and pulled him into her arms. "Oh, Sam. It is a lovely name, and you say it beautifully."

He leaned back so that he could see her speak. "Will you come back someday so we can see the baby?"

"I'll try, Sam."

"Will you send me pictures?" He knew she wasn't coming back. He'd already been conditioned by his mother to the kind of white lie she'd just told him.

"I'll send pictures every week. I promise. Cross my heart."

He nodded. He didn't hug her back. He just turned around and left without another word. Just as Mitch had done. Caleb didn't even stop to say goodbye. The Sterling men had joined ranks and shut her out, and she had no one to blame but herself.

She put the last of her packages in the car and went back into the apartment to get her purse and the notes she'd written for Maggie and Lily. She'd post them on her way out of town. In the end she hadn't even been able to reach Kate to say goodbye. She'd left a message on her machine at the store, including Ruth and Rachel in her halting message of explanation and thanks for their kindness and friendship the weeks she'd been in Riverbend.

She was only a few miles out of town when the first weather bulletin broke into the oldies channel she'd picked only because it wasn't WRBN. She'd deliberately left her radio off for the past few days. She didn't want to hear Mitch's voice advertising the store's pre-Thanksgiving sale. She didn't want to hear who'd had a baby and who had died. She didn't want to know when Santa would be arriving at Killian's in the town's brand-new fire engine, or what the menu for the Thanksgiving buffet at the country club would be.

Callie had told her they were getting a ton of snow in Albany when she'd called last night, but Tessa had assumed the roads would be cleared by the time she got there. What she hadn't counted on was a big storm out of Canada heading her way. The farther she drove, the worse the details became.

She listened in stunned silence. Cleveland airport was already socked in, stranding thousands of holiday travelers. Detroit and Toledo would be shutting down by midnight, due to ice on the runways. The storm was expected to be more moderate by the time it hit the Indiana border, but holiday travelers heading for Indianapolis and Chicago and points west should prepare for sleet and freezing rain, black ice and possible electrical outages caused by ice on power lines.

She pulled her car off to the side of the road, laid her head on the steering wheel and wept. She couldn't drive into that kind of weather. She was exhausted and woozy from too many nights without sleep. Her back ached constantly. She was going to have to go back at least as far as the motel out on the highway. But when she got there fifteen nerve-racking minutes later, the No Vacancy sign was prominently displayed. Travelers were getting off the highway right and left. The harried clerk had turned down three cars of stranded holiday travelers before she pulled in, he told her. There might be a room left at the River View Hotel in Riverbend. Did she know the way to town?

She turned the car around and drove slowly back the way she'd just come. She didn't have snow tires and the car fishtailed every time she stepped on the brakes. It was fully dark by the time she turned onto Main Street. The sidewalk in front of the hotel had been salted, but it was still treacherous with freezing rain that had glazed every surface in sight with a thin layer of ice. Tessa knew the moment she stepped into the River View there were no rooms available. People sat on the couch and chairs in the small narrow lobby. A young couple were camped out in sleeping bags against the wall. She had never seen the man behind the desk before.

"Is there someplace I can spend the night?" she asked. Even if she had to sleep in her car in the park, she wouldn't ask Mitch to let her back into the cottage.

"We're full up here," the man said. "But they've opened the fellowship hall at the Community Church. I just sent a carload of people over there. It's three blocks over, on Elm. They're putting up cots and they have coffee and sandwiches. It beats getting stuck on the side of the road all night."

"Yes, it does. Thank you." She turned and made her way carefully back to her car. Lynn Kendall's church. She could stay there and leave as soon as the roads were clear tomorrow. With any luck Mitch would never know she was back in town.

She'd be spending Thanksgiving Day in Riverbend, but she didn't have much to be thankful about.

LYNN KENDALL was helping a tired-looking young mother spread sheets and blankets over the thin mattress of a fold-up cot when Tessa arrived. Half-a-dozen ice-coated cars were parked in the church parking lot. Small groupings of more cots and folding chairs were scattered around the big low-ceilinged room. Luggage and pet containers were piled beside the beds. Fifteen or twenty people sat around talking, playing cards, listening to music on headphones or milling around the long tables set up in a row near the large pass-through window into the kitchen area.

Reverend Kendall left the young mother and children she'd been helping. "Tessa? What are you doing here?"

"Hello, Lynn. Do you have room for one more stranded traveler?"

"Of course, but—"

"It's a long story." Tessa felt she owed the minister some explanation. "I planned to leave Riverbend today to be with my sister. I didn't realize the weather was so bad...." She shrugged helplessly, her eyes burning with tears she was too proud to let fall.

With ministerial tact Lynn didn't ask why she wasn't going back to Mitch's boathouse. Tessa knew it would be common knowledge around town that she wasn't working at the hardware anymore, and that she hadn't left town with her baby's father. She didn't care what they said about her. But for Mitch's sake she hoped no one linked her name with his after she was gone. "Yes, of course we have room. There's a cot right over here where you can put your things. Do you have anything that needs to be refrigerated? Medication? Food?"

Tessa shook her head. "Nothing."

Lynn pointed to an empty cot a few feet over from the ones she'd just been preparing. "Make yourself comfortable. We'll be open until everyone can get back on the road to wherever they were going."

"Is there anything I can do to help?"

"Are you kidding? I'm holding down the fort almost single-handed right now. Anything you can do will be most appreciated."

"I'll get my things put away and freshen up, and I'll be right with you." Her back and leg muscles were screaming for rest, but Tessa knew her mind would never allow her the oblivion of sleep. She might as well be doing something useful.

"Take all the time you need. Have a sandwich. They're from the Sunnyside. They're bringing over more cold meat and cheese and milk for the little ones from the grocery later. Oh, and there's coffee on the counter and soft drinks in the cooler by the table."

"I'll find my way around the kitchen," Tessa assured the young minister as Lynn hurried to the doorway to greet another trio of refugees from the storm.

Three hours later Tessa finally got her sandwich. By then she was almost too tired to eat. The two-year-old girl on the next cot was fussing while Tessa took off her coat and folded it over the end of her bed. She'd laid her purse beside it and looked around for the ladies' room. Just as she'd spotted it at the far end of the hall, the little girl had let out a moan and vomited all over the cot and her older brother's shoes.

Tessa had taken the little boy to the bathroom to wipe off his shoes. Then she'd helped the beleaguered young mother change the sheets on the cot and find another blanket, a softer one, from the storage room behind the kitchen. By the time they had made the bed, found some Tylenol for the girl's fever and got both little ones settled on their cots, ten more people had arrived to take shelter in the church hall, and a fresh delivery of food arrived from the grocery.

Tessa had made sandwiches and coffee until everyone was fed, leaving the kitchen only long enough to call Callie and tell her the storm had forced her to turn back. The sleet continued, and the radio started reporting power outages here and there around town. She was sitting at a table, staring into her cup of luke-warm apple juice and wondering how fast it could take to catch a stomach virus, when Reverend Lynn's fiancé, Tom Baines, came by.

"You look beat, Tessa," he said. "Why don't you take a break after you finish your sandwich?"

"Thanks. I think I will. Do you expect many more people?" she asked, pushing her hair behind her ears. She decided she should make some more sandwiches before she went to her cot. She was so stiff and aching that she was afraid if she lay down, she wouldn't be able to get up again. She picked up a knife and a jar of peanut butter, but when she reached for a loaf of bread, Tom took it away from her.

"I'll do that," he said. "The rush seems to be over. I doubt anyone's still out on the road. It's almost eleven."

"I didn't realize it was so late." Tessa wasn't wearing a watch, and there wasn't a clock in the church hall. No wonder she was tired. It had been a long day.

"Go get some rest, Tessa. You've got a baby to think about, you know." He pulled her chair back and she put her hand on the table to help herself stand. A sharp pain arced across her back and around to her middle. Tessa gasped with the force of it. "Are you okay?" Tom asked.

"Yes. Just have a stitch in my side." Her words sounded breathless and thready even to her own ears. Tom was watching with concern in his eyes.

"If you need anything, give me a call," he said in a tone that made it an order, not a request.

She nodded and watched as he headed for the kitchen. Then she dragged herself to the ladies' room and over to her cot. The mother and her two little ones were all asleep. The little girl hadn't thrown up again. Maybe it had just been the excitement and anxiety of being stranded in a strange place.

Tessa lay down, but her mind refused to shut down in sleep. Someone on the other side of the room was snoring. A knife clattered in the kitchen and Tom growled a muffled curse. She heard Lynn scold softly and then laugh. The only light came from the kitchen and the streetlamps through the windows where the curtains didn't quite meet. She closed her eyes and eventually, amazingly, fell asleep.

The dull ache in the small of her back grew in intensity. Tessa awoke to pitch-blackness. For a moment she lay quietly, panting through the steadily increasing pain across her middle, fighting confusion. She'd been dreaming about Mitch, the sadness in his eyes, the tightness of his mouth as he'd turned and walked away from her, leaving her to face the sterility of her lonely life.

She lifted her hand to her face. Her cheeks were wet. She'd been crying in her sleep. Was that what had woken her? She heard others stir around her and remembered where she was. The Community Church hall. The storm. And now, it seemed, the lights had gone out.

She sat up. The little ones on the cot next to her still slept. Their mother was awake, though. Tessa could hear her fumbling in the dark to see if her children were still covered. The room was cold. Tessa shivered, and another sharp pain tightened around her middle. False labor, she told herself. She'd read about it in the booklets that Annie Stevens had given her so that she would have a better understanding of the process of childbirth. Surely that was all it was. It was more than three weeks until her due date.

"What happened to the streetlights?" the young woman beside her whispered. Tessa tried to recall her name but couldn't.

"The storm must have brought down a power line or something."

"It's cold in here."

Tessa swung her feet over the side of the cot. She'd been so tired she hadn't even bothered to take off her shoes. Now she was glad. It would have been hard to find them in the darkness.

A flashlight beam pierced that darkness. Lynn Kendall's voice came from behind it. "Tessa? Are you awake?"

"Yes, Lynn. What happened to the lights?"

"They've been out for about an hour."

"What time is it?" she asked groggily.

"Almost six. It will be daylight soon, thank the Lord."

Tessa had slept longer than she thought. She felt as if she'd barely closed her eyes.

"Ethan Staver stopped by a little while ago," Lynn continued. "It's the transformer on the main line south of town. It's going to be a while before they fix it. Mitch is bringing over a generator from the hardware. Ethan says we'll probably be getting townspeople coming to the shelter now, too. They're going to start announcing it over the radio. Ruth and Rachel and some other members of the church will be coming in as soon as it's daylight. They're bringing food. Turkeys. Pies. The works. We're going to cook them here. Thankfully we have a gas range.''

A little voice in Tessa's head kept talking over Lynn, getting louder, shriller and more insistent. Mitch was on his way to the church. She had to be gone before he got there.

''Tessa, are you all right?'' Lynn whispered so as not to wake those sleeping nearby. She shone the flashlight beam full in her face. Tessa closed her eyes, as much against the new onslaught of pain as the bright light.

''I'm fine. Just a contraction. Braxton-Hicks, aren't they called?'' She was whispering, too. But she doubted she could have spoken any more forcefully at the moment if she wanted to. It wasn't a lie. She really was having contractions, strong ones.

''You mean false labor? I've heard of it, but I've never been pregnant.'' Tessa couldn't quite see the other woman's face in detail, but she could hear the worry in her voice.

''Dr. Stevens said to start expecting them. I'll just lie back down. They should pass in a few minutes.''

''Okay,'' Lynn said. ''I'll go back into the kitchen and wait for Mitch and Tom to get here with the generator.'' She turned away.

''Lynn?''

''Yes.''

''Do me a favor.''

''If I can.''

"Please don't tell Mitch I'm here. And ask Tom to do the same."

SAM AWOKE in the pitch-darkness. What had happened to his night-light? To his clock? He sat up, his heart pounding. He hated being in the dark. He couldn't tell what was going on around him when he couldn't see. He sat up straighter and tried not to be scared. The power was out. That was all. He knew there was a storm. Ice or wind must have downed the power lines. Too bad it wasn't a schoolday.

He felt around for the flashlight he'd put on his bedside table and turned it on. It worked. Just barely. He hadn't changed the batteries for a long time. He swung his feet over the side of the bed and raced to the window. The floor was freezing. There was ice on the window, but only at the bottom. He shone the beam out into the yard, toward the boathouse. The driveway was empty. Nothing there but his dad's truck. His prayers hadn't been answered. Tessa hadn't come back.

The reflection of another flashlight beam alerted him that his dad was awake and coming to his room. "I'm over here," he said, switching his own light back on as he turned toward the door. His dad was dressed to go out, he noticed.

"I didn't think you'd be awake." Mitch held the flashlight under his chin so Sam could read his lips.

"It's too dark to sleep."

He could see his dad's lips stretch in a smile. "Yeah. I thought that might be the case. Chief Staver was just here. I'm going to the store to get a generator for the church hall. Reverend Lynn has a bunch of stranded people there, and they don't have any lights, either.''

"What time is it?'' It seemed like the middle of the night it was so dark.

"Almost six. Granddad's got a fire going in the fireplace, and there's still hot water, so you can get washed up.''

"Will the electricity be back on in time to cook the turkey?''

"I don't know.''

"It's Thanksgiving. We have to have a turkey.''

"We'll think of something. But first I have to get the generator to Lynn. There are cold hungry people in the church hall.''

Sam nodded. "Can I come with you? Maybe there's something I can do to help. I'm old enough.''

"It's early yet. Don't you want to go back to sleep for a couple of hours?''

"Nope. I'm awake now.''

"All right. Hurry and get dressed. We'll swing by the church and pick up Tom Baines. He can help me load the generator.''

Sam washed his hands and face and got dressed while his dad cleaned the ice off the windshield of the truck. His granddad was bundled up in two sweaters and rummaging in the kitchen cupboards for candles when Sam came downstairs. Caleb found a couple of Christmas ones Sam's class had sold to raise money last year, a half-burned Santa Claus and a snowman whose hat was melted all down his face. Caleb lit them and set them in the middle of the kitchen table. They didn't burn very brightly, but at least it was already starting to get light outside.

Sam ate a cookie and drank a glass of milk and grabbed his coat and hat. "I'm ready, Dad," he said when Mitch stuck his head in the door.

"Be careful. It's slippery out."

"I've got my snowmobile boots on." He stuck out his foot to show Mitch.

"I don't know when we'll be back, Granddad."

Sam was standing close enough to catch Caleb's response. "Don't worry about me," he said. "I'll see if I can bypass the electronic ignition and light the oven for the turkey. Wish me luck."

"Be careful, Granddad. They don't make those things like they used to."

"I've been working with propane stoves since way before you were born. I'll get it hot. Don't worry."

Their truck had four-wheel drive, so it wasn't too hard driving. At least his dad said it wasn't. They picked up Mr. Baines outside the church hall and headed for the store. There were a lot of cars parked around the church. A lot of people must be inside. The hair on the back of Sam's neck stood up and a chill ran down his backbone that had nothing to do with the cold.

He thought he'd seen Tessa's car, but he couldn't be sure.

"Hi, Sam. You're up early," Mr. Baines said.

"Hi." Sam squirmed around in his seat, knocking his leg against his dad's.

"Sam, sit still," his dad said, tapping him on the

knee to get his attention. "What's so interesting back there?"

"I thought I saw Tessa's car in the parking lot."

His dad's mouth pulled into the kind of straight line that meant trouble for someone. "She's gone, Sam. There are lots of little red cars around. It's not hers."

Mr. Baines went on talking about the storm and how they were going to feed all those people at the church. He knew who Tessa was. If she'd come back to the church for some reason—any reason—wouldn't he tell them?

His dad was right. She was gone. Just like his mom. Sam had to face up to that. She wasn't going to fall in love with him and his dad. He wasn't going to get to be a big brother. He wasn't going to get a miracle like they read about in Sunday school, even though he'd prayed for about an hour last night that she'd have to come back to Riverbend because of the storm—and even crossed his fingers and toes and wished on a star he couldn't see, to boot.

# CHAPTER SEVENTEEN

THE GENERATOR STARTED on the second pull. Mitch hunkered down and checked the level of gasoline in the tank. Only half full, but enough for a couple of hours of running time. When everything was functioning, he'd go back to the store and fill a jerrican with fuel from the storage tank at the back of the lot.

He turned up the collar of his coat against the drips of icy water from the eaves spout above his head. He'd already gotten one or two down the back of his neck, but at least they meant the ice was melting. The temperature had been rising steadily the past couple of hours. Patches of starlight glimmered here and there through the clouds. Dawn was a gray streak on the horizon. With any luck the stranded travelers Lynn and her flock were sheltering could be on their way by early afternoon. He hoped the citizens of Riverbend would be as lucky getting their power restored.

Another cold drip found its way into his coat. He swore softly, although the cold water on his skin couldn't make him any more miserable outside than he was inside. Tessa was gone. He still couldn't quite believe it. She had simply packed up and left as he'd always feared she'd do. No goodbye call to the store, no forwarding address in a note left with the keys to the boathouse apartment. Nothing. She had simply gotten in her car and driven off into the storm.

He stood up, his knees protesting the change in position. He felt old and defeated after too many sleepless nights. He couldn't stop trying to figure out where it had all gone wrong. He loved Tessa. He'd thought she loved him. But something inside her kept fighting that love. He'd been a damned fool to believe what he felt for her, what he knew instinctively she felt for him would be enough to overcome all her doubts. She'd told Delaney to take a hike, but whatever demons drove her had commanded her to do the same to him.

And he hadn't been strong enough to fight them off for her. And in his misery he'd turned his back and let her go.

If he'd been fighting real dragons, instead of Tessa's imaginary ones, maybe—

"Dad? Are you ready for Reverend Lynn to turn on the lights?" Sam was signing. The generator was noisy enough for even him to realize he couldn't be heard over the engine.

Mitch reached for the extension cords that would allow them to restart the furnace and turn on the lights in the big kitchen. The generator he'd brought wasn't big enough to run everything in the church hall, but it would allow everyone to stay warm and provide enough light for Lynn to get coffee started without scalding herself.

"All set," he signed back. "Don't turn everything on at once."

"Right." Sam disappeared.

Mitch followed him inside. The noise of the generator subsided when he shut the door behind him. They were at the back of the hall, in a room where the furnace and hot-water heater were located. Tom Baines was waiting for him with another extension cord. He took it and plugged in the furnace, while Tom held a flashlight to light his work. The fan on the furnace chugged into life, the pilot caught and the burner lit with a *whoosh.*

"Heat," Tom said. "That's good. We've got a dozen kids and old people in there."

"You should be able to use the stove, too. Running the refrigerators and all the lights in the common room is pushing our luck, though."

"I'll make sure Lynn tells everyone that. It'll be daylight in another hour or so. We won't need the lights then. When do you suppose the roads'll be clear?"

Mitch shook his head. "I don't know, but I imagine Ethan or one of his men will stop by and give us a report as soon as they get out and inspect them."

"Right." Tom's answer was abrupt and he seemed anxious for Mitch to be done and gone. Mitch couldn't blame his old River Rat pal. He hadn't been good company for anyone this past week. But since he'd come home from work last night and found Tessa gone, he had to admit he'd been downright impossible.

"I have to go back to the store and get some more gasoline for the generator. It's out of my way to take Sam home. Is it okay if he stays here?"

"Uh, sure." Mitch couldn't see Tom's face in the gloom of the musty-smelling room, but he sounded even more anxious than before to have Mitch gone from the church hall. "The kid's probably hungry. We've got doughnuts and cookies and fruit. I'll get him something to eat."

"Thanks. He had breakfast before we came, but he's always hungry. I should be back in twenty minutes or so. You'll tell him where I've gone?"

"No problem," Tom said, but he didn't sound as if he meant it. Mitch gave up trying to figure out his old friend's odd behavior. He had too many other things on his mind.

He hoped it would be no problem for Ethan Staver to track down Tessa's whereabouts for him. Because sometime during the cold dark hours of the stormy night he'd made up his mind to go after her. No matter if it took weeks and every cent he had. Even if he had to go door-to-door through the streets of Albany, New York, looking for her sister's home. He wasn't going to rest until he found her and brought her back to Riverbend—where she belonged.

TESSA FOLDED her blanket neatly at the end of her cot and picked up her coat and purse. She didn't dare stay in the church hall any longer. It was full daylight outside. Sam was still there. In the kitchen, helping Lynn put doughnuts on trays, pouring milk into pitchers. She'd been watching him from the shadows, and the pain in her heart at having to stay hidden was almost as sharp as the pain in her back.

*Surely this can't be labor, is it?* She asked herself for the hundredth time.

Her heart beat fast with apprehension. The pain was

everywhere. In her side, her back, her stomach. It was steady and unrelenting. There was no respite, no easily timed contractions, or so it seemed. Something must be terribly wrong with her—or the baby. Tessa hadn't felt her move in hours.

She needed to get out to the hospital. Townspeople were coming in now in a steady stream. Those without heat in their homes or loved ones to take them in, church members bearing dishes and casseroles, even a turkey to cook in the huge gas range.

The ice was starting to melt. Droplets had been splashing on the windowsills. She could see them from where she sat. That meant the streets were probably passable, if still treacherous. If she could get to her car, it was only a few minutes' drive to the hospital. She could do it. She would do it. On her own. The way she meant to live her life from now on. She couldn't even stop and say thank-you to Lynn. Sam was standing right beside her. Another new friend she would leave with a bad impression. It couldn't be helped.

She dared not wait any longer and hurried into the hallway that connected the addition to the church sanctuary. The only illumination came from the double glass doors leading to the parking lot. She walked toward the murky gray rectangle of light. She'd expected ice on the windshield, but she hadn't considered the possibility that she couldn't get her car unlocked. The keyhole was iced over. She almost gave in to the urge to cry. The pain was unrelenting. But she was going to have to go back inside and find something to thaw the lock. She pivoted carefully, retracing her steps across the glazed surface of the parking lot, then froze in her tracks as a familiar four-wheel drive pickup swung into the driveway.

Mitch. There was no way he could miss seeing her. And no place for her to hide. She stayed where she was, leaning against the fender of her car for support, and waited. He turned off the engine and dropped out of the cab, crossing the icy pavement with long, distance-eating strides, as though it were dry as a bone, not as slick as a skating rink.

"Tessa? Sam told me he saw your car in the parking lot, but I thought he was just imagining it. What are you doing here?"

"I spent the night in the church hall."

"You what? Why the hell didn't Tom tell me that?"

"I asked him not to." The iron band of pain in her middle eased for a moment. She straightened. "The roads were so bad when I left town that I turned around and came back. The hotel was full—"

"You have a home here, Tessa. Why did you come to the church like some stranded traveling salesman?" She'd expected anger and outrage in his voice; she heard only gentleness and disappointment.

"I couldn't come back. I couldn't do that to Sam." She took a deep breath, or tried to. The pain had eased, but it wasn't gone.

"What about me?"

"Oh, Mitch." Her carefully thought-out arguments had flown from her head like birds flying away from a storm. *You can't trust your heart. You have only yourself to rely on. You'll never have the strength to stand on your own again if you give in to this terri-*

*fying need to throw yourself into his arms.* Why did putting up such a struggle for independence seem so meaningless when she was looking into the hurt and the longing in his eyes?

"Does Sam know you're here?"

She shook her head. Another contraction snaked across her middle. She tried to breathe through it, the way she'd read about in the book Annie Stevens had given her. It didn't help. Maybe because only half the pain was in her body. The rest was in her heart. "Lynn's keeping him busy in the kitchen. That's why I'm leaving now. Before it gets light enough for him to see me in the common room."

"You can't go anywhere. The roads are still a mess."

She was in too much pain to argue with him. She didn't want to argue with him. She wanted him to wrap her in his arms and hold her, tell her everything was going to be all right. That she and her baby were going to be all right, because she was suddenly terrified something was very wrong.

"I wasn't running away," she said in a voice that was barely more than a whisper. She put her hand on her stomach and almost doubled over with the force of the pain. "I was trying to get to the hospital. Oh, Mitch, help me, please. I think I'm in labor. I'm going to have the baby now. And it's too early." The contraction tightened mercilessly. She clutched at the fender of her car, but the icy surface slid away beneath her grasping fingers. Her knees buckled. She began to slide to the ground. Mitch moved so quickly she didn't see him coming. In a moment she was where she longed to be. In his arms.

"How close together are the contractions?" he asked, turning her around. She closed her eyes against the pain.

"They're just there. Constant, almost. I...I can't time them."

He held her against his chest and opened the door of the truck. "I'm taking you to the hospital now."

"I was going to drive myself," she panted.

"Damn it, Tessa. Stop that. You can't do every god-damned thing for yourself. When will you get that through your head? Let me help you."

She waited for him to say. *I love you,* but he set his jaw and slammed her door closed on whatever else he might have been going to say. She laid her head against the cold glass of the passenger-side window and let the tears come. What had she expected? She'd thrown his love back in his face countless times. She couldn't blame him for finally taking her at her word.

IT WAS LESS THAN TWO MILES to the hospital, but for Mitch the ride seemed endless. He felt as if he were moving through some sort of time warp. Everything was happening in slow motion. He almost couldn't believe that Tessa was here beside him in his truck, when less than five minutes ago he'd thought he was going to have to move heaven and earth to find her again. He was having less of a problem believing she was in labor. Every bump in the road, every extra-slick patch of ice they hit wrung a little whimper of agony from her lips.

"We're here, Tessa," he said at last, easing the truck into a space outside the ER entrance. "Hang on. Everything's going to be okay."

"I believe you," she whispered as he swung her up into his arms. "I can walk," she insisted, sounding more like her stubborn lovable self than she had since he'd first seen her in the parking lot of the church.

"Sure you can. But I'm not going to have you slip and fall on the sidewalk."

"What if you fall?" she asked, wrapping her arms around his neck.

"I won't fall."

"But if you do, I'll squash you flat."

"Wanna bet?"

The bantering exchange got them inside the door. Mitch was relieved but not surprised to see Annie Stevens standing behind the nurses' desk in the reception area of the ER. Maggie Leatherman was there, too, and Barb Baden, the mayor, along with her husband, Gary, Riverbend's postmaster, and Wally Drummer, the old high-school basketball coach, and his wife. Maggie was the president of the auxiliary, and the others were members. The hospital administrator had probably instituted the facility's emergency plan when the power went off, calling in every doctor, nurse and volunteer who could get out of their driveways.

Annie came toward them, one hand shielding her eyes. The whole area was illuminated by huge emergency lights bolted to the wall just below the ceiling. Their light was harsh and concentrated on work areas and doorways. The rest of the place was in shadow.

"Tessa? I thought you'd left town to be with your sister."

"I tried."

"She's in labor, Annie," Mitch said.

Annie grabbed the handles of a wheelchair and pushed it forward. "Put her here."

Tessa pressed a hand to her distended stomach. Her face was white and pinched, her eyes enormous pools of pain and anxiety. Mitch straightened with an effort. He didn't want to let her go, even if she was more comfortable sitting in the chair. "It's too early. I'm not due for three weeks."

"Your baby's not interested in what day the calendar says it is," Annie said briskly, helping Tessa out of the sleeves of her coat.

"But what if something's wrong?"

"Don't borrow trouble. Let's get you checked out and then we'll worry if it's warranted, okay?"

"Okay." Tessa's hands were knotted into fists on her lap. It took every ounce of self control Mitch possessed not to go down on one knee beside her and take her hands in his.

"Mitch, you wait here while I examine her. Tessa, is there anyone you want me to call?" Mitch wasn't sure if Annie had been told Delaney had left town. The discreet question only underscored his own lack of place in her life.

Tessa looked up at him and managed a small smile that slammed into his heart like an arrow in the center of the bull's-eye. "No. No one else." She gasped as another contraction hit her.

Annie dropped to the balls of her feet beside the

wheelchair and took Tessa's wrist in her hand to check her pulse. "Breathe through it, Tessa. Small breaths. Pant. That's the way." The contraction went on for a long time. Tessa seemed spent and weakened in its aftermath. Mitch's heart beat slow and heavy with dread. The contractions seemed so hard already. What if something was wrong with the baby? Or Tessa? Annie stood up and prepared to wheel Tessa away.

"I'm going with you," Mitch said. He could feel the blood pounding in his ears. Here was another dragon to fight, and this time he was going to come out the victor. Tessa was the woman he loved. She was facing the most difficult situation a woman could endure. He wasn't going to let her do it alone.

"I'm sorry, Mitch. We're operating under emergency conditions here until the power's back on. If you're not Tessa's husband or her assigned labor coach, I can't let you come back."

"Don't go spouting regulations at me, Annie. I'm not leaving her for a minute no matter what the emergency regs say."

"Mitch, do you really want to stay with me?" There was a world of longing in Tessa's voice and despite his fear for her safety, Mitch's heart soared.

Maggie and the others were listening with rapt attention, but despite his audience, Mitch hunkered down on the other side of the chair. "Every step of the way."

Ethan Staver came through the ER doors bringing a swirl of wet cold air with him. "Lynn Kendall called me. She said Rachel and Ruth were on their way to the church to help out and saw you carry Tessa to your truck and head this way with her. Thought I'd better check it out.''

Mitch paid no heed to the chief's arrival. The world had narrowed down to two people. Him and the woman he loved. He held her blue, blue gaze with his brown one, covered her hands with his. "I love you, Tessa. I won't leave you unless you tell me you don't want me by your side through this whole wonderful terrifying business.''

"I—''

"Shh, Tessa. Don't tell me you've got to do this on your own. You don't.''

Tears filled her eyes, but she blinked them away. "I want you with me every step of the way,'' she whispered. "I'm so scared there's something wrong with my baby.''

Annie laid her hand on Mitch's shoulder. "To hell with the rules. My patient needs you, and that's good enough for me.''

She wheeled Tessa into an exam room, and Mitch helped her onto the high table. He held her hands and her eyes with his and told her over and over again what a beautiful healthy baby she was going to have. He delved into his memory of the night Sam was born and coached her through a contraction that hit in the middle of Annie's examination. "Easy, Tessa. Breathe through your mouth. That's the way. Still think it's a girl?'' he asked, brushing her hair back off her forehead as the contraction eased, striving for a note of lightness to keep his own fear at bay.

"It's a girl,'' Tessa said, panting, but resolute. "I know it.''

"Okay," he said with a smile. "I'll take your word for it."

"And she's going to be here before it's time for kickoff, or I miss my guess," Annie said. Completing her exam, she pulled off her rubber gloves and went to the sink to wash her hands again. "You're doing fine, Tessa. Nothing's wrong. This baby has just decided she's going to be born today, and nothing we can do will change her mind."

"You're sure?" Tessa asked as Mitch and Annie helped her to her feet. Another contraction caught her and she clutched at Mitch for support.

"Absolutely." Annie brought the wheelchair back to the exam table. "I was going to ask you if you felt like walking to the birthing suite, but maybe you should ride."

"Everything's really fine? I didn't do something to hurt the baby and make her come early?"

"You haven't done anything wrong, Tessa," Annie assured her.

Tessa was crying openly now. "I've made such a mess of things. I tricked myself into believing Brian was the kind of man I'd always dreamed of, when he wasn't. I followed him to California. I ran away, instead of trying to work out some kind of arrangement with him for the baby. I was going to take him back for all the wrong reasons. I—"

Mitch touched her lips with his fingers, silencing her litany of regrets. He caressed her cheek with the palm of his hand and laid the other one across the roundness of her stomach, cradling the baby she carried inside her. He kissed her softly, quickly, but with all the love he held in his heart. "You're going to marry me for all the right reasons."

She opened her mouth, closed it, then opened it again, but no sound came out.

"Why did you come back to Riverbend yesterday, Tessa?" Now that he knew the baby was okay, that Tessa was okay, he intended to make them both his forever as quickly as he could manage.

The question surprised her. "The weather..."

"It wasn't only the weather, was it?"

She held his gaze. He let her see inside him, into his soul. "No," she whispered after a long moment. "It wasn't only the weather."

"Now tell me why you turned around and came back?"

"I couldn't leave. I...I belong here. You knew that before I did." A little of the darkness left her eyes, reminding him of the gentle blue of an April sky after a thunderstorm.

"Do you love me?"

"Yes," she said simply. "With all my heart."

He smiled, held her eyes captive with his. "Why?"

"Why? I..." She seemed confused.

He kept pushing. He had to make her see what was in her heart, bring it out into the open and make it strong, or her fears might get the best of her again. "Tell me why, Tessa."

"Because I want to spend the rest of my life with you." She grasped one of his hands between her own.

"And I want to fall asleep with you beside me every night," he said, "and wake up with you every morning." He leaned forward and kissed her lightly on the mouth. "I want to raise your daughter as my own, Tessa."

Her breath caught on a sob and her eyes were bright, not with pain, but with joy. "Oh, Mitch, that's the most wonderful thing you could say to me." She leaned forward to kiss him back. "And I want Sam to love me as his mother."

"No more doubts?"

"No more doubts. But I'm still scared, Mitch. I'm not ready for this. Don't leave me."

"I have to leave you, love. For a few minutes, just while Annie gets you settled in. There's work to be done."

"What work?"

He took the handles of the wheelchair from Annie Stevens and wheeled Tessa back into the hallway. "Maggie!" he called. "Does being the mother-in-law of the county clerk carry any weight?"

Maggie laughed, but her eyes were suspiciously bright as she came out from behind the nurses' station. "You bet it does. And you don't have to tell me what you want her for. I can guess." She reached for the phone on the desk and started to punch in numbers.

"I don't understand?" Tessa murmured, turning in the chair.

Mitch dropped to the balls of his feet to bring her face level with his. "The marriage license." He smiled. "We're going to get married. Here and now."

"Oh, Mitch. Can we?"

"Ethan? Can you get Shannon Leatherman to the courthouse to pick up a license and get it out to us?"

"Consider it done."

"But what about blood tests? Waiting periods? A preacher?" Another contraction was beginning to ripple across her belly.

"Shh, stop asking so many questions. Breathe through it, Tessa. Just like we did in the exam room." She watched him, matched her breathing to his. "That's it. Keep focused. That's the way."

"Okay," she said, relaxing against the back of the chair. "It's okay. But we can't get married now."

"Yes, we can. There's no waiting period in Indiana. And no law against a marriage certificate that's written in longhand that I know of."

"That's right," Maggie said, shooing Ethan toward the door. "I'll come with you to get Shannon. And we'll pick up Sam and Caleb on the way. They can't miss this. We'll be back in two shakes of a lamb's tail with the license."

"And I can marry you." Barb Baden peered over the top of the high counter, her round face beaming. "I'll just go and fetch a Bible from the chapel." As good as her word the rotund little mayor hurried off down the gloomy hallway.

"We'll hold down the fort here," Wally Drummer assured Annie and a surprised nurse who'd just come on the scene.

"It's that easy?" Tessa asked.

"It's that easy." Mitch kissed her once more. "In thirty minutes you'll be my wife, and the position comes with a lifetime guarantee."

## *CHAPTER EIGHTEEN*

TESSA WATCHED the sunset fade from coral to pink to pearl as twilight deepened outside the window of her hospital room. She was sore and aching in every bone and muscle, and so tired she could barely hold her eyes open. But she was far too excited to sleep.

She had a child. A daughter. A beautiful little girl, all six pounds, three ounces of her.

And a husband.

She lifted her hand and ran her fingers over the worn surface of the wide gold band on the third finger of her left hand. It had belonged to Caleb's wife. He had carried it with him every day since her death ten years before, he'd told her as he'd handed it to Mitch. The ring was his gift to welcome her into the family. She'd even had flowers, courtesy of Wally Drummer and his wife, who had opened the hospital gift shop and confiscated a handful of roses and daisies for her impromptu bouquet.

And then, the baby who had been in such a hurry to make her appearance, decided to stay put for a while. A very long while, in Tessa's estimation. She hadn't been born until the middle of the afternoon, just after the electricity was restored. In time for Annie and her staff to head home for their turkey dinners and the second half of the Detroit Lions and Chicago Bears game. A true Thanksgiving baby.

She turned her head to the chair by the bed where Mitch sprawled, his long legs stretched out, the baby resting on his chest. Her beautiful perfect daughter. *Their* beautiful perfect daughter.

She couldn't have done it alone. Nothing she'd read about had prepared her for the rigors of childbirth. It was truly a miraculous awe-inspiring event. It was also a frightening, painful and exhausting ordeal. There had been times when she was ready to give up, let the darkness take her away. But every time she wavered Mitch had been there to urge her on. She had clung to his hand like a lifeline. Made his quiet encouraging voice the center of her universe. Drawn on his strength and unshakable faith that she was going to bring their baby into the world safely. And she had.

A little girl. She would have welcomed a son, of course. But a daughter was even more special to her.

Because she already had a son.

She smiled and closed her eyes on a sudden rush of happy tears. Hormones, she told herself. And excitement. And pure unadulterated love for all the Sterling men.

"What are you smiling about?" Mitch asked, his voice very soft so as not to disturb the baby sleeping in his arms. His big hands cradled the infant against his strong chest. He held her so surely, so comfortably.

"Everything," she said, leaning back against the pillows. She didn't know how she was going to stay awake long enough to eat the turkey dinner with all the trimmings that Sam and Caleb had gone off to fetch for her. She held out her hands. "Can I hold her?"

Mitch chuckled. "I don't know. I'm pretty comfortable here. I don't think I want to give her up yet."

"Do you think she'll be hungry when she wakes up?"

"Probably." His eyes narrowed as he straightened slowly from his lounging position in the chair. "You'll do fine at that, too."

She felt color rising in her cheeks but didn't look away. They hadn't yet made love, but they had shared an intimacy that far transcended even that joining—the birth of a child. Talk of breast-feeding shouldn't make her uncomfortable. And it didn't. Only a little anxious. "I didn't think I'd get to breast-feed her. I...I thought I'd have to be looking for a job as soon as I could."

"You have a job. Full-time wife and mother. It's yours for as long as you want it, Mrs. Sterling." Mitch stood up, still cradling the baby against his chest. He came and sat down beside her on the bed. "Although I don't imagine it'll be all that long before you'll want to be adding to your résumé."

Her eyes widened in momentary dismay. "You mean another baby?"

He laughed softly and the little one stirred and rooted against his collarbone, then settled back to sleep as Tessa took her in her arms. "No, I didn't mean another baby. But one or two more would be nice."

"Yes, another baby would be nice. In a few years."

"I meant getting your degree. Teaching."

Her tears spilled over, and she made no attempt to stop them. "Oh, Mitch. I've put that dream aside."

"There's no reason to."

"But the expense. I can't ask..."

His hand stilled for a moment as he traced the outline of the baby's fine ear. He looked up at her. "Who else would you ask? What's mine is yours. It's an investment in our future and a damned good one. I want you to have your dream, Tessa."

"I've always wanted to teach. And that way I can give something back."

"A lifetime of teaching children to honor the past and use it to build on the future."

"A lifetime in Riverbend. I like the sound of that." The baby stretched and mewed, her tiny mouth pursed in a pout. Her eyes opened. Eyes so blue they were almost black. Tessa wondered if they would stay that way, always reminding her a little of Brian. She didn't want to think of him, but she had to.

"I tried to call Brian," she said, speaking her thoughts aloud without hesitation. She could tell Mitch anything, everything. "A friend of his answered. He's already left for Honduras. I don't know when he'll get back to me." She sighed. She couldn't help it.

Mitch lifted her chin with his knuckle. "He's a fact of life, Tessa. Just like Sam's mother. They're going to weave themselves in and out of our lives for a lot of years to come and probably cause some trouble and heartache, but we can handle it."

She nodded. She looked into his warm brown eyes and saw the depth of love reflected there, and felt she could take on the world. "I'll make mistakes," she warned him.

"We all make mistakes. Parenting is a learning curve. Just about the time we get it right, they grow up on us and leave home."

"You make it sound so easy."

"It won't be easy. But together we can take on the world."

"I think you just might be right."

He leaned forward and kissed her. "I know I'm right. Have you decided what we're going to name this little beauty?"

He cupped his palm gently to the baby's cheek and she covered her hand with his. "I thought I'd let Sam do that," she said.


EVERYONE WAS ASLEEP but him. Sam looked around, wondering if he'd dozed off for a while, too. A whole plate of turkey and stuffing and mashed potatoes and gravy on top of a long, weird, scary, happy day could do that to a guy. His dad was stretched out on the hospital bed with his arm around Tessa. She had her head on his shoulder and they were holding hands. Granddad was sleeping with his chin on his chest in the only comfortable chair in the room. He was sitting on one with a hinged seat that lifted up. He hadn't wanted to look and see what was underneath—he was afraid he already knew.

The baby was asleep in a little see-through plastic crib beside him. He looked over at her. She was starting to move around, kicking her little feet, waving her tiny hands. Was that what had woken him? He stood up and bent over the crib. Her face was all screwed up and getting red. She was going to start crying any second.

He wondered what to do. He saw movement reflected in the dark glass of the window and turned around. Tessa was beckoning to him.

"Pick her up," she mouthed. He knew she wasn't making any sound so his dad and granddad wouldn't wake up.

"Me?" he signed. He'd held her already, sitting in the good chair with his hand on the arm so her head didn't flop or break her in two or anything. He hadn't lifted her. Or carried her.

Tessa—his stepmom. He'd prayed and he'd wished on a star for extra luck, but he hadn't expected to get his wish so soon.

Yeah, it was a miracle, all right.

And now he had a brand-new baby sister into the bargain.

He wouldn't dare miss Sunday school any more after this.

"Bring her to me," Tessa signed.

"Carry her?" he asked, just to be sure.

Tessa nodded, smiling. "Yes." She held out her hands.

He picked his little sister up as carefully as if she were made of glass. Spun glass, the sparkly kind that hung in shop windows. He slid his hand under her neck and cradled her head. He slid his other hand under her bottom and lifted her up a little bit.

She didn't break in half or roll out of his hands. He lifted her a little higher. She was light as a feather, even wrapped up in a blanket and wearing a little knitted pink cap. She didn't have any hair at all that he could see.

She opened her eyes. Babies couldn't see very well when they were so little. He'd learned that in school. But she sure looked like she was staring right up at him.

"Hi," he said in a whisper, working very hard to make sure he wasn't talking too loudly. She squirmed a little in his hands and he held his breath, but didn't drop her. Then he straightened. "Hi, little kid." She opened her eyes wider. Now he was sure she was looking at him. "I'm your big brother, Sam. Who are you?" She was going to have to have a name. He wondered what Tessa was going to name her. He hoped she remembered how much he liked Laura Marie.

He turned toward the bed and deposited his sister gently in her mother's arms. He didn't know how his dad had talked Tessa into marrying him so fast, but he was glad he had. Now she was his mom, too.

"She's cute," he said, still whispering. His voice was just right. He could tell by Tessa's encouraging smile. "What's her name?"

"I don't know," Tessa whispered back. There were bright tears in her eyes and on her lashes. Happy tears, Sam knew they were called. Tessa reached out and laid her hand on his arm and smiled straight into his eyes. "Your dad and I thought we'd leave that very important decision up to you."

# HARLEQUIN®
# SUPERROMANCE®

## *You are now entering*

WELCOME
TO
**RIVERBEND**
POPULATION
8793

Riverbend…the kind of place where everyone knows
your name—and your business. Riverbend…home of
the River Rats—a group of small-town sons and
daughters who've been friends since high school.

The Rats are all grown up now. Living their lives and
learning that some days are good and some days
aren't—and that you can get through anything
as long as you have your friends.

Starting in July 2000, Harlequin Superromance brings
you Riverbend—six books about the River Rats and
the Midwest town they live in.

**BIRTHRIGHT** by Judith Arnold (July 2000)
**THAT SUMMER THING** by Pamela Bauer (August 2000)
**HOMECOMING** by Laura Abbot (September 2000)
**LAST-MINUTE MARRIAGE** by Marisa Carroll (October 2000)
**A CHRISTMAS LEGACY** by Kathryn Shay (November 2000)

*Available wherever Harlequin books are sold.*

# HARLEQUIN®
*Makes any time special* ™

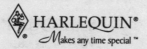

This Christmas, experience
the love, warmth and magic that
only Harlequin can provide with

# Mistletoe Magic

a charming collection from

# BETTY NEELS
## MARGARET WAY  REBECCA WINTERS

*Available November 2000*

HARLEQUIN®
*Makes any time special* ™

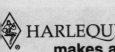

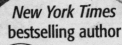

Presenting...

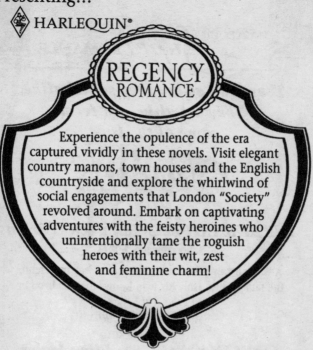

HARLEQUIN®

REGENCY ROMANCE

Experience the opulence of the era
captured vividly in these novels. Visit elegant
country manors, town houses and the English
countryside and explore the whirlwind of
social engagements that London "Society"
revolved around. Embark on captivating
adventures with the feisty heroines who
unintentionally tame the roguish
heroes with their wit, zest
and feminine charm!

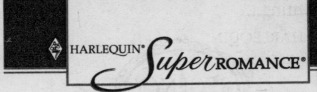